# THE GROVE

*The Legend of Tena, Book 1*

## KARRI THOMPSON

REIGN PUBLISHING

Editing by Jennifer Murgia
Proofreading by Appalachian Proofing

ISBN (Paperback): 978-1-7323731-2-9
eISBN: 978-1-7323731-3-6

Library of Congress Control Number: 1-10574345522

*For John and Kyle*

# CHAPTER 1

A chill crawled up my spine, tightening the muscles in my neck as I froze, listening. Beneath the light of the full moon, the forest was visible, even at midnight. A sugar maple, spellbound by the wind, wagged its upper limb until a smaller branch tore from its trunk and teetered to the ground.

I stepped forward, my heartbeat strong. The trees stirred in unison as if sap pulsed through their stiff veins by means of a wooden heart. Swaying to-and-fro in my direction, each branch enticed me forward, until I entered their flora and fauna world. A snapping sound followed, stirring a crisp crackling of leaves behind me.

I gasped, spinning on my heels, shuddering as forest foliage crumbled beneath my feet. Stumbling, I fell to my knees.

"Is someone there?" I asked and caught my breath by inhaling slowly through my nose.

The end of a crooked limb poked through the forest floor. Pulling it from the thick layer of leaf debris, I pushed myself up and stood, wielding it in front of me like a sword.

"Laura," came a voice in an elongated whisper.

The hair on my arms rose. My heart thumped hard, the blood pulsing through my chest into my throat. Looking left and right, I felt my muscles tense to run or fight.

"Who's there? What do you want?" I said at the same low whisper, my voice shaking.

A shimmering blur disappeared behind a tree—a featureless something, flashing in indistinguishable color as quickly as a silent whip.

"Laura," someone said again, gentle and feather-light, drifting between the largest trees in front of me.

I held my breath.

"Laura." My name resonated through the humid night air, echoing through the sugar maples before it thinned and died.

It was a male voice, full-bodied, but lacking malevolence and hostility. Strangely, it put me at ease. There must be a boy somewhere out here in the woods. I was sure of it. The voice sounded young, maybe my age of seventeen.

Or maybe it was a ghost. My Uncle Dean had told me the locals believed these woods were haunted. But ghosts couldn't kill. At least that's what I believed.

"Who are you?" I asked, relaxing my stiff muscles just enough to take a step forward. My shoulders dropped as I exhaled a pent-up breath. Broadening my stance, I leaned forward, raising the branch, and squeezed my eyes shut, hoping to hear it again.

"Laura," it repeated. The word lingered through the dead of night, ringing softly in my ears. I opened my eyes.

"How do you know my name?" I asked, moving toward the direction of the voice. As a cool breeze rustled my pajama shorts, I wrapped one arm around myself.

A bird chirp rode the wind, followed by several more, weaving into a rhythm of tweets and trills. I looked up. Within the tousle of leaves and sway of thin limbs, perched a gathering of birds, flexing their wings for flight.

I took a step backwards, my eyes fixed on the canopy of leaves.

The bird calls increased, one squawk overlapping the other until their unique melody collapsed, twisting into an eerie song and wing beats.

"A–are you still there?" I breathed, eyeing the woods ahead of me and taking another step back.

A smear of color flashed to my left, and a cloud of leaves rose from the forest floor.

"Don't go," I said, breaking from a whisper.

The woods resonated with angry bird speak, their unnatural song thumping in my ears.

"I want to see you," I shouted above the rising mad twitter.

A shadow skated across the ground at my feet. Wings flapped overhead, and a bird beak met my scalp with a hard peck.

"Ouch!" I ducked, shielding myself with my arms as another beak hit, striking my forearm. I rubbed out the sting.

A series of wings pounded, flashing silvery blue in the moonlight. The flock formed overhead, blocking the light of the moon. Blindly, I dashed right, covering my face with one hand and swinging the branch over my head with the other.

Like miniature warplanes, they swooped, blocking my path. I scrambled in the opposite direction. The manic flock followed, dove, and struck again with a screeching barrage of pecks upon my bare arms.

"Get away!" I screamed, beating the air with my fists. I tripped, falling forward, rolling onto my rear.

A loud, moaning howl rumbled nearby, twisting into a prolonged growl. With a frantic flap of wings and frenzied shrieks, the birds scattered, ending their uncoordinated dance of torment.

I sat, my palms pressed to the ground, listening over the pounding pulse in my neck for another wolf-like howl. A summer fog rose from the forest floor, a soft veil of white, thickening as it moved ghost-like, shrouding the trees in front of me. My arms prickled. The woods became silent. I fumbled to recover my weapon, found it, and stood.

The howl was closer this time, a single high-pitched yelp, dwindling into a whine that reverberated in all directions.

I broke into a sprint, dodging tree limbs as I pushed through the last row of birch and maples. My house appeared, glowing in the porch light, its white exterior contrasting sharply against the black sky.

Slowing to catch my breath, I jogged across the lawn of neglected grass between our property and the woods and continued up the driveway, the crunch of gravel and chirp of crickets the only sounds. Powering down to a brisk walk, my heartbeat slowed.

"Laura?" came a woman's voice.

"Oh my god, Mom! You scared the crap out of me!" I gasped, dropping the branch and smacking my free hand against my chest.

Mom stepped from the shadows of the porch, tightening the belt of her thin robe and squinting from the glare of the bare light bulb shining above her head.

"What in the world are you doing out here? It's after midnight." Her eyes shifted to the branch at my feet. "You get in here right now." Her glasses flashed as she disapprovingly shook her head.

I looked over my shoulder at the woods. A deep yearning, an unexplainable need to explore, tugged at my curiosity as if the trees were taking one long, collective deep breath, trying to pull me from the front yard and back into the woods. It was the same sensation I'd felt earlier when I couldn't sleep and sat up to look out my bedroom window. The pang of want, an unexplainable craving to explore the unknown, had pumped through my veins.

"I, um . . ." I said, brushing the hair from my eyes and giving the hem of my pajama shirt a quick tug to free it from where it clung to my sticky, sweaty skin. "It was too hot in my room, so I came outside to sit on the porch for a while."

"Well, get inside. For all we know, there are murderers and rapists hiding in the forest. When I was a kid, a band of no-gooders camped out there for weeks before they were found and arrested."

The boy I heard couldn't be a murderer or rapist. He had the perfect chance to confront me, but he didn't. If he'd wanted to hurt me, he would have done it right then and there.

I took a step toward my house and stopped, glancing back at the woods. The tree line was still, but the dead leaves near my feet fluttered, brushing passed the toes of my tennis shoes. The boy's soft voice reentered my mind, his words calm and unnatural but with substance, reminding me that what I'd heard had to be real and not a figment of my imagination.

"Laura, honey. Come on." Mom waved for me to get inside.

I climbed the porch steps to the front door and wiped my feet on the faded "welcome" mat left by whomever had rented the house before us.

Mom moved inside the doorframe to stand in the kitchen. "You weren't on the porch when I came out there. And why are you wearing tennis shoes? You didn't go in the forest, did you? You know you're not allowed."

"I know. I didn't," I said, diverting my eyes from hers. "I just went to the end of the driveway to cool off for a—"

A breeze swept from my left, sending my mother's wind

chimes to tinker and ting. Moths played tag around the porch light, forcing me to sidestep passed my mother. Just as I cleared the front door, I thought I saw something move near the end of our driveway. I spun to take a look, squinting against the porch light, my heart beating in my throat.

The driveway was empty, but from the corner of my eye, I saw something move again. *What the —?*

"Laura, what are you doing? Close the door," Mom scolded.

Rushing to the kitchen window, I threw the curtain aside, fighting to see beyond the glare of the ceiling light reflected in the glass. I heard my mom shut and lock the door.

"What are you looking at?" she asked.

From the forest rim, an elongated shadow emerged from one tree, retreated behind another, and vanished. I pressed my forehead against the pane, longing to see the figure again. The urge to investigate resurfaced, pulsing through my brain.

"Laura, talk to me. What's wrong? You're acting weird," Mom said.

"Nothing's wrong," I answered, my eyes still focused on the woods.

"Get over here. We need to talk. Right now." I heard Mom stamping her foot.

I gave the forest a last scan, hoping I'd see something to explain what had happened. There were no shadows or blurs. I dropped the curtain and watched it swing back into place.

"Mom," I groaned as I followed her into the living room. "I told you. Nothing's wrong."

She plopped onto the couch and tapped the cushion next to her. "Sit."

"Mom. Really, there's nothing going on. Let's go to bed." I could watch the forest through my bedroom window.

"Not until we talk."

"There's nothing to talk about. I just got hot. I'm not used to the humidity here like you are. I prefer Albuquerque's dry heat." I shot a glance at the kitchen window, but I was too far away to see between the curtain panels.

"Just because I grew up here in Berkshire County, doesn't mean I'm used to it either." She wearily leaned against the arm of the couch and fanned her hand in front of her face. "The landlord promised to fix the air conditioner next week." She tapped the cushion again.

"Let me get something to drink first," I groaned.

I got a glass from the cupboard and filled it at the tap, my eyes glued to the crack between the curtains. By leaning over the sink and bringing my face inches from the pane, I could just make out the tree line from under the glare. There was no movement, no shadows.

It seemed so real, but maybe I had just imagined the whole thing. Or maybe no one called my name at all. Maybe it was just the whistling of the wind and what I'd seen was a squirrel or a deer. I returned to the living room with my drink and dropped down on the cushion next to Mom.

"Isn't that good news?" she said.

"What?"

"The air-conditioning being fixed."

"Oh, yeah. Yeah, that's great news."

"And you'll get some relief from the weather when school starts," she added.

"Don't remind me," I grunted.

"Uncle Dean said the high school has air conditioning. My graduating class wasn't so lucky. We suffered through every heat wave."

"What about registration? I still don't know how I'm going to get there and back."

"I'll drop you off and go into work a little late. I'm sure

Uncle Dean will pick you up. Don't worry about it. It'll be figured out before the end of the week."

I set my drink on the end table but missed placing it directly on the coaster. Water splashed across the back of my hand as I repositioned my cup. "Crap," I said and wiped the drops onto my pajama shorts.

"Why are you so on edge?" Mom asked.

"I'm not," I said.

"I know you better than that, Laura. Spill it."

"It's late. And really, there's nothing to spill. Can't we just go to bed?" I had to look for whatever it was again!

"It's never too late to have a needed conversation with my daughter. And I won't be able to sleep until I know what's bothering you. Now, tell me. Why did you really go outside? I mean, come on, Laura. Tennis shoes? And why were you carrying that big stick?"

There was no way could I tell her the truth about someone calling my name, especially since I still wasn't one hundred percent sure it had even happened.

"I told you. I was hot. That's why I went outside."

"And what else?" she said, raising her eyebrows.

"And . . ." I tapped my fingers against the top of my thigh. I had to tell her at least some of it, so we could go to bed. "And then I heard a noise," I quickly said. "So, I put on my shoes to check it out. That's what happened. I'm just still a little freaked out by it, that's all."

"Laura! If you hear a noise, that's the time to come back in the house and lock the door—not investigate it on your own, and at night! Being an only child, you're mature and independent. Too independent. You take risks, and I don't like that. What were you thinking?" She dropped her hands in her lap.

"That's why I grabbed the stick. So I'd have something to protect myself with just in case."

"A stick wouldn't protect you against someone with a knife or a gun."

"It wasn't that kind of noise."

"Then what kind of noise was it?"

"It . . . it was just a howl. I wanted to see if it was a wolf."

"A wolf?" She lifted an eyebrow. Deep shadows formed under the lines on her forehead.

"Yeah, a wolf. Didn't you hear it when you were outside? It happened again just before you called my name. It was pretty loud."

"Nope, not with these old ears."

"So, you didn't hear anything?"

"No. But no matter what, you shouldn't have left the porch." She shook her head again, and her lips thinned. "It couldn't have been a wolf, but it could've been a stray dog—a stray dog that bites and has rabies!"

"How do you know it wasn't a wolf?" I asked, remembering the creepy, canine-like wail.

"There hasn't been a timber wolf in Massachusetts since the eighteen hundreds. All were killed off by hunters. The only thing we need to watch out for is the eastern rattler."

"So, no bears or mountain lions or anything like that?"

"Nope. Lots of deer, though."

"But I heard a wolf."

"Laura, it wasn't a wolf," she insisted.

"But it didn't sound like a dog. It was different. It had to be a wolf."

"Fine, it was a wolf—in your imagination." She winked. "So, besides the heat and the howl, what else is bothering you?" She yawned. "There has to be something else," she persisted.

Her yawn was infectious, and although I was pretty wide-awake at this point, I yawned, too, arching my back and stretching my arms. "There's nothing else, really," I maintained.

The woods just felt like a place I'd needed to be tonight. How could I explain that?

I picked up my water glass and snuck a peek at the kitchen window, my eyes yearning to see beyond the curtain and the glare.

As if hit by a cool breeze, the sweat on the back of my neck chilled. A trail of goose bumps rose across my shoulders and down my arm. My hand trembled. Bringing the glass to my lips, I took a sip and closed my eyes.

In my mind's eye, a face materialized, a male face with piercing blue eyes and lips as red as a candied apple. A face framed with flowing brown hair curling slightly at its ends. It was handsome and delicate, but strong. Its blue eyes twinkling, its lips close to mine. He whispered my name—*Laura*.

"What the—?" I sucked in a deep breath and opened my eyes.

"Laura," Mom snapped.

I jumped in my seat, straightening my back, and spilling water in my lap. "I'm sorry. I meant to say something else." I set down my glass, ignoring my wet PJs. "I'm going outside—just to the porch this time—I promise. I want to see if I hear that howl again."

"No way. You're staying right here. Forget about the dog," Mom said.

I sunk back into the couch with a grunt-like sigh, trying to dismiss my over-active imagination as my mind tried to make something of nothing.

"I know what it is," Mom said. "You're worried about starting a new school, aren't you?"

"No. Yeah, I guess," I said, not knowing which answer would lead to us going to bed sooner.

"It's your senior year. You have so much to look forward to. Homecoming. The prom."

"Come on, Mom. Not this conversation again." I kicked off my shoes and put my feet on the ottoman. "As if I'll ever get asked to a dance. Or have a boyfriend to even take me to one."

"You can't always predict the future by looking at the past, sweetie. The world, and what's in it, is constantly changing." She pulled me in for a side hug. "This is your year, Laura. I can feel it."

"Well, I can't," I grumbled.

"I have to admit," she sighed. "I had a great time at prom with your father. That's where we fell in love. Who knew twenty-two years later, he'd be exploring Alaska with his new girlfriend, and we'd be here in the middle of nowhere barely making the rent?"

She stared at the ceiling and took a big breath. "Jeffery Butternut. He was cute and had a fast car. I should have gone to the dance with him. But then again, you wouldn't be here if I had, right?" She held me tighter. "Sometimes you can't have a rainbow without a little rain. Or in your father's case, a big storm," she snickered. "If he hadn't been so pig-headed—"

"Mom, please." I crossed my arms.

"I know, I know," she said, letting me go but keeping one arm over my shoulder. "Your father just makes me so mad." She shook her head. "He promised to call you at least once a week, but how many times has he actually called you this month?"

"Once. But I'm not mad about it. He knows I don't have a signal half the time, and during the other half, he's at sea, so—"

"Don't give him an excuse, Laura! He could call on the house phone and crab-fishing season doesn't start until October."

"I know, but either way, it doesn't matter. He was hardly around when you guys were married, and he's hardly around now. I'm used to it." I leaned my head on her shoulder, and she brought her hand around to smooth my hair.

"Well, you shouldn't be because your father shouldn't be acting like this in the first place." She kissed the top of my head. "But don't think his behavior has anything to do with you." She shifted closer. "He might not show it as much as he should, but he does love you."

"I know," I sighed, nestling my head under her chin. "He just has an itch he can never scratch." That's how he'd explained things to me when he and Mom told me they were getting divorced.

My dad, the ultimate adrenaline junky, left home almost every weekend to mountain bike, camp, fish, rock climb, bungee jump, ski, or scuba dive with his buddies—anything to feed his need to explore and take chances with his life. Being so-called "guy trips," Mom and I were never invited, not even to stay at base camp while he was doing his thing with the guys.

Sometimes I'd sit in the garage watching him prepare for his big adventures, but he'd never let me help or answer my questions about his gear or his trips. Making fly-fishing lures was something I especially wanted to do. It looked fun, affixing colorful feathers to hooks and winding them with thread. But according to Dad, at ten, I was too young and would just make a mess out of things.

I'd fled the garage crying that day in hopes he'd come after me, apologizing and saying he'd changed his mind. But he didn't. I should have known better than to assume he would. That was the last time I hung out with him the night before one of his stupid trips, and the first time I realized he didn't care about me.

The second time happened last year when Mom and I ran into him at the grocery store. He was there, grabbing a few last-minute things before going on one of his camping trips, and he wasn't alone. A box of granola bars fell from Dad's hand when he saw us.

The woman next to him wore tight, khaki cargo pants, a white tank top, and hiking boots. She tightened her messy bun, rocked her hips to one side, and said something like, "Are you kidding? This is your wife and daughter?" She was thin, tanned, and toned, and her lips glistened with a smear of clear gloss that flashed when she laughed at us.

Mom and I were twins in our oversized sweatpants, T-shirts, white socks, and slides. It was a casual, no makeup day for both of us, not that Mom ever wore a lot of makeup in the first place. Leaving our cart in the aisle, she grabbed me by the arm, and we went straight to the parking lot and drove home.

"I'm not surprised," Mom sniffled as she pounded the steering wheel with an open hand. "Suspected it for a long time. I just wish you didn't have to see that." She smacked the steering wheel again. "Son of a bitch!"

Back then, Mom never cussed. Tears flooded her cheeks, and as I tried to hold my own, my throat tightened, and my bottom lip protruded and trembled. She filed for divorce the next day, and Dad never returned home from that camping trip. We could only assume he started staying with the woman we'd seen him with.

Since that day, Mom's communication with Dad has been strictly business concerning the divorce and child support, and mine has been filled with broken promises about him spending time with me. I did make one thing clear to him, though. I'd told him I wanted nothing to do with his girlfriend. Moving to Massachusetts has helped make that possible.

I stared at the kitchen window for the millionth time, wondering if what happened to me in the woods was real or in my imagination.

"This has been such an emotional change for both of us, especially for you," Mom said.

"I thought you loved this town." I gave her a squeeze.

"I do." She kissed the top of my head again. "I just wish you did, too."

"It's not that I don't like it. It's a cute town. The people are nice. It's just boring, and I don't know anyone here who's my age. There's no one to hang out with and nowhere fun to go."

"What about the coffee shop?"

"A bunch of old people hang out there," I whined.

"I saw some high school kids in there the other day. They looked like they were having fun."

"And how would I get there, Mom? It's not like you'll let me ride Molly into town."

"Honey, you know how I feel about that. If you fell off her and were unconscious or badly hurt and couldn't walk, no one would know."

"She's a sound horse, and I'm an experienced rider."

"Any horse can be unpredictable and throw a rider."

"So I'm stuck here all day without a car or the internet, and I can't even ride Molly around the yard when you're not home."

"I'm sorry, honey. But that's the way it is right now." She sighed, dropping her shoulders.

I slid my feet from the ottoman, and they fell with a clunk to the dingy area rug. The ottoman wobbled, and one of its pegged feet popped off and skated across the floor.

"This furniture sucks," I said.

"Be grateful the landlord agreed to rent this place to us fully furnished or we'd be sitting on the floor and using sleeping bags." A two-inch strip of gunky duct tape repaired a tear in the couch arm. She flattened one of its peeling corners with her fingertips. "It's not so bad."

"I know. I'm sorry, Mom." I leaned up against her again, resting my cheek on her upper arm.

We couldn't afford to take anything with us or buy new furniture when we got here. But it was hard for me to enjoy using things that were half broken and only put here out of pity.

Unbeknownst to Mom, before the divorce, Dad had refinanced the house twice, pulling money out both times to pay for his "boy trips" and buy his girlfriend a brand new, Barbie-pink Jeep. Because of this, my parents owed more money on their house than it was worth, so selling everything we had after they split was the only way to make up for it.

Dad wanted me to sell Molly, too, but Mom wouldn't let him.

"She's being completely unrooted because of you," she screamed, the night I ran to my room crying. "And now you want her to give up the one thing that will give her at least some sense of stability?"

I'd spent plenty of evenings with my ear pressed against the wall listening to their post-divorce fights. Stuff about how Dad cared more about his trampy girlfriend than his own daughter, and how she'd never forgiven him for wanting her to get an abortion instead of having me.

Mom broke down, sobbing until she choked and coughed, and Dad ended the argument by shouting, "The biggest mistake I ever made was marrying your dumb ass. I did it out of guilt instead of love and look where that got us." He slammed the door when he left.

I've never quite forgiven my dad for what he'd said to my mom that night, and to this day she still doesn't know I'd heard everything. Dad's behavior has made it hard for me to miss him. And when I do miss him, I think it is mainly from guilt, too. I mean, he's my dad. I'm supposed to miss him, right?

"I wish things were better, sweetheart," Mom said.

"Someday, they will be. Did you talk to any of your friends back home today?"

"I tried, but like always, my calls drop after thirty seconds and most of my text messages aren't delivered," I huffed. "But it doesn't matter anyway. Mariana and Deb are spending twenty-four seven with their new boyfriends. They don't have time for me anymore, anyway."

"I'm sorry, babe. That's what happens. But you'll make a lot of new friends soon." She gave me a soft jab in the ribs with her elbow. "And maybe even meet a nice boy, too."

"Yeah, maybe." I stopped myself from rolling my eyes.

"Look, you have nothing to worry about when it comes to school. You're a good student. You're beautiful, and you have an amazing personality. You won't have any problem fitting in. I know it."

"Thanks, Mom," I said. We hugged, and I gave her an extra squeeze.

A deep hum rattled through the wall behind us. The skin on the back of my neck prickled. My shoulders shook. Wood creaked, followed by a muffled pop and dull scrape. I broke away from my mom's hold, listening for more.

"What was that?" I asked, eyeing the kitchen window. Mom hadn't even flinched.

"Honey, it's just the wind hitting this old, rickety house. It's cooling off outside. As the temperature changes, wood contracts and expands. You know that."

I wiped my damp forehead. "It doesn't feel any cooler to me. Are you sure? Maybe we should check." I pushed up from the couch.

"There's no reason to. This house has been making those same noises since the first day we moved in. Besides, a dog, or even a wolf, wouldn't make that kind of sound."

I dropped my shoulders and slouched back into the couch

cushions. She was right, and a boy or a ghost wouldn't make that kind of noise either.

"So is there anything else you aren't telling me?" Mom asked. She yawned again, patting her hand over her mouth.

"Nope, but there's still stuff you're not telling me."

"Like what?" She rubbed her eyes.

"Like you. And Jeffrey Butternut. And his fast car?" I teased. "But you don't have to tell me more about it tonight."

"Good thing. Cuz you wouldn't be able to sleep if I did." She winked, and we both laughed. "I guess we're doing okay, right sweetheart?" She slapped her hand on my thigh.

"We're doing great, Mom."

We walked down the hall, fanning our sweaty faces with our hands. When we were halfway to our rooms, I stopped mid-step and listened, cupping my hand around my ear.

"Now what?" Mom asked. "Still stuck on that stray dog?"

"Um, nothing." Although I could have sworn I'd heard another howl, a distant bark, echoing.

The muscles in my neck and shoulders tightened, and the voice calling my name consumed my imagination, its delicate, muted tone resonating through my mind.

I closed my bedroom door and rushed to the window. The moon glowed just enough for me to make out the blackish-blue silhouette of the tree line. I stared at the woods, my elbows perched on the sill, hoping to hear or see something to prove the voice and the wolf were real.

Something moved, a dark blotch of black darting from one tree to another. Or was it? I blinked, my eyes watering as I held back a yawn. Resting my forehead on the cool glass, I strained to see more. Shadows shifted as the wind rose, and spindly clouds streaked across the moon, playing tricks with my eyes. I finally gave up and went to bed.

# CHAPTER 2

The forest looked different in the morning, its grand trunks and canopy of green exuding a benign aura and innocence opposite from the night before. But I had a can of pepper spray with me, nonetheless. I kept it clipped to my keychain.

I fed Molly and sat on the porch with a cup of green tea. It was muggy outside but not yet hot enough to break a sweat. Mom was at work.

A gentle breeze shook the treetops. I set my tea on the empty cable spool we used as a table and got up from my chair, shoving the pepper spray in my back pocket of my shorts. Shading my eyes against the sun's glare, I peered more intently, concentrating on the spaces between the distant trees.

Stepping down from the porch, I took deep breaths, filling my lungs with the warm, woodsy air. Mist rose from the thin patch of dead lawn below our house. I cut through it, the tranquility of the forest beckoning me to search for any signs that the boy or the wolf existed.

I stopped at the forest rim where I thought I saw the

unusual shadow the night before. I yanked the pepper spray from my back pocket.

Miles and miles of trees lay ahead, plumed with silvery leaves and dusty bark, their limbs reaching up into the morning sky while their roots bulged like arthritic toes at the base of their trunks. Sheets of sunlight sliced through the clouds, projecting ghostly images upon the forest floor, making everything magical and surreal like being in a dream.

Taking a step forward, I broke through the forest rim, twigs cracking beneath my feet. A limb bounced, a bird shot from a cluster of leaves, and I jumped. My heartbeat surging, I shuffled backward, taking aim with my pepper spray just in case. But the bird flew upward without a tweet or attack and disappeared.

I lowered my arm and exhaled, trying to calm my nerves. A series of deep breaths did little to settle the pounding in my chest, but I moved on, my index finger poised on the spray head.

The daylight dimmed, and the air grew cooler as I passed through the first row of trees. Their numbers increased, obstructing the sun. Creeping forward, I watched the shadows for movement. I continued, my pace steady, and my want for wonder at its peak. Every sound, the snap of twigs and the rustle of leaves, were magnified, my senses heightened.

As I entered the small clearing I'd found the day before, the trees thinned in number and size. Young saplings dominated the open land. Sunlight skipped across my shoulders, and my body finally relaxed, a veil of calm settling into my being.

Two boulders lay ahead, one slightly bigger than the other, but both as flat as a park bench and of the same height. I dusted off the smoothest section of the bigger one and sat down, taking in the soft, earthy scent of damp, decomposing leaves.

The wind died and the woods silenced, the play of shadows

the only movement as the clouds shifted above me. With my ears and eyes tuned for wolf noises, bird mischief, blurs, and the call of my name, I took a big breath and waited, my pepper spray at the ready.

A black beetle the size of my thumb nail rounded the top of my boulder and marched toward me, its tiny legs clambering. I blocked its path with my hand, nudging my nail under its tiny legs until it clung to my index finger. Keeping the bug upright while I moved, I set it on the ground and watched it crawl into the forest mulch.

"There you go, little guy," I said as it disappeared. "Don't worry. I won't step on—"

A keen, mysterious awareness swept through my core, and the sound of breathing, something heavy and rhythmic, filled the air next to me. A chill cut across my shoulder blades, and I tensed, holding my breath. As I turned, a throaty growl pricked the dry air.

A gray wolf stood in front of me, it ears clamped to its head. The hair down the center of its back stood on end. Pushing up from the boulder slowly, I readied my legs to run if it attacked, shifting my weight to my feet. As I moved, gripping the sides of the boulder with my fingers, the can of pepper spray slipped from my hand, landing at the wolf's feet. I reached for the can but missed as the wolf stepped closer. I lowered back to the rock.

"Hello, there," I said as coolly as I could, my words soft and soothing. Keeping my eyes from his, I smiled without showing my teeth.

The wolf sat, bringing it ears forward. I saw it was a male. He panted, his pink tongue hanging from its mouth, and his tail wagged, disturbing the dirt.

"Good boy. Good boy," I said.

He stretched his neck toward me, and I leaned back, keeping my face far from his. With his nose, he nudged my hand, and I made a fist and held it up for him to smell.

"Nice wolf. Nice wolf," I said, relaxing my jaw and continuing to speak in the same mild tone.

He sniffed my knuckles, licked the underside of my wrist and forearm, and tucked the top of his head under my closed hand. I uncurled my fingers and gave him a gentle pat.

"Good boy," I said again.

His fur gleamed in the sunshine, a combination of browns, grays, and white, running thickest around his neck and along his back while thinning down his legs. It was soft, not matted, and clean, leaving my palm dry, not oily or dirty, something I wouldn't expect from a wild animal. I ran my fingers around his neck and found nothing. He stood and came closer, rubbing his body against my legs.

"I knew there was a wolf out here," I told him as I stroked his side with my fingertips. "It was you. So, if you're real, then maybe a boy who said my name is real, too."

He barked, a low whine, and stared into a thick band of trees at the far side of the clearing. A flash of gray caught my eyes, something featureless but more than just a blur this time. It was shadow-like but solid and three-dimensional. As it moved, I distinctly saw the silhouette of a tall, lean body.

I rose from the boulder and bent at the waist, snatching up my can of pepper spray. The figure skirted behind a tree, its arms swinging delicately at its sides. What I had seen was definitely not in my imagination. It was a real boy who'd been moving so quickly within the shadows that he'd been hard to see clearly.

"Who are you? What do you want?" I asked, sliding my finger to the top of the spray can nozzle.

The wolf dashed from the clearing toward the spot where the boy disappeared, the animal's movements effortless and graceful.

I followed, leaving the bright comfort of the clearing, my skin prickling as I entered the shade. The open sky shrunk as the forest grew dense and the canopy of leaves thickened. A squirrel scampered across my path, and a pair of birds burst from the foliage ahead, shooting upward to another limb. My heart beat wildly, and I took small breaths to quell my unease and contain my nervous excitement.

"How do you know my name?" I asked.

The figure revealed himself, facing me, the silhouette of the wolf at his side, their features too shadowed for me to see them clearly.

"Your wolf is beautiful," I said, daring to take another step forward.

The figure turned, and in one swift movement, vanished into a thicket of skinny trees, the wolf following.

"Wait! Come back. Please? I want to meet you," I said sprinting forward, pushing the saplings aside and entering another small clearing.

I stopped to catch my breath, my pulse pounding. One tree looked like the next. I was afraid I wouldn't be able to find my way home if I went any farther.

"Hello!" I shouted. "Are you still there?"

I walked to the next cluster of trees and waited, my eyes and ears ready for any movement or sound.

"Hello," I said again, but the woods remained quiet, holding its mystery. I waited a few more minutes and finally turned toward home.

An engine puttered. Tires rolled to a stop. The mailbox rattled open with the repeated turning of a key. The car resumed its trek, tires crunching upon the gravel driveway. A car door opened and closed, and the front steps clicked with my mother's footsteps.

"I'm coming, Mom!" I shouted, running to the door and opening it. She entered, a bag in each arm.

"Today was my boss's birthday," she said. "Turns out he believes in giving instead of getting. Handed out fifty-dollar gift cards to Carter's."

Carter's was the only grocery store in town. "Here, let me take those." I set the bags on the kitchen table.

"I checked the mail. Nothing important. Just junk." She pulled a handful of envelopes from her purse and tossed them on the kitchen counter next to the grocery bags.

"No bills. That's good," I said. "What's wrong with the mailbox? The lock broken?"

"Yeah, it's old. It started acting up yesterday. Takes a few wiggles and a couple of turns to open it now." She put a carton of orange juice and a half dozen yogurts in the fridge. "Did you try to get the mail today?"

"No. Why?"

"Because you knew the lock was acting up?"

"I heard you fumbling with it."

"From all the way down the road?"

"Yeah, it was pretty loud." I pulled a box of granola bars from one of the bags. They were my favorite. "Thanks Mom. I love these."

"Don't eat 'em yet. They're for your lunches." She tossed a package of hotdogs into the meat keeper. "Must be your young ears. I ruined mine listening to the radio too loudly in the car when I was a teenager. Apparently, you haven't destroyed yours yet. But you will if you keep wearing those thingamajigs all day long."

"They're called earbuds. And I lost mine during the move, remember?" I put a bag of apples in the crisper.

"Your ears deserve the break." She folded an empty grocery bag and shoved it in the space between the refrigerator and the broom closet. I unpacked two containers of fresh pasta.

"Don't put those away," she said. "We're making spaghetti. Uncle Dean's coming over for dinner. He'll be here in less than an hour."

I set the boxes next to the stove.

"So," Mom said. "How was your day? And don't say boring. You say that every day." She leaned against the counter below the flickering florescent light. The shadows under her tired eyes deepened.

"I say it every day because it is." I didn't dare tell her I broke her rule about entering the woods, and I certainly wasn't going to tell her what I saw.

"When I get paid next week, I'll buy an outdoor antenna for the TV. Uncle Dean said we might be able to pick up a few more local stations with it than we can with our indoor, digital one. He even offered to install it for us."

"I doubt it will do any good," I moaned.

"Don't blame me for our TV situation." She drew her hands to her hips. "If your dad paid his child support like he's supposed to, we could afford satellite."

"Okay, I know. I'm sorry. Enough about Dad." I closed the pantry door—hard.

"I know I shouldn't keep bringing him up," she added, "but it's true. What I need, until he gets his head out of his ass, is a raise."

Mom worked at the local mom-and-pop sporting goods

store, Rutner Sports. The thirty-minute commute to and from the town made her fifteen-dollar-an-hour job hardly seem worth it, but with her lack of a college degree, it was the only employment she could find that paid more than minimum wage.

I'd wanted to get a summer job to help out financially, but since we'd arrived here halfway through the season with only a few weeks left before school started, all the short-term jobs were taken. She wouldn't allow me to work during the school year. With only one car between us, it would have been difficult anyway.

"You should ask for one. You deserve it."

"If your father," she continued, "gave a rat's ass about how we're doing out here, then—"

I emptied the last grocery bag, bringing a canister of coffee to the counter with a bang. "Mom! Please."

"Okay. Okay. I'll stop." She took a long breath and adjusted her glasses. "So, besides being bored, what else did you do today?"

"Um, besides being bored? Let me think." I tapped the side of my head and imagined the crisp, shadowy outlines of the boy and the wolf. "I finished my book, took a nap, and read a mag—"

A faint howl came from outside, so faint, I could barely hear it.

My heartbeat sounded in my ears. I dashed to the kitchen window and looked outside. The dead, empty lawn glowed silver with the wash of evening moonlight. I pressed my forehead against the glass, squinting to stretch my vision, my pulse rising, but there was no sign of the wolf or the boy.

Mom parted the curtain next to me and held her hand up to block the kitchen light. "What are you looking at?" she asked.

"Nothing," I said.

She let go of the curtain and gave me a playful slap on the rear end with her dish towel. "I told you there aren't any wolves around here," she teased and walked to the kitchen counter.

"I know," I said.

The howl came again, a little louder this time. Maybe the boy and the wolf were on the road. I glanced behind me. Mom was at the sink washing her hands.

"Can I borrow the car? I need to go to the library. I don't have a book to read for tomorrow," I said in one breath while stepping away from the window.

"Tonight? It's thirty minutes from here."

"It doesn't close until eight. I have plenty of time. Please, Mom. Plus, I think my book's overdue." It wasn't. I'd only had it for a week.

"I know money's tight, but we can afford a ten-cent-a-day fine. Besides you know I don't like you driving all alone on these country roads at night. What if the car breaks down?"

"You just had the car fixed."

"A new battery and spark plugs. But that didn't stop the funny noise the transmission's been making."

"Then I'll call you, and I'll keep calling until the call goes through."

"And how I am I supposed to come get you if you have the car?" She pulled a saucepan from the cabinet and set it on the stove.

"Mom, please. Nothing's going to happen. I'll be fine."

"No, Laura. You'll just have to wait until the weekend. Besides, what about Uncle Dean? He'll be here any minute."

I groaned. I didn't mean to, but it happened.

"Laura, come on. I thought you liked your uncle. He's done a lot for you. Molly wouldn't have a stall if it wasn't for him."

"I know. I'm sorry. I love Uncle Dean. I just want a new book to read, that's all."

"You can go to the library on Saturday. I promise."

"That's three days from now."

"So, it'll cost me thirty cents. We can spare thirty cents." She pulled a jar of spaghetti sauce from the cabinet. "Or, if you want, I can put it in the drop slot tomorrow on my way to work."

"It's totally out of your way to go to that end of the town. And that won't get me a book for tomorrow. Please, Mom. Just let me take the car. Uncle Dean won't mind if I show up late for dinner."

"No. You'll just have to wait until Saturday," she said. A sly smile spread across her face. "Or maybe sooner if you're lucky."

"What do you mean?" I asked.

"Well." Her smiled got bigger. "I was going to wait for Dean to tell you, but you know how bad I am with surprises." She clasped her hands.

"What?" I asked.

She lifted one eyebrow and put her hands on her hips. "Your Uncle Dean called me during my lunch break. His neighbor, Phyllis, the librarian, has an old car she wants to sell, and Uncle Dean said that if you like it, he'll buy it for you."

"What? Really? That's great!" I jumped in place. "Do you know what kind of car it is?" Not that I cared. Anything with an engine and four wheels was fine at this point.

"He told me, but I don't remember. When he's here, I'm sure he'll tell you all about it. Now," she said, taking a breath, "I don't like the fact that it's old, but Dean said it has low miles for its age, and it's in really good condition. Phyllis is getting it ready to sell. She said it will be done tomorrow afternoon, so we'll take a look at it when I get home from work."

"Thanks, Mom," I said and gave her a big hug.

"You're welcome, sweetie." She slid a bag of lettuce toward me. "Make the salad. And try to act surprised when your uncle tells you about the car."

There was a heavy knock at the door as my mom poured the sauce into the pan. I opened it to find Uncle Dean ready to give the door another rap.

"Hi, Uncle Dean," I said.

"Howdy, little lady. How's that corral and stable holding up?"

"They're prefect. Thanks again for building them for me." I gave him a hug, and he handed me a plate of homemade cookies. "Did you make these?"

My uncle was not the kind of man I could picture in the kitchen making cookies, even if they came from a tube. He was short and husky, and working in the sun for so many years had made him look older than my mom, even though he was younger than her by four years.

"Oh, no, not me. Phyllis, the lady who lives next door to me, made them." He blushed.

"Uncle Dean, do you have a girlfriend?" I gave him a poke on the upper arm and set the cookies on the counter.

"Nope. I'm done with women."

"Sure you are, Dean." My mother laughed from the kitchen, her wooden spoon knocking against the side of a saucepan.

"She's just a nice lady, that's all," he said.

Mom appeared in the kitchen doorway holding the spoon. "That's all, huh."

"Yes, Margie, that's all. She knows I like to read, so she brings me books, and sometimes cookies. She works at the library."

My mom cracked a smile and nodded toward me. "There you go, Laura. If you're so worried about paying a fine, give

Uncle Dean your overdue book. He can give it to his friend." Mom made quotes in the air with her fingers when she said "friend." "And she can turn it in for you tomorrow." She pointed her finger at her brother. "That will give you an excuse to see this nice lady again tonight."

Uncle Dean chuckled. "Yeah, I can do that for you, Laura."

"Okay, that would be great. Thanks," I said. "She does sound like a really nice lady."

Uncle Dean shook his head. "Your mom told you, didn't she?"

Mom and I exchanged glances.

"You were never one for keepin' a secret, Marg. I had a feeling you'd tell her before I had a chance to," Dean continued.

Mom lifted her shoulders in agreement, and he chuckled.

"So what kind of car is it?" I asked.

"A 1970 Dodge Challenger RT."

"I've never heard of it."

"I figured that'd be the case. It's a classic. Built before you were a twinkle in your momma's eye." He winked. "But that's all I'm gonna tell you about it. Any description I have couldn't give it justice. You're just gonna have to see it for yourself tomorrow night."

"Thank you so much! I can't wait!" I gave him another hug.

Uncle Dean took a seat at the dining room table while I prepared the salad and ran fresh cloves of garlic across the top of crusty bread. "Do you ladies need any help?" he asked.

My mom was quick to answer. "No, Dean. We're just fine. All we need is your company." Steam from the boiling pot of vermicelli fogged up her glasses.

"Well, it sure is nice having you two here in town with me. I missed my big sister, and now I'll get to see her all the time and watch my lovely niece graduate from high school." He winked at me. "Just remember that any young man you decide to date has to be approved by me first. I know these local boys, and some of them aren't worth knowing."

I pulled a drawer open, looking for salad tongs. "Uncle Dean, don't you dare ever do anything to embarrass me, especially when it comes to boys." Not that there'd ever be any boys for him to embarrass me with.

"I'm not going to let anyone take advantage of my niece. A guy might look nice and act sweet and innocent, but in reality, he's only after one thing."

My mother dropped the wooden spoon back into the simmering sauce. "Dean!"

"Well, it's true. Anything you want to know about boys, Laura, I can tell you. Come to me for advice, and I'll explain what they're really all about." He looped a finger through the right strap of his overalls.

I flashed my mom a please-change-the-subject look, my eyes wide and lips pursed.

"You know, Dean," she said, "Laura swears she heard a wolf howl last night."

Uncle Dean leaned back in his seat, stretching his legs under the table. "There haven't been wolves around here in over a hundred years. If there was a wolf, or even a hybrid roaming about, I'd know about it. This town's too small, and I've lived here too long not to know everything that goes on."

True. If anyone knew the history of this place, he did. I put the garlic bread in the oven and took a seat across from my uncle.

"What about an animal sanctuary? You know, the kind of place that takes in wild animals that people tried to keep as pets." Maybe the boy worked there.

"Nope, I'd know about that, too."

"What about the people living in the forest? Maybe they own wolves."

"Much of those woods are state owned. There shouldn't be anyone living in them."

"Have you seen people coming out of the woods?" Mom asked. "Because if you have, I'll call the police right now. People camping illegally are probably no-gooders, and I certainly don't want any no-gooders near our home." She set three plates on the table.

"No, I haven't seen anyone," I said. "I just thought if there's a wolf out there, it was probably somebody's pet."

"Your great, great, great grandfather raised his family in Appalachia. Created his own town up there. Lived off the fat of the land. For years, outsiders didn't even know their little mecca existed," Uncle Dean said. "But that was a long time ago. These days a family couldn't get away with living anywhere around here without being discovered."

"So you don't know anyone in this town who owns one?"

My uncle tucked a napkin into his shirt collar and laughed. "Nope. Haven't seen any. Haven't heard any." He leaned across the table, interlocking his fingers and smiling. "What you heard was an old hound dog."

My detective work ended there when it came to Uncle Dean. I'd have to find out more about the boy and his wolf on my own. "Yeah, I guess you're right," I said.

"But like I told you before, some people think these woods are haunted. That the trees play tricks on your eyes and spring up from out of nowhere." Uncle Dean spoke slowly, his eyes wide and gleaming. "Maybe they play tricks on ears, too." He chuckled.

My mother crossed her arms. "Dean, what are you trying to do, scare her again with those silly folktales? She's home all alone during the day. And this whole wolf thing has made her all jumpy."

"I'm sorry. I don't mean to scare you, Laura."

"Don't worry. I'm not scared. I like hearing about supernatural stuff."

I twisted in my chair to look out the kitchen window. The moon was full, casting its silvery glow, turning the trees gray as their leaves shivered in a wash of wind.

"Then you've moved to the right place. At least once a year, some unlucky devil ignores the town's talk and trapes into that packed acreage of trees right over there and gets lost." He thumbed toward the window. "And aren't found for days. Claim they was tormented by ghosts and mean birds."

I sucked in a quick breath, trying to hold in an obvious gasp. The mean birds were totally real, although I figured they were just protecting their territory or something. The boy didn't look like a ghost—not that I knew what a real ghost looked like. But he was solid. I couldn't see through him, and I doubted a real wolf would be hanging out with a ghost. But still . . .

"Tell me more about these ghosts," I asked, turning to face my uncle.

"Well, people claim that they've seen figures deep within the woods; dark figures with featureless faces. One minute they're there, and the next minute they're gone. And if you try to follow one, you lose your sense of direction and get lost. Apparently, this has been going on for hundreds of years."

"Have you ever seen one of these figures?" I asked.

"No, not me." He chuckled.

"And I haven't either," Mom said from over her shoulder. She held the pot of pasta over the sink and poured the noodles into a strainer. "I don't believe in ghosts and neither should you."

She bustled to the window and drew the curtains closed. A

slender beam of moonlight snuck between the cloth panels, illuminating the table. Uncle Dean folded his arms, kicking back in his seat, withdrawing his face from the light.

"Do you believe it, Uncle Dean?" I asked him. "Just because you haven't seen one doesn't mean they aren't real."

"Nope." He made monster hands, curling his fingers like claws and pawing at the air. "But I do believe in werewolves and vampires!" He tried to howl, but his voice cracked, and he coughed into his hand.

"Is that what you heard, Laura?" my mom asked. "Maybe your uncle's been prowling around the neighborhood trying to keep the legends alive." She threw a noodle at him, and we all laughed.

"I'm just kidding, Margie. I don't believe in anything I haven't seen for myself. We won't talk about ghosts anymore." He plucked the sticky noodle from his dingy T-shirt and chucked it into the sink. "Let's talk about your senior year, Laura. You must be excited about it."

"I'm excited about graduating," I said.

"What about after graduation? What are your plans?"

"I'm not sure," I said.

"Well, you don't have a lot of time to make a decision. Phyllis just posted information about college applications on a bulletin board in the library. They're due in a few months."

"I keep telling her that, Dean," Mom said. She set a basket of garlic bread in the center of the table.

I picked up a slice and took a bite. "I might apply to UNM," I said through a chew.

Mom brushed a crumb from the table. "You know we can't afford that even if you did get some kind of partial scholarship."

"Yeah, I know. I really don't know what I want to do." I sighed and set my garlic bread on the edge of my plate. "But sometimes when I really think about it, I get this weird feeling inside that . . . never mind. It's stupid."

"No. Tell us," Uncle Dean urged. "Please."

I looked down and stared at my milky reflection in my plate. My stomach stirred in a good way, and I smiled.

"I just get this weird feeling inside. And there's also this little voice in my head that keeps telling me there's something else out there for me to do, something bigger than cracking open a text book. Something that will make a difference, something with a real purpose."

"You have a calling, Laura. That's what that little voice is." Uncle Dean folded his hands on the table. "You just need to find out what that calling is. What about joining the military or the Peace Corps? There's a purpose for you."

"Don't give her any ideas. That could put her in danger and on the other side of the planet, Dean," Mom said. She smacked his shoulder with a kitchen towel. "The local junior college is your calling, honey. That's what we can afford."

"Yeah, that's probably what I'll end up doing," I said even though I knew going to a JC, or any college for that matter, would be the total epitome of unfulfilling for me.

While we ate, Uncle Dean told a few jokes I'd already heard, and soon my mom and I were hugging him goodbye. He left with my library book under his arm, telling me how excited he was to show me the Challenger tomorrow evening.

That night, I lay in bed, the sheet pulled to my chin, listening to the tick of my ceiling fan and thinking about the mysterious boy in the woods. It wasn't like the boy was trying to scare me on purpose. At least I didn't think so. It was just like he didn't want to be seen yet, or something like that. I mean, if his goal was to terrorize me, he would have of done a lot more than call my name and hide behind trees.

If he was around my age, like I suspected, there was no way

he was the so-called ghost that's been scaring people over the last hundred years. And I still didn't know where the wolf came from or why the birds sometimes attacked people, like they did me.

"Who are you," I whispered toward the window.

I had to find out. Maybe having my own car would make that easier. The building excitement when it came to both made it hard to sleep.

# CHAPTER 3

The grass was swampy from last night's rain. The musky, earthy scent of damp soil wafted up with my footsteps, and the sick, sweet smell of wet, rotting leaves drifted on the breeze as if suspended from invisible balloons. Gnats rose from the grass, circling my ankles as I entered the barn.

Molly whinnied as I approached her stall with her bridle slung on my shoulder. I'd already broken one rule by going into the forest, twice. I might as well break another. With Molly, I could cover more ground and make a quicker escape if I had to.

"Good girl," I told her as I slipped the bridle over her ears and eased the bit into her mouth. I positioned the pad and saddle on her back, wrapped and tightened the cinch strap, and secured the back cinch. Playing it safe, and not knowing how long I'd be gone, I clipped my pepper spray key chain to the saddle horn and strapped my bag of supplies across the back of the saddle.

At the front of the house, I mounted her slowly, keeping my eyes focused on the forest. She was sound and solid, calm but eager, without a shift or bobble of weight from hoof to hoof as I rode her across the driveway to face the trees.

The woods were warm and welcoming, as harmless as the glow of summer as the sun accentuated the golden foliage of beech trees. But when we reached the end of the driveway, Molly hesitated. She stopped and shook her head, yanking at the reins as she shuffled from one side and then the other.

"It's okay, girl, come on." I gave her sides a tap with my heels. She took a few steps and stopped again. Maybe it was a sign. Maybe something bad would happen, I thought, as I took my uncle's silly superstition and turned it into something real. No, I wasn't going to talk myself out of this.

"Good girl. It's okay. Come on." With a click of my tongue and anther kick, Molly walked forward, and we passed through the first fringe of trees.

Molly didn't spook easily, and she was used to dogs. At our old house in Albuquerque, the neighbor's dogs were constantly in our yard and Molly's corral. She pretty much ignored them. I didn't think a wolf would be any different. I could only hope we wouldn't run into a flock of over-protective birds.

I reached down and stroked the left side of her neck. She was a beautiful animal, and at times I regretted keeping her given name when I'd purchased her. Molly was a cute name, a pony's name, not the name of a black, fifteen-hand quarter horse.

"Good girl. Let's wait here for a bit," I said when we reached the boulder where I'd encountered the wolf and saw the dark figure of a boy. The only sound was Molly's hooves crushing the forest floor as I brought her to a stop.

"Hello, is anyone here?" I shouted. The sun broke through the treetops and shadows danced across the forest floor. "Hello!" I said again through cupped hands, my voice breaking as I strained to speak louder. My words came back as an echo, dying against the silvery tree trunks.

"Let's keep going, Molly," I said, prodding her deeper into the woods.

The light dimmed as the leafy canopy thickened. Something about this part of the forest was different. A moist coolness covered the ground like a thick, weighted blanket. The trees were dense, concentrated in clusters, with larger trees between them. A chill encompassed the back of my neck, spreading until my upper body shuddered. I tightened my grip on the reins.

A bird's squawk pierced the air, followed by the flapping of wings. I flinched, shielding my face with my hands and looking toward the sky. A ray of sunlight split through the leaves. Blinded, I turned my head. Molly increased her speed, side-stepping.

"Damn it. Not again," I mumbled to myself while working the reins. "Whoa, girl."

Like a recording on a continuous loop, the chirping increased, piercing my ears with the fervor of their chaotic song. A row of birds took flight from a low-lying limb, and the forest filled with twisted bird whistles and wicked peeps.

Molly galloped forward, the birds at our backs. Holding the reins with one hand, I protected my head and face with my other. Weaving through the trees, she cleared fallen tree limbs and large rocks. And as she changed directions, their torturous ballad of evil continued as they dove, pecking my arm and hands.

Molly slowed and reared, the song-maker's banter driving her mad. I grabbed the saddle horn, digging the heels of my boots in the stirrups. Molly lowered her front hooves and jerked her head, shuffling backward. The birds scattered, peppering the gray sky.

"Steady, girl. It's okay. They're gone," I said, pulling the reins to steer her in the opposite direction, but the more I pulled, the more she fought the force with her neck, throwing her head and side stepping.

"Molly!" I tightened my grip as she refused my commands.

Skirting left and right, she rose onto her back legs, kicking as her front hooves lifted from the forest floor. Lowering her head, she rotated and bucked. The saddle bag flew from her back.

I grabbed the saddle horn, squeezing my legs hard against her sides, trying to hold on. But she was too fast, too strong. She burst forward, turning sharply to the left and stopped. I shifted from the saddle, the reins and the saddle horn slipping from my hands, and fell to the ground.

At first, I couldn't breathe. Gulping for air, I peered past my chin to a stomach refusing to contract. A second later, the air released from my lungs, and I took a big breath, inhaling deeply.

Pain rose from the base of my spine. Moving my arms and legs slowly, I moved onto my side. Molly was far in the distance, darting between trees. I lay steady for several more minutes, catching my breath and watching a cloud of dust and leaf debris settle to the ground as she disappeared.

"No! Molly! Come back!" I cried. Warm tears rolled down the side of my face to my ear. I wiped them away and held the next set at bay.

My shoulders hurt, hands stung, and my head spun. I blinked until the landscape stopped spinning, and twisted, rising onto my palms to sit with bent legs, wondering which way was home. My bag of supplies lay crumbled by my feet.

A horse's sense of smell can not only lead them to water, it can also lead them home—at least that's what I'd been told. My best bet was to start walking in the direction Molly had run.

Mom wouldn't be home until after five, so I had plenty of time to find my way back.

I pushed up with my raw, burning palms and stood, my legs unsteady. Hooking my bag with one finger, I slung it over my shoulder and walked. As I scaled the uneven earth, pain burst from my left hip to my thigh, and my lower back ached. But I trucked forward, telling myself Molly had made it home safely, and I'd find her standing outside the barn when I got home.

When I'd walked longer than I thought it would take to reach the clearing with two boulders, I stopped to survey my surroundings. I was surrounded by a thick, unrecognizable cluster of trees. The clearing should have been just ahead, but it wasn't.

My heart pounded in my chest, my confidence to get home before Mom dwindling. A sense of panic pushed through my being, and I sniffled and blinked, trying to hold back tears while hopelessly trying to convince myself that I wasn't totally disoriented and had no idea in which direction to go.

"Maybe it was this way." I turned left. "No, it was this way—I think," I said, turning back to the right.

Nothing looked familiar. I was utterly and completely lost. I sunk to my knees and screamed. "Molly! Where are you, girl?" Dead silence was the only response.

I had two options—stay put and wait to be found or try finding my way home and risk becoming even more lost than I already was. I wished I'd had my pepper spray, but it was with Molly, attached to her saddle. I could only hope I didn't run into any no-gooders like my mom had talked about.

Waiting to be found meant being put on restriction, since Mom would find out I'd broken her rules. She'd also be incredibly disappointed in me for doing so. Trying to find my way home gave me about seven hours to become unlost, and in the process, I might find the boy and the wolf. I went with option two.

Of course my cell phone didn't have any reception, but I tried using it like a homing device. Taking my best guess at which way was home, I picked a direction and walked, hoping to find a signal. If I did, I'd head in the direction where it was strongest. That would at least lead me toward civilization. From there, I'd figure out how to make it back to my house before Mom.

My shoulder and left side were killing me. Holding my phone with my head down while looking at the screen only made it worse. No signal. I turned and walked another twenty minutes. No signal. I turned and walked for thirty minutes more. Still no signal. The pain in my hip doubled, causing me to limp.

I stopped to take another good look around and dug through my bag for my water bottle. I unscrewed the cap and took a sip. The trees, the foliage, a birch branch drooping to the ground like a broken arm—everything looked the same. Maybe it was the same. Had I been walking in circles this whole time? Is this what my uncle meant when he'd said the forest was unpredictable?

I kicked a birch branch with the toe of my good leg. The branch cracked from the tree and dropped. Three leafless twigs poked through the peeling bark at its center. I could remember this unique branch and this tree, but I couldn't remember them all. I had to do something to make them memorable.

Digging through the fallen leaves at my feet, I found a sharp rock. Using the corner of my fingernail, I peeled a layer of bark from the next tree, creating a smooth, eye-level patch of beige trunk, and with the rock's point, scrapped a large "X" into it. My plan was to do the same on every tenth tree I passed.

With each "X" I carved, I studied my surroundings and

tried to predict whether I was traveling east or west—not that I exactly knew which direction lead toward home. Remembering the sun always set above the tree line past my driveway, I finally decided I needed to go east.

The canopy above thinned just enough for me to catch a glimpse of the sun, but it was almost noon. The sun had already risen, and it wasn't ready to drop, so I couldn't figure it out that way. But even if I could have, wandering east wouldn't necessarily mean I'd end up at my house. It just meant I'd be getting kind of close.

The dead signal on my phone hadn't changed, but I held it up, moving it up and down and back and forth. Nothing! With stiff legs and hurting hip and shoulder, I moved on, munching on a granola bar and carving the next X. Rotating my bum shoulder helped, but my side continued to twinge with each step.

Heat beat through the treetops with the afternoon sun, and the welcomed coolness rising from the forest floor was replaced with a cushion of almost intolerable humidity. Sweat ran down the sides of my face, between by breasts, and down the center of my back. My forehead was hot and wet. The more I walked, the more my side hurt, and I wondered how long I could keep going without the pain becoming unbearable.

Using the rock like a pointer, I continued to count, ready to brand the tenth tree. ". . . six, seven, eight, nine, ten."

I lowered my arm. My bottom lip quivered. An "X", oxidized brown by the air and heat, already marked the tenth tree. But I'd walked in a straight line! Or at least I'd thought I had! I'd been walking in circles this whole time!

Chucking the rock as hard as I could, I whipped it Frisbee-like and dropped to my rear. The foreboding X stared back at me, mocking my ignorance and vulnerability. Pressure built behind my eyes, and I swallowed and squeezed them shut to stop my tears.

I wasn't worried about not being found and dying out here all alone. A search party would find me if it came down to that. I was more concerned about my mother. I imagined the look on her face, her lips parted and face growing pale when she discovered I wasn't home tonight.

She'd panic, calling first my Uncle Dean and then the police. I couldn't put her through that kind of worry and heartache because I was determined to find a mysterious boy. And I certainly couldn't tell her the reasons why I'd entered the woods in the first place. She'd never leave me home alone again if she thought there was a strange guy and a real wolf lurking near our house, especially when the guy knew my name.

I checked my phone again for the umpteenth time. Of course, there wasn't a signal. Tears threatened as I held my face in my hands and forced myself to take long, deep breaths and exhale them slowly. The swish of my pulse sounded in my ears.

A twig snapped. Something rough, warm, and wet hit the side of my face. My heart leaped into my throat, and I gasped, batting a furry something away with my hands while pushing off with my feet to scoot away from it.

"Oh, thank god! It's just you," I said, bringing my hand against my chest.

The grey wolf stood next to me, his tongue dangling to give another lick. He made another pass, and I turned my head and closed my eyes; when I opened them, the wolf was gone.

"Hey, where did you go? Come here, boy," I said, clapping my hands. He was nowhere in sight, but it was a good sign. I'd previously seen the wolf when I was close to home. I could only speculate I was near my house now.

Rolling onto my knees, I got up on one foot to stand. A

deep pain tugged at my hip, lingering, and I lowered back to the ground to stretch it out and try again.

The leaves rustled, and the forest floor whispered with soft-soled feet. The sun cut across my eyes, forcing me to blink. Ignoring the pain, I got up on one knee, bringing my line of sight above the sun beams.

Shading my eyes with my hand, a shadowed face brightened like a full moon, and its features became visible.

# CHAPTER 4

I t was a face I knew—the face my imagination had constructed from the shadows I'd seen, the face that had called my name—pale, with blue eyes and red lips, framed by the flow of brown, wavy hair. The face I saw in my head was his. But I'd never actually seen him until now. How was that possible? There was only one explanation. I *had* actually seen him, just a glimpse, and it had been enough for me to weave a picture of him in my mind.

I peered deeply into his intense but soft eyes. He smiled with lips slightly parted, and I smiled back unblinking. My heartbeat steadied, my chest rippling with excitement, and my fright of being injured, lost, and alone eerily faded. It was unlike me to put down my guard so easily. As calm and gentle as he appeared, I moved away from him, bringing my weight to one foot, so I could jump away if necessary.

"You are in pain," he said.

The tendons in my neck and jaw relaxed just enough for me to speak. I pushed myself up and stood. "A little," I admitted.

"And I'm . . ." Maybe it was better he didn't know I was lost, something making me incredibly vulnerable at that moment.

"You are unfamiliar with this section of the woods," he said. Though his pronunciations were clear, he spoke with an accent I didn't recognize. His tone, soft yet masculine, flowed with a melodic flare that made it seem magical.

"Yeah, a little," I stuttered.

His facial features were both delicate and bold. Thin, arched brows rose above his large, wide-set eyes, and his full lips lay between prominent cheek bones above a square jaw. His lightly tanned, flawless skin complimented the golden-brown highlights in his hair, and a loose strand, twisted almost braid-like, hung independently at one side of his face.

A leather bandana rode across his forehead, covering the tops of his ears and tying at the back of his head in a neatly fixed knot. It was primal but oddly elegant at the same time.

His clothes were also a bit unusual. He wore tight pants, kind of like leggings, with boots rising almost to the knee. His shirt was of the same hue, the color of fall leaves, and it billowed across his chest like the sail of a ship when he lifted his arms.

He offered his hand and I took it. With his gentle tug, I contracted my leg muscles and rose onto my feet. I shoved my phone in my back pocket.

"Thank you," I said. I became aware of my appearance, my face without makeup, and my clothes full of dust. I lowered my head and licked my lips.

"Where does it hurt?" he asked.

I took a step backward and winced while trying not to limp. "I'm fine. I just need to walk it off," I said even though all the walking I'd already done hadn't helped a bit. "My shoulder is already better than it was," I said as I rotated it twice.

"Is it here?" he said, pointing to his own hip.

He came closer. I held my next breath, releasing it slowly. He moved, graceful and smooth, the cling of his pants accentuating the thick muscles in his thighs.

"Yeah, but I'm fine. Really."

"Can I touch you?" he asked, continuing in the same rhythmic accent. The choice of his words and the way in which he spoke were deliberate yet controlled.

"Um." I swallowed, shifting my eyes to his empty hands.

His fingers were long and slim, his nails trimmed to the end of each finger, instead of bitten to the quick like every guy I knew.

"I will not hurt you." He smiled, and when I smiled back, the tightness in my neck melted.

There was something strange and unique about this boy, something I couldn't explain, but it was something that kept me from being frightened of him, his innocence immediately putting me at ease.

"Okay," I said.

He came closer, and with a light touch, set his hands on my shoulders. My chest fluttered.

Leading with his fingers, he ran his palms down my arms. When he reached my elbows and moved his hands to my sides, I drew in a sharp breath and stiffened.

"It is okay," he said. His lips curved into a delicate yet masculine smile.

Exhaling slowly through my nose, I stood still, following his gliding fingertips with my eyes. Trailing from my waist to my hips, he hit the point where my pain developed and radiated. Pressing firmly, he closed his eyes, his hand clamped tightly against my side. I flinched and held my breath.

An indescribable, sweet euphoria swept through my body as the warmth of his hand penetrated the thin fabric of my jeans, the heat settling through my skin and the muscles beneath it.

My heartbeat slowed as he kept his hand there for several minutes. I remained speechless while studying his innate beauty.

"It is done," he said, bringing his hands to his sides.

"Done? Um . . . what did you . . . Oh," I said, testing my leg by putting all of my weight on it. There was barely any pain. I lifted my leg and lowered it. "Wow. Thank you." The pain was gone and he . . . I'm not sure what he did. "That was definitely a Mr. Miyagi moment."

"I do not understand," he said. "Mister . . ."

"It's from a movie. It's old. You've probably never seen it. It's from way before we were born. A karate master makes his hands hot by rubbing them together. He touches a kid's injured shoulder, and the heat makes the pain go away. Like using a heating pad except it's his hand."

The corners of the boy's mouth lifted in a soft smile. "Yes, it is like that."

"Thanks." I rose up on my toes and scanned the woods. "I'm looking for my horse. I think she ran home, but I'm not exactly sure. Did you happen to see a black horse—?"

Leaves crunched, hooves hit the earth, and Molly appeared through the trees.

"Molly," I gasped. "Thank god."

She galloped toward us, her ears forward and mane flowing. Slowing to a trot, she stopped a few yards away from us. I took her by the reins, pulled them over her head, and gave her a hug.

"I um, fell off her. That's how I got hurt," I admitted, too embarrassed to add that some birds had freaked us out.

The boy patted Molly's neck, and she nudged his shoulder with her muzzle.

"So, do you live around here?" I asked.

"Yes, I live close."

"Do you go to Forest View High?"

"I do not. My education is complete." So he graduated and wasn't going to college.

"How old are you?"

"I have seen nineteen winters."

That was a weird way to put it. "Then you're nineteen?"

"Yes, I am."

"What's your name?"

"I am called Brell." His rhythmic accent, his choice of words, and the way in which he spoke was so unusual.

"I've never heard that name before," I admitted. "My name's pretty common. I'm Laura, but I think you already know that." Brell parted his lips. "That was you I heard, right?"

He tilted his head to one side and his eyebrows came together.

"I heard someone call my name," I continued, imagining the blur I'd seen becoming his face, and the hollow, yet vivid voice, a gentle whisper, repeating my name. "That was you, wasn't it?" It had to have been him. I pressed my lips together and took a small breath.

His eyebrows came together a second time, making smooth wrinkles between them. "You *saw* me before this day?" he asked.

"Yeah, but I couldn't really see who you were," I said, looking him up and down. "It was too dark. I could only tell it was a person."

Brell lowered his head, and the corners of his lips turned upward. "Yes, it was me."

"And the wolf I've seen. Is he yours?"

"He does not belong to me. He chooses to be my companion."

It was probably illegal to own a wolf in Massachusetts.

He clapped his fingers twice against the palm of his other hand. The wolf emerged from a cluster of thick trees and sat down next to him. He patted the top of the wolf's head, and the wolf lifted his nose and licked the underside of his hand.

"He's beautiful," I said.

"His name is Bay," Brell said.

Wind rustled through the forest and, like a gentle spatter of rain, light illuminated through the cover of leaves above us, creating patches of soft light against Brell's face. He lifted his chin, and I studied his features: a strong, cut jaw, full lips, distinct cheek bones, and thin nose. His blue eyes were unique, their light-blue irises rimmed a darker shade and speckled with the same hue.

"How did you know my name?" I asked.

"Many days ago, when I was at the edge of the woods, I saw you outside your dwelling. Someone called you by name." He smiled wider, revealing perfectly straight teeth.

"So you know how to get to my house from here?" I asked, bringing my hands together palm to palm.

"Yes, I do."

"Good. Because I don't. I'm totally lost, and there's no reception out here so . . ."

"Your dwelling is not far from here. I shall take you there now."

"Thank you," I said.

We walked through the forest side by side. I led Molly, and Bay followed at Brell's heels. Brell looked straight ahead, easily scaling the uneven earth, while I kept one eye on the trail to avoid large rocks and fallen branches.

"Do you always dress like this?" I asked and then immediately regretted it, hoping he wouldn't take it as an insult. "I mean, it's cool and everything. It's just not something I usually see guys wearing."

"My attire is practical for one who lives as I do."

"Oh," I said, at a loss for what to say next about it. "You said you knew my name because you heard someone say it when you were at the edge of the woods."

"Yes, it was a woman."

"That would have been my mom. Do you go to the edge of the forest a lot?" I asked. He nodded. "At night?" He nodded again. "Then it must have been you who I saw from my porch and from my kitchen window."

"Yes, that was also me." He lowered his head.

"Why were you in the woods by my house?" I asked.

"That is something I—"

Molly whinnied and Bay yelped, dancing in a trot at Molly's feet. Through the trees, I saw the clearing with two boulders.

"What? We're already here?" I gasped. "But we've only been walking for a few minutes. I thought for sure we were a lot farther in the woods than this. How could I have been lost? I'm such an idiot!" I shook my head. "My house is straight ahead!"

"I will leave you here," Brell said. He turned his head left and right, drawing back his shoulders.

"I don't need to go home yet." I shifted my eyes to the boulders. His beauty, his grace, his naivety—everything about him made me want to sit on the boulders with him until it was time for Mom to come home.

"I cannot stay," he said. "But I would like to see you again. That is, if you would like to see me again, too?"

"Yeah, I would."

"Then it will happen very soon," Brell said. "But now I must return to the Grove."

"When do you want to meet?" I asked. "I don't even know where you live or how to get a hold of you." I pulled my phone from my pocket. "Don't you want my—?"

"I will come for you. At your home." Brell turned to walk away. Bay scampered to catch up with him.

"Wait. Before you go, can you at least answer some of my

questions? Why were you watching me? Why did you call my name?" I asked almost in a panic as Brell and Bay pushed through the trees. My heart raced and Molly's reins became slippery in my sweating palms.

"That is something I will explain at another day's turn," he said over his shoulder.

"Another day's turn? What is that supposed to mean? I don't get you, Brell. Please don't leave me so confused," I shouted as he and Bay left the clearing and disappeared into the thickness of the forest.

I rushed after them at a jog, pulling Molly with me, but they were gone, and the woods were still. "Brell!" I shouted. But there was no answer. "What the hell?" I muttered to myself.

Keeping Molly's reins loose, but holding them tightly, I left the clearing and headed toward home, my nerves still pumping with confusion at Brell's words.

Why would a boy call my name and watch me at my home without announcing himself or telling me why he'd done it in the he first place? He kind of pissed me off for being so elusive and not answering all of my questions, but at the same time, my heart thumped with the want to see him again and get to know him better.

He mentioned a grove. Was the Grove a small forest or wooded area? If he lived in one, there were no signs he slept on the ground. He was too clean, and too well-groomed to live like a hermit or be a runaway kid. Besides, like Uncle Dean said, the forest was government owned. That meant it was a designated open-space area, so no houses or buildings.

Maybe "The Grove" was the name of a condominium or apartment complex—or maybe a housing development. A row of old apartments called "Forest View" lined the street near the high school, and "Wilton Village," named after the town's first mayor, was the only other housing development in our community. If "The Grove" was a small neighborhood or building, it wasn't located in this town. It could be something else, but without the internet, I'd have to wait until I was at the library to do a search and check it out.

Molly whinnied as we approached the house. As I led her to her stall, I imagined Brell before me, smiling sweetly, his handsome face and gentle touch ingrained in my memory like a tattoo. My body warmed, and swirls of sweet bliss funneled through my chest as I inhaled. My anger toward him dissipated.

I continued my fantasy, picturing him as if he was part of the forest, a tree come to life, descending upon me stealthily, magically, graceful but strong, relaxed and confident, holding my hand, leading me deep into the woods to reveal all his secrets.

A boy with a pet wolf, strange clothes, and healing touch. A boy that did exist, and more than anything, he wanted to see me, and I wanted to see him again, too.

# CHAPTER 5

Mom was due home any minute. I waited from my window, and finally, after what seemed like forever, I heard her car putter down the road and watched her pull up the driveway.

"Laura," she said as she came through the door. "Dean's ready to meet us at his neighbor's and check out the car." She caught her employee badge with her hand and pulled the lanyard over her head. "Now, honey, I hope you don't have your heart set on getting that car because if it's not going to be dependable, we're not going to buy it."

"I know, Mom. Don't worry."

"Okay, then let's go."

Uncle Dean lived in a small, white farmhouse. He was out front, a big smile on his face, one hand lifted, pointing to the house and barn next door. A trio of chickens pecking near his feet scattered as he broke into a jog to run alongside our car. He met me at the car door when we parked.

"So what do you think, Laura?" he asked.

The barn door was open, revealing a semi-shiny white car

that was longer, wider, and older than my mom's Accord. I'd never seen a car of that make or model before, but it looked cool and fast.

"It's great," I said.

A woman approached us. "Welcome," she said with open arms, "I'm Phyllis." She gave my mom and me a hug. "Dean told me all about his niece and his big sis."

"Really." My mom laughed. "I hope those stories included the pranks Dean used to play on me and how they always backfired."

"Nope." Dean grinned. "I only included the ones that made me look good."

Phyllis was tall, taller than my uncle, and very thin. Her long, gray hair was pulled back in a flat ponytail, and when she turned her head, I saw that the top of her ponytail was held tightly and pinched together at her skull with a tiny, wooden dowel woven through a thick round-shaped piece of leather painted with a floral design. Her skin was smooth and tight, leaving me wondering if she'd had a face lift. Her slim lips curled in a soft smile, raising the apples of her pink cheeks.

Uncle Dean held out his arms like he was showing the prize behind the door on a game show. "Well, here it is, Laura. What do you think?"

The evening sunlight poked through the barn's weathered roof slates, creating vertical spotlights of sunshine against the car's hood. "It's cool. What kind of car is it again?" I asked.

"A 1970 Dodge Challenger RT," Uncle Dean announced, his face aglow. He lifted the hood and smiled broadly, his eyes squinting from the sun's glare as it glinted against the orange metal plate covering the air cleaner. "It's a four, forty."

He opened the driver's door, slid into the seat, and rolled down the window. Phyllis handed him the key, and he tuned the ignition, grinning like a kid in the toy aisle at a big-box store.

The Challenger started immediately, polluting the air with exhaust and its guttural roar.

My mom pressed her hands over her ears. "It sounds like it goes fast—maybe too fast for Laura," she said.

"You liked Jeffery Butternut's fast car," I countered. One side of my mom's face creased as she smirked.

"Oh, that's just the muffler making it sound fast," Uncle Dean said. He winked at me when my mom wasn't looking. "Remember this car is thirty plus years old. It's not even fuel injected." He drummed his fingers against the steering wheel. "Your turn, Laura. Let's take it for a spin." He stepped from the driver's side, and I quickly took his place.

The black vinyl dashboard was dry and dusty with a thin crack running vertically from the windshield to the speedometer. The plastic window covering the gauges was smudged and yellowed, and the woodgrain surrounding them needed a good wipe of wood conditioner. But the seats were comfortable, the vinyl surprisingly supple, and it didn't smell like an ashtray. The minute I curled the fingers of one hand around the steering wheel and the other on the odd-looking stick shift, I knew I wanted this car to be mine.

"That's called a pistol grip," Uncle Dean said sliding in on the passenger side. "Pretty cool, huh. Your mom told me you learned to drive on a stick."

"Yeah, I did. We had an old Mustang 5.0 before my mom sold it and bought the Accord."

"Well, it's no different. It just looks like it. Now put it in first and give her a try."

I stalled it twice, but eventually we were riding down the dirt road leading to the two-lane highway.

"Just stay on here for the next half mile, and then we'll turn around." Uncle Dean leaned back, crossing his arms and stretching out his legs. "It doesn't have power windows, air-conditioning, or cup holders, but it's a classic. They don't make 'em like this anymore." He shook his head. "They tried. My buddy bought a new one last year, but it's not the same as the original. Couldn't come close."

"I love it," I said, easing back on the accelerator when I realized I was going faster than I thought.

"Your mom told me you would. Said you were a practical girl. Said you weren't drawn in by fancy advertising and gimmicks. Didn't need anything too pricey or brand-named clothes to be happy." He twisted a nob on the radio and the fuzzy sound of static pulsed through the speakers.

"That's true," I said.

I was practical, but I was also creative, finding ways to make a thirty-dollar outfit look expensive by glamming it up with accessories. Even before my parents' divorce, we'd lived on a tight budget.

"Your mother said Molly would be your primary mode of transportation if there were hitching posts and water troughs in town and at the high school."

"She would," I agreed. I was more comfortable in a saddle than a bucket seat.

"Phyllis is the same way. She's a horse lady like you." He pointed to the road. "Go ahead and turn around here."

"She has a horse?" I asked. There was no traffic. I made the U-turn, the Challenger bobbing as the front passenger wheels met the dirt.

"She *had* a horse," Uncle Dean corrected. "Lost Jessup two weeks ago. Lived a long life though—fifty-nine years."

"Fifty-nine years? That's impossible." I threw one hand into the air and let it drop to slap the top of my thigh. "The average lifespan of a horse is like twenty-five to thirty years. There's no way it lived that long."

"I thought the same thing. But I saw the photos. Phyllis, at age five, riding the same horse. Said Jessup was ten at the time. A black and white pinto. The patches of white on that horse were identical to his, so there's no question it was Jessop."

"I don't know, Uncle Dean. That's hard to believe."

"Phyllis is a nice lady, a good lady," my uncle continued. "She wouldn't lie. And guess what?"

I shrugged my shoulders.

"She's only going to charge me what she knows I can afford." He drew in a deep breath. "I told her she could get a hell of a lot more money for this baby, selling it to someone else, but she said she wanted my niece to have it. Materialism isn't in Phyllis's blood either."

Mom dropped her crossed arms as I pulled into Phyllis's driveway and parked in front of the barn. She poked her head through the driver's side window before I could open the door.

"You like it, don't you?" she asked, frowning.

"Sorry, Mom, I do. But can you blame me?" She didn't answer.

Uncle Dean got out of the Challenger, pulled a rag from his back pocket, and wiped his forehead. "It's in good shape, Margie. I spent an hour under the hood yesterday checking it out for myself."

She backed away from the car, refolding her arms. "No airbag," she said.

"Nope, no air bag, but this car ain't no tin can either. They don't make them like this anymore." I pushed open the door and stepped from the car. Uncle Dean kicked a front wheel. "This is a solid, heavy car," he said. "Hey, these wheels look brand new."

"They are," Phyllis said. She set her hand on the hood. "I had them replaced this afternoon when the oil was changed."

"Phyllis," Uncle Dean said. Soft lines formed between his

eyebrows. "I told you I'd take care of the tires and the oil change."

"I know," she said, "But as the owner, it was ultimately my responsibility. I wouldn't feel right selling Laura a car that already needed work."

"Thank you," I said.

"Yes, thank you," Uncle Dean said. He set his hand on Phyllis's shoulder. "Laura likes the car, so I guess it's up to you Margie."

"That's a lot of money to spend on your niece," my mom said. She tapped her index finger against her chin. "So I say it's up to you."

Uncle Dean clapped his hands. One corner of his mouth lifted. "I've already written the check," he said, pulling it from the center pocket of his overalls.

"Dean!" my mother said, giving him a playful smack on his upper arm.

I ran to him, giving him a hug. "Thank you so much!"

"You're welcome, sweetheart," he said and kissed the top of my head. "Just don't expect a Christmas present this year."

"Or a birthday present for the next twenty years," Mom said. "Or maybe more."

Uncle Dean laughed while patting my back. "I'll tell you what," he said. "If it's okay with your mom, we'll stay here and take care of the paperwork, and you can go ahead and drive it home."

My mom nodded. "It's okay with me."

"Congratulations on your first car, Laura," Phyllis said.

"And now you can take yourself to registration tomorrow," Mom said.

After a quick round of hugs and more "thank you's," I was on my way home.

The radio reception sucked. I could only get AM, but I

found a song I knew and sang along while tapping the beat on the steering wheel with my thumbs.

Maybe I'd run into Brell on the road or at the tree line by my house. Maybe then he'd answer my questions. As weird as the whole thing was, I smiled, and a sweet shiver ran down my spine as I thought about him.

The setting sun burned orange, disappearing behind a fringe of trees in the distance. I pressed my shoulders against the seat, straightening my back and shifting into forth gear. The moon was visible, hanging low in the sky. I turned up my driveway and parked. No Brell. No Bay.

At the porch steps, I fumbled through my purse for the house key, and in the process, dropped the keys to the Challenger. They landed in a potted, half-dead bush we'd inherited from the previous renter. There were two keys on the ring. I held it in my palm and brushed way the spider web it had caught on the way down.

Squinting, I eyed the keychain. Dots and soft strokes etched onto its surface outlined a couple, a boy and a girl, dancing on a patch of grass encircled with trees. The ears of both figures pointed at their tips. Tiny crisscrosses represented stars and a glistening circle, the full moon. It was absolutely beautiful. Surely Phyllis wanted this back. I'd have to remember to ask her about it.

# CHAPTER 6

The high school was just inside the city limits, anchored on a half-city block like a welcoming committee of red bricks and white-trimmed windows. I pulled into the parking lot, parked near the entrance, and followed a group of kids passing through the front gates. A guy wearing a blue baseball cap, white T-shirt, and jeans peeked his head around one of the trees I passed. When I looked at him, he ducked away.

The registration tables were set up in the small quad by the counseling office. There were four tables, one for each grade. The line for seniors was the longest. Why couldn't we just do all of this online like my old school did?

Looking at my feet, I avoided eye contact, and only looked up because I was able to hear a trio of girls whispering about me, saying they didn't recognize who I was, and I must be new. There was a lot of waving and hugging going on between the students, having reunited after the summer months, and I stood there, feeling stupid with my manila registration envelope pressed against my chest.

The guy I'd seen earlier was at the side of the building leaning against the wall. I caught glimpses of him from the corner of my eye, and every time I did, I could have sworn he was staring at me.

I finally flashed him a quick glance, trying to make it look unintentional by flipping my hair at the same time. When our eyes met, I politely smiled, expecting him to smile back. Instead, he lowered his head, his eyes narrowing as the bill of his baseball cap enclosed his face in an elongated shadow. The hair on the back of my neck rose. I looked away and stepped forward as the line moved.

A pair of boys in front of me turned around and smiled. "Hey," one of them said.

I peered over my shoulder to see who they were talking to.

"Hey," one of them said again.

"Me?" I asked.

They were about the same height. One had brown hair and the other blonde. Both were skinny, but the boy with brown hair had a prominent Adam's apple that was hard to ignore when he swallowed, and the other had really bad acne. Two zits were white and ready to be popped.

"Yeah, you. Were you here last year?" the boy with brown hair asked. The top of his nose was in the process of peeling from a sun burn, and the pink, raw skin underneath was shiny.

"No. I moved here a month ago."

"From where?"

"New Mexico. Albuquerque."

"I'm Robert." His smile was crooked, but his eyes were friendly.

The blond boy put out his hand. "And I'm Chris." His T-shirt read: "You're pointless" and had a picture of a triangle with a face and hands pointing to a frowning square.

"I'm Laura." I smiled and shook their hands.

"Hope you don't mind the cold," Robert said. "We get our first snowfall in November." His Adam's apple bobbed.

"I prefer the heat—dry heat, but I guess I'll get used to the weather here. I'm totally not used to this humidity." I patted the sweat from my forehead.

"What classes did you sign up for?" Robert asked.

"English, calculus, physics, American government, Spanish, and, um, journalism."

He laughed. "Calculus? You must be really smart. I'm in algebra II." He waved his registration packet in front of his face like a fan.

"What year Spanish?" Chris said.

"AP," I said.

"Damn. Are you fluent?"

"Yeah, pretty much."

"Hey, there's my step-sister," Robert said. "She's also a senior." She was a tall brunette. A girl with hair the color of a Tabby cat's walked with her. "Sandy, come here for a minute!" he shouted to his sister.

"What do you want?" she said, annoyed, and shoved her phone in her back pocket. The two joined us.

"I want you to meet someone. This is Laura. She's a senior. Just moved here from New Mexico."

"Hi," Sandy said. "This is Jill." She motioned to the red head.

"She's taking calculus," Robert said. "Sandy's taking basic algebra for the second time, or is it the third?"

Sandy punched him in the arm. "Don't be a dick."

"Ha, look who's on his way over here," Chris said.

He motioned toward a lanky boy with messy, dirty-blond hair, pulling a suitcase-styled backpack behind him. With the boy's next step, his backpack's wheels stuck against an uneven seam in the concrete, and he jerked the long handle to get it free.

Robert and Chris laughed, and Sandy scrunched up her face.

"Sandy wants him," Robert teased. "Oh, Odd Ninja Todd," he continued in a high-pitched girly voice with his hands folded under his chin. "You're so hot. Will you go out with me?"

"Shut the hell up!" Sandy gave her brother another punch. "Everybody knows I can't stand him." Robert acted like he was going to hit her back but rubbed his arm instead.

"Odd Ninja Todd?" I asked.

"Yeah, he's a weirdo," Jill said, "and he claims to be a black belt in Karate, but no one believes it." Her green eyes slanted upward at the outer corners as she wrinkled her thin, freckled nose. "He's had a thing for Sandy since the sixth grade. He doesn't have any friends. The only thing he's got going for him is a scholarship to Stanford when he graduates."

Our circle became quiet as Todd came up to Sandy's side. "Hey, what's up?" he asked and pushed his glasses higher up his nose. His voice was deep and husky, a lot more masculine than he looked.

Sandy crossed her arms and answered. "Just standing in line. What did you think we were doing?" She kicked his rolling backpack with her toe. "Why did you bring this thing?"

"To pick up my books. I want them early. Get a head start," Todd said. "Who's this?" he asked, nodding his chin in my direction.

"I'm Laura," I said.

"She from New Mexico," Robert added.

"Oh, I've been there," Todd said. "Went to Las Cruces junior year for a robotics competition."

"Next!" the lady manning the registration table called.

Robert went forward with his packet.

"Hey, did anyone else see that cool Challenger in the parking lot?" Todd asked. "It looks like Mr. Dobson's old car."

"What do you know about old muscle cars?" Chris challenged.

"A lot more than you," Todd said boldly. Chris rose up on his toes and stuck out his chest, but Todd didn't even flinch.

"Next," another counselor shouted, and Chris handed him his packet.

"The Challenger's mine," I said.

Todd sucked in a small breath like he'd accidently swallowed a clump of gum and scratched the top of his head. "Really? Where did you get it?"

"I bought it from a lady who works at the public library."

"It is Mr. Dobson's old car!" he announced. "Wow! I'd heard his ex-wife put a brick on the gas pedal and ran it into a lake."

"Nope," I said. "It's been sitting in her barn."

"If I had known it was still around," Todd said, "I would have tried to buy it. Will you let me drive it sometime?" Sandy and Jill snickered in their hands.

"Um, I don't know," I said, shifting my eyes from him.

"Come on up!" a counselor announced.

I stepped forward and handed over my manila envelope. She pulled out the paper listing the classes I'd picked and the emergency contact card and student health information sheet my mom had filled out and signed.

"Hey, Laura. I'll see you around." Todd winked and waved as he walked away, his smile wide enough to show both rows of teeth.

When he was out of ear shot, I heard Jill say to Sandy, "Poor Laura. It looks like Odd Ninja Todd has a new girl to stalk." Her orange hair bounced against her shoulders as she laughed.

"I hope so," Sandy said. "I am so over his crap."

The counselor handed back the manila envelope and my

class selection sheet with all of the teacher's names and periods filled in.

"You're all set," she said. "You got all the classes you wanted. Looks like you're ahead in credits and are meeting all the requirements to attend a four-year. Welcome to Forest View, Miss Brooks."

"Thank you," I said and walked from the table. Robert and Chris followed me.

"Where's your locker?" Robert asked.

"Let me check." I fumbled through my envelope and found the pink card with my locker assignment printed on it.

Something flashed to my right, a smudge of blue and white. That same kid in the baseball hat was now just a few yards away, glaring at me again from under his cap. He folded his arms and stood with his legs shoulder width apart.

"Hey, Laura. Are you okay?" Robert asked.

"Um, yeah. Why?" I asked.

"You look pissed," Robert said. He waved his hand in front of my eyes. "What's wrong? What are you looking at?"

"Nothing," I said, shifting my eyes to Robert. "I'm fine. Just a little overwhelmed, I guess. Being at a new school."

"Is your locker in building two?"

"Yep, building two."

"So are ours," he said, gesturing to Chris, "but my sister's is in building four, which sucks for her because it's on the other side of the school. Ours are next to the gym." Robert folded up his class schedule and shoved it into his back pocket. "Let me see your classes."

I handed Robert my schedule, and from over his shoulder, I glanced at the guy with the hat. He was still eyeing me. He leaned against the building behind him and crossed his ankles.

"Oh, you got Mr. Parker for English!" Robert laughed a low-pitched cackle.

"What's wrong with Mr. Parker?" I asked.

"He's just kinda weird that's all. I had him last year."

"What do you mean by kinda weird?"

"I think he's into aliens and stuff. I heard he belongs to a cult that thinks a spaceship is going to land here when the world is about to end. Supposedly, every weekend, Mr. Parker and the other whack jobs from his cult try to make contact with the aliens, using all kinds of homemade devices they build in their garages. They even bought a piece of property and put a landing pad on it."

"Really?"

"Yep. I saw a documentary all about it."

"Was Mr. Parker in it?" I asked.

"Nope, but that doesn't mean he's not a part of the cult. When I was in his class last year, he told us he believed in Big Foot and the Loch Ness monster. If he believes in that crap, then he must believe in aliens, too, right? So the rumors have to be true."

"I don't know, but as long as he's a good teacher, I don't care what he believes."

Robert handed me my schedule. "Do you want us to show you where your locker is?"

"Sure," I said.

The school consisted of a series of long, rectangular, two-story buildings with double doors at each end. The red brick was old and crumbling in places. The white trim was in need of a fresh coat of paint, but its age only added to the beauty of the school's history having been built in the early twentieth century.

I read the plaque above the door to building two. "Through these Doors Walks Scholars and Champions."

"Yeah, cheesy, I know," Robert said.

"I don't think it's cheesy. I think it's cool. My old high

school was only five years old. This is a proud school with traditions. I can feel it." I closed my eyes with my next breath. "I know I'm going to like it here."

Chris chuckled. "You can feel the pride? What, are you psychic or something?"

"No, I just sense it. I mean . . . I don't know what I mean."

"Robert, Chris! We're leaving right now!" Sandy shouted from the other side of the quad.

"Hold on!" Robert yelled back. "We're going to show Laura where her locker is!"

"She can find it herself. I'm not waiting," she spat.

"She can be such a bitch." Robert shook his head. "We better go," he said to Chris. He turned to me. "Sorry, Laura. The lockers are numbered. It'll be easy to find yours. Just go straight through those doors." He pointed.

"That's okay. I don't need to find it today. I think I'm going to go, too."

Robert cupped his hands around his mouth. "Wait for us! We're coming!" he shouted to his stepsister.

We left the quad, Sandy and Jill ahead of us laughing at who-knows-what. At the parking lot, Sandy said something in Jill's ear, and the two of them looked at me and laughed. A few seconds later, I understood why. Odd Ninja Todd was next to my car.

"Damn! I wish this was mine," he said, patting the roof of the Challenger as the four of us walked up to him.

Robert peered through the driver's side window. "Yeah, it's pretty sweet."

"Hey, Todd," Sandy said. "Laura didn't get a chance to check out her locker. You should show her where it is." She hit Jill's arm with her elbow.

"Sure, I can do that," Todd said. He smiled showing teeth and gums.

"Actually, I really don't have time right now," I said, having absolutely no desire to get to know him better.

"How about Thursday? No wait, Friday?" He sniffled, wrinkling his nose and rubbing under it with his index finger.

"He goes bird watching on Thursdays," Sandy explained with a smirk. "With a group of senior citizens. I know because my grandmother belongs to the same bird-watching club."

"I go with my grandfather," Todd shot back. "It's a way for us to spend time together." He turned to me, apologetically. "His memory's starting to go. Sometimes he can't remember how to tie his shoes, but he can spot and identify birds faster than anyone in the group." He lowered his head.

"You can show her where all of her classes are, too," Sandy threw in with a devious grin.

Todd lifted his head, smiling wider than he had before. "Yeah, and I can introduce you to your teachers. They'll be here next week prepping for their classes."

"That's a great idea," Jill said, her eyes wide and sincerity fake. "How can you say 'no' to that, Laura?" She drew in her lips, trying not to laugh, but failed, and spun around to hide it.

I dug in my purse for my keys. "I'm not sure what my plans are, so . . ."

"So, you'll have to text her, Todd, and find out when," Sandy boldly suggested.

"The reception at my house is terrible," I told Todd. "So if you text me, I might not be able to respond right away."

"Then let's set a day and time now," Todd said. "Let's plan for Friday at eight. Meet in the lower quad by building two."

That was a bit early for me, but oh well. "Okay," I said. Todd pulled out his phone, and I felt like I had no choice other than to exchange numbers with him.

"See you soon," Todd said, waving good-bye with his whole arm.

"Yeah, see you," I said, trying to sound a little bit enthused. Sandy and Jill walked away laughing. Chris shook his head.

"Sorry about my sister," Robert said. "I told you she was a bitch."

"You were right. But oh, well. All I can do it make the most of it."

I slipped into the Challenger and drove from the parking lot, passing the kid with the baseball hat who was standing on the corner.

# CHAPTER 7

The next morning, I found Mom in the middle of her Saturday-morning ritual, sitting at the kitchen counter sorting coupons and drinking a glass of orange juice.

"Tell me about the new friends you made yesterday," she asked.

I sat down and put on my shoes. "I don't know if you'd call them friends. I just met them at the registration table," I said while tying my laces.

"Well, friends or not, I know you, and you'll make the most of it." She threw a wadded up kitchen towel at me. I snagged it with my foot like a soccer ball and kicked it back.

"I'll try," I said.

"Hey, I have an idea." She set down her scissors. "How about we take your new car into town? It'll give me a chance to see how reliable it really is before you start driving it to school."

I really didn't want to go anywhere. What if I missed seeing Brell if he decided to make an appearance?

"I know," I said. "How about *you* take my car into town, and

I'll stay here and get some chores done? Then you can see for yourself how reliable my car is."

"Nope, you need to be there," she said, smiling with eager eyes, one eyebrow bending higher than the other.

"Why?"

"I'm working on Sunday. The whole crew's going to be there doing inventory."

"That's a bummer."

"No, it's not," she sang like it was a happy little song in a commercial. "Because it counts as overtime, which means time and a half, and that means I'll have a little extra money on my next paycheck. Which means I can buy you some new clothes for school," she squealed.

"Aw, Mom. You don't have to do that. My clothes from last year still fit."

"I know, but I want to make you feel a little more confident and less nervous on your first day of school. Wearing something new will help."

"Thanks, Mom." I half stood and leaned over to give her a hug.

"There's a cute little boutique across the street from the hardware store. I went in there yesterday during my lunch break, and the salesgirl, I think she's your age, she goes to Forest View, pulled some stuff she thought you'd like. They're holding them for me. Everything in the store is on sale, and the sale ends today."

"I don't need someone to pick out my clothes," I said. I'd seen the boutique, and there had never been anything intriguing enough hanging in the window for me to want to go inside and check out the place. And I certainly didn't want a girl I didn't know and who went to my high school to select things for me to wear.

"I know, but she offered. Come on. Feed Molly, and let's go."

She gave the table a drum beat with her hand.

I fed Molly, peering through the morning haze, hoping to see Brell, but the woods remained quiet and still. When Mom and I loaded into the Challenger, there was still no sign of him or his wolf.

The Challenger started easily with a rumble, and soon my mom and I were headed down the dirt road. We hardly spoke during the long drive. Mom primped her hair and applied orange lipstick using a travel mirror from her purse (the Challenger's visor didn't have a mirror), and once I pulled into a parking stall in front of the boutique and turned off the engine, she undid her seat belt and announced, "What a nice drive. It's a little loud, but it feels solid."

Thankfully the salesgirl who'd set clothes aside for me worked the evening shift, so I didn't have to be awkwardly steered into buying everything she'd thought I'd like. Overall, the merchandise was better than I'd expected. We bought two shirts, two pairs of jeans, and a pair of leggings at twenty-five percent off, and next we were off to the grocery store, my mother driving, so she could experience her first muscle car.

"Hey, Laura, look who's here," Mom said. I looked up to see Phyllis standing next to her.

"Your first drive to town in the Challenger. What did you think?" Phyllis asked.

"I love it. Thanks again for selling it to me."

"You're welcome."

"Oh . . ." I looked down at my key. "Did you want your keychain back?"

"No, honey. You can keep it."

"Thank you. It's so beautiful and unique."

"I made it myself. Hand etched," she said.

"Their pointed ears are so cute. Are they supposed to be elves?"

"Yeah. I guess you could call them that." Phyllis laughed. "I just think of them as magical woodland people." She shifted her shopping bag to her hip. "I planned on making more of them to sell at the library's annual craft fair, but I never did."

"Well, if you ever do, I'd buy another one," I said.

She smiled and moved the bag to her other hip.

"Well, we better let you get to your car," Mom said. "That bag looks heavy."

"Yep, and I have a busy day ahead of me. Enjoy the car and the keychain." She winked at me. "Have a great weekend, ladies."

"Let's divide and conquer," Mom said as we entered the market. "You pick out something for breakfast. I'll grab the detergent, and then we'll meet back at the frozen food."

As good as a bowl of sugar-coated puffed corn sounded, I knew Mom would only say "yes" to something healthier. I rounded the corner to the cereal aisle, stopping when I reached the shredded wheat.

Something flickered in the corner of my eye. Goose bumps riddled my arms, something that usually only happened when I was in the refrigerated section. The muscles in my neck tightened and tingled, the sensation traveling to my shoulders.

Someone was watching me.

I shuddered, glancing over my shoulder and rubbing my arms. A woman to my right pushed her toddler in a shopping cart and an old man at the end of the aisle held up a jar to read the label. Neither one looked at me.

I grabbed a box of toasted oats and headed to the frozen food section. As I passed the next aisle, that strange sensation of being stared at hit me again. My pulse pounded in my ears. My heart jerked in my chest. I took a deep breath, releasing it slowly.

A mucky blur of shapeless color dashed across my peripheral

vision and stopped. I turned to see who it was.

The boy in the blue baseball cap stood at the end of my aisle, wearing the same clothes he wore at registration. Tufts of blond hair poked from under his hat, curling at his chin, framing his pale, delicately chiseled face. He lifted his chin. Our eyes locked, and neither one of us moved.

My mom pushed passed him with her cart.

"I'm craving ice cream. What about you?" she asked me.

"Yeah. Sounds good," I answered, shifting my eyes to look at her.

"What's wrong? You look like you've seen a ghost."

"Nothing," I said. "I'm just cold." When I looked back, the boy was gone.

"Yeah, it's kind of chilly in here," Mom said. "My waistline doesn't need it, but go ahead, Laura, pick out any flavor you want."

"Chocolate sounds good." I opened the glass door and grabbed a carton of Rocky Road. "But so does cherry vanilla."

"I'll get some frozen fruit. It's been a while since we've made smoothies." She moved to the other side of the aisle.

"I can't decide. Which one do you . . .?" I gasped, choking in a quick breath.

The boy was next to me by the popsicles, peering at me through the glass door he held open. With an evil glean in his eyes, his lips curled, and with each breath, a circle of fog developed against the cold glass. His grin widened, revealing his teeth. The carton of rocky road slipped from my hand. He let go of the door and walked away, rounding the end of the aisle without looking back.

"Laura," Mom said. "Don't just leave it there."

I reached down for the carton. "What a weirdo," I said. "Something's wrong with that kid."

"Who?" my mom asked.

"That boy who was just here."

"I missed him. Was he one of the kids you met yesterday?"

"No. I saw him there, but I didn't talk to him or anything."

We continued to shop, and I inspected each aisle before we entered it, hoping I wouldn't run into that boy again. My mother stayed on budget, adding up the prices under her breath, and when the cart was half full, she announced she was done and so was her wallet.

"Be careful. There's a carton of eggs in that bag," Mom said when I set the last bag of groceries in the trunk and shut it.

My face grew warm and my palms hot and sticky. He was watching me again. I could feel it deep in my gut. Squinting under the glare of the sun, I stood on my toes and scanned the parking lot. From over the roof of my car, I saw him.

He nodded, his eyes sparkling devilishly. His thick brows furrowed above his thin nose and pursed lips. I didn't move.

"Laura, come on, honey. Let's go." Mom said.

I got into the car and started the engine. Mom took her time, smoothing a wrinkle on her shirt before sitting down. I pulled from the lot, entering the street. The light turned red, and I slowed to a stop.

The boy was at the corner, leaning against a street pole, his icy stare and creepy smile giving me the chills. Acting like he wasn't there, I pushed the buttons on the radio, trying to find a decent song.

"The light's green," Mom said.

I stepped on the gas too hard, and the Challenger jerk forward into the street.

"Laura!"

"Sorry, I'm just not used to this clutch yet."

I checked my rearview mirror and couldn't see him. And I thought Todd was supposed to be the stalker. I'd have to ask Robert about this bizarre boy.

# CHAPTER 8

Mom was already gone by the time I woke up. She'd made a full pot of coffee, like she always did on Sundays, the extra caffeine being needed for the laziest day of the week. At least that's what she'd always said.

I poured myself a cup, dousing it with a spoonful of sugar, and sat at the kitchen counter. Since Brell hadn't come by, as far as I knew, I could look for him instead, playing it off like I was just out for a walk if I ran into him. I wouldn't go far, just to the clearing with two boulders.

I dressed and did my hair, torturing myself with hot blasts from my blow dryer in a house that was already eighty-seven degrees, and curled the bottom of each hair strand with the turn of a barrel brush. Keeping my makeup light and natural looking, I choose eye shadows in shades of brown and blushed my cheeks and lips in pink and headed outside.

A blue jay was perched on the railing at the far end of the porch. Turning its head left and right, it flapped it wings, lifted from the porch, then darted toward the row of trees at the end of the driveway, before landing on the limb of a large sugar maple.

The base of my neck warmed and prickled, working down through my chest, and I was struck once again with the sensation of being watched. But this feeling was different than it had been with the boy at the grocery store. Instead of wickedly creepy, it was wildly welcomed. I squinted, readjusting my gaze.

Next to the sugar maple stood Brell, his feet spread shoulder-width apart and arms folded.

I waved, ready to skip from the porch steps. The roar of a diesel engine stopped me.

Uncle Dean's blue pickup headed up the road. He'd never approve of me having a boy over when Mom wasn't home, and he certainly wouldn't allow me to hang out with one in the woods either. His "some of these boys aren't worth knowing" talk told me that.

Trying to make an inconspicuous gesture with my hand, I swished it in the air, signaling Brell to hide, but he didn't move. I held my breath as Uncle Dean drove past the fringe of trees and turned up the driveway. Thankfully, Uncle Dean kept his eyes on the road, never turning his head. He rolled his truck to a stop next to the feed shed and stepped out, smiling.

"Hi, Uncle Dean," I said, hopping down from the porch to meet him.

"Good morning, Laura. I got a present for ya." He motioned to the three bales of alfalfa in the truck bed.

"Thanks. You didn't have to do that. You know we can have it delivered." We hugged, and I looked over his shoulder. Brell remained at the tree.

"I know, but I don't mind. And why pay a delivery fee when I've got this ole truck that can haul it for ya?" He patted the side of his ancient Ford.

"How much do we owe you?" I asked.

"Awe, don't worry about it." He shooed the air with his hand.

"Uncle Dean, you know Mom will get mad if you don't take any money." She put funds aside each week to pay for Molly's feed. I ran up the step, into the house, and returned with an envelope of cash.

Brell was still at the tree, leaning one shoulder against its trunk. As Uncle Dean unloaded the bales of alfalfa into the shed, I side-stepped left and right, bobbing to block Uncle Dean's view of Brell and keep my uncle from facing the tree line.

Uncle Dean dusted off his hands. "Nope," he said when I tried to give him a handful of money. "I'll be fine with that one," he said, pointing at a five and winking. I handed him a ten, and he reluctantly shoved it in his pocket.

"I'm going into town. How 'bout I take us to lunch?" Uncle Dean said. "And Phyllis, too." His exhale was more like a snort, making me laugh. "I still can't believe she sold you the Challenger. Guess what she's driving instead?" he snickered.

"What?"

When Uncle Dean wasn't looking, I held up my index finger, letting Brell know I'd just be another minute or so.

"An electric car. A two door. Not very fast. Not a lot of get-up-and-go, but I guess it's enough for her," my uncle said. "Wouldn't be for me, though. She doesn't like to leave town. Just goes to work and back." He nudged my shoulder with his fist. "So what do you say about lunch?"

"I wish I could, but I've just got too much I need to do today. But don't let that stop you from taking Phyllis out on a date."

He dug his hands in his pockets and his cheeks flushed. "A date? Aw, we're just friends."

"Right now, you are. But it's not going to be that way for much longer," I teased. "I have a feeling she likes you more than just a friend. And I know you feel the same way about her."

"Really?" he said, his pale lips lifting in a light-hearted smile.

"Yep, so you should drive back to town right now and ask her out before she's already eaten."

"Ha," he laughed. "I guess your mother's right about you."

"About what?" I glance passed Uncle Dean. Brell was at the same tree, standing so still that at first glance, I couldn't see him.

"About you being extra perceptive. When you two decided to move here, one of the first things your mother told me was that there was no point in hiding my emotions when you're around because *you* can read people like a book. Better than anybody she knows."

"Really? She's never told me about that."

"Well, that's what she said, and I believe her. You're a special gal, Laura Brooks." He opened the truck door and slid inside. "Sure you don't want to go?"

"I'm sure," I said, and took another look at Brell.

When the truck became a blue dot in the distance, I walked to the edge of the woods. Brell moved to greet me as my uncle's truck entered the road.

"Hi," I said.

"Hello, Laura." Brell smiled, and the bird perched above him flew away.

He was draped head to toe in shades of spring, apple green to a crisp, canary yellow, his shirt glistening with threads of gold. His supple, brown leather boots clung tightly to his calves, folding down below the knee. He looked princely, like someone from a storybook.

"Sorry you had to wait so long," I said.

"That is okay. I do not mind waiting if it means seeing you

again." His blue eyes warmed like a fire had been lit behind them.

Heat flooded into my cheeks, and I smiled, lowering my chin. "Thank you," I said.

"Your uncle seems like a very nice man."

"He is. He's been a big help to my mom and me. But . . ." I titled my head, and my eyebrows came together. "How did you know he was my uncle?"

"Because that is what you called him—uncle."

"You heard that from way over here?"

"Yes."

That didn't seem possible. I glanced over my shoulder. My house was at least fifty yards away. But then again, I was used to living in a bustling city where a voice couldn't travel more than a few feet before it was overcome by the noise of traffic, airplanes, and construction work, making it impossible to distinguish one sound from another.

"Did you hear our whole conversation?" I asked.

"Yes, I am sorry. I did not mean to eardrop."

"Eardrop? I think you mean eavesdrop." I laughed and Brell cocked his head to one side. "I was afraid my uncle was going to see you. He wouldn't have approved of me hanging out with a boy when my mom isn't home."

"I made sure he didn't see me," Brell said.

One side of his mouth rose in a half-smile and an eyebrow lifted as he moved closer. Shadows in shades of blue swept across his brow. His smooth skin, firm and flawless, was like that of a porcelain doll.

"Come," he said. He held out his hand and I took it. A pleasant shiver radiated up my arm, and we entered the forest, our footsteps in tandem and my heart beating slowly yet strongly.

"So you're nineteen," I said to break the silence.

"Yes. Nineteen winters have turned since my beginning."

"Your beginning?" I asked slowly.

"Yes," he said. "My day of first breath?"

Though his clothing, accent, and answers to my questions were odd, I was intrigued and fascinated instead of frightened.

"I'm seventeen," I said. "I'll be a senior at Forest View High. Did you go there?"

"I did not attend that institution of learning," he said.

"Where did you go to school?"

"I was educated among my family, my people."

"So, you were home schooled?" I asked.

"Yes," he said. "In the Grove."

"How long have you lived in Berkshire County?"

"Since first breath."

He definitely had an interesting way of explaining things.

We entered the clearing with two boulders, and he led me to the larger one. He let go of my hand as we sat down. "I like this spot. It reminds me of you." I smiled at the sentiment and my chest filled with warmth.

"Where's Bay?" I asked.

"He is in the Grove."

"What exactly *is* the Grove?" I asked. "I mean, honestly, Brell, no offense, but from everything I know about you so far, it sounds like you live in some kind of commune, and you're part of a cult or something."

Brell shifted his eyes upward as in deep thought. "Would you not want to see me again if that were true?" he asked, bringing his eyes back to mine.

"Honestly, that would depend on what the cult was all about. You know, what your group's beliefs were and stuff like that. So, tell me. What's the Grove?"

I didn't care how hot he was, but if he was part of some weird sect living their lives based on conspiracy theories or a made-up religion, that would be a deal breaker for me. Robert had said my soon-to-be English teacher belonged to a group of people who believed in aliens. Maybe Brell and his family were a part of that, too.

He straightened his back and took a deep breath. "I would like to ask you out on a date," he said.

"You're changing the subject." I crossed my legs, and with fingers laced, rested my hands on my knee.

"I know it is common for humans to go on 'dates,' social engagements," Brell said. "And I know it is customary for the male to organize these events."

I couldn't help but smile. "It is, but before I see you again, I need you to answer my questions. The last time I saw you, you said you would."

His shoulders dropped.

"Come on, Brell! Why do you talk the way you do? Why do you dress like this?" I motioned to his billowing shirt sleeves and boots fit for a medieval cosplay battle. "Why do you hang out in this forest? And why did you wait so long to show yourself to me?" I folded my arms. "Please tell me."

He scooted closer. "Yes, I did tell you I would answer your questions, but today is not the turn of day to do so. But until then, I want you to understand that where I come from is a secret place of peace, and everything I am works to maintain that harmony."

Okay, that sounded way too cultish to me. "You're creeping me out, Brell. I really think I should go." I started to push up from the boulder.

"No. Please." He set his hand on my arm. The strange euphoria I'd felt the first time our eyes met returned, and in my head, I heard his sweet voice calling my name. "Say 'yes' to our date," he continued, "and when I see you then, I promise I will tell you much more."

His unimaginable beauty, his soft touch, his gracefulness, and his innocence—everything about him at the moment, coupled with the mystery of his existence, fed my desire to know him better. His strange naiveté gave me a confidence I'd never felt with any other boy.

"Please, Laura," he said, slipping his hand to the top of my hand.

"Where would we go on this date?" I asked softly. I couldn't picture him bowling or even taking me to dinner or a movie dressed like he was now. But maybe he wore regular clothes when he was in public.

"A place not far from here," he said.

"Not the Grove," I said, shaking my head. If it was a cult, I didn't want to be surrounded by a bunch of people who'd try to convert me the whole time.

"No," he said, "but it is in these woods."

"Tomorrow?"

"Yes."

"Okay, I'll go, but I'll need to be home by five."

"You will." Brell smiled, his lips lifting softly. "Thank you."

"What time do you want to meet? I'd say just text me, but you know how terrible the reception is here." I pulled my phone from my pocket to check the time. Brell moved his head, blinking as my phone's screen caught the sunlight.

"I will come for you when the sun is at its highest point in the sky."

"That translates to noon, right?"

Brell nodded. "Yes, it is noon."

"Your cult doesn't believe in clocks?" I joked, though I totally wondered if they did or not.

He shifted his eyes from me and blinked. "I must return before I am missed," he said, "but there is something I would like to give you first."

He raised his chin, and I caught the sparkle of something gold, a chain half hidden within the collar of his flowing shirt. He lifted it from his chest and pulled it over his head.

Like fluid flowing within an invisible shell, the metal changed hues as it glistened in his hand, from copper to gold, then silver. The charm was round, quarter-sized, and carved with an intricate design resembling a cluster of leaves. Around its edge, cryptic symbols appeared as it sparkled in the sun.

"Please, take it," Brell said.

I held out my hand, and he laid it across my palm, the mysterious charm winking.

"It's beautiful," I said in awe of its eerie craftsmanship. "I've never seen anything like it. What's it made from?"

"It is called lithel."

"I've never heard of it." I slipped the chain over my head and the charm dropped against the middle of my shirt. "Thank you."

Brell rose from the boulder. "You are welcome, Laura. We will see each other again soon. I will leave with sweet memories of this time together."

I watched him walk away, disappearing behind a cluster of trees, before I turned toward home. Accepting a date from a strange boy who probably belonged to a cult was definitely *not* something I was going to tell my mom when she came home.

# CHAPTER 9

"I've got some exciting news," Mom announced when she came through the front door bursting into the kitchen.

"What?" I asked as I topped off my glass of iced tea.

"Dean and Phyllis were going to go to the movies tonight, but they had a change of plans, so he forwarded his tickets to me while I was at work, so we could use them."

"Tonight?" I asked. "Aren't you tired from taking inventory all day?"

"Yeah, but it's been a long time since you and I have gone to a movie together. And I have that gift card for the Burger Den, so I figured we could get some dinner, too."

"That sounds great, Mom," I said.

The Burger Den wasn't very crowded. The hostess seated us by a window next to the street. Our waitress brought us menus and glasses of ice water, and with a big country smile, scribbled our order on a notepad and bustled away. I checked my phone. Every text and call I couldn't receive at home had come through, including one from Todd reminding me about when we were meeting.

"See that antique store?" Mom pointed out the window. "We'll have to go in there some time. In fact, they're having a week-long anniversary sale soon, and on one of those days, I think they're having a buy-one-get-one. I have the flyer for it somewhere in here," she said and started rummaging through her purse.

I turned to look. On the sidewalk, the boy with the baseball hat, the grocery store boy, stood with his arms folded. He saw me and grinned, the arch of his eyebrows becoming sharp points. His blood-red lips thinned into a broad smile. He lowered his chin, his upper lip raised above his gum line, and his smile turned sinister.

A low chuckle broke from his throat, penetrating through the glass. His blue eyes narrowed, becoming tight slits. With a high-pitched laugh, the boy threw back his head, bolted into a sprint, and ducked between two buildings.

"Here it is," Mom said. She pulled the flyer from her purse and readjusted her glasses. "The buy-one-get-one's next week. We should come back for that."

"What the . . ." I gasped.

"What?" Mom asked. "You don't want to go?"

"No. I do," I said, my pulse pounding.

The waitress set our plates on the table. During dinner, I watched the street, ate only half my burger, and picked at my coleslaw and beans.

"Are you okay, Laura?" Mom asked. "You're not coming down with something are you?" She reached across the table to press her palm against my forehead.

"No. I'm fine," I said, slouching to dodge her hand. "I'm just not that hungry."

The theater parking lot was packed. In a town with only two entertainment choices besides dining, bowling or the movies, it was no surprise. We parked behind the building, walked to the front of the theater, and got in line.

The grocery-store boy was at the front of the ticket booth! Two other boys I hadn't seen before were with him. They were similar to one another in height and build. All three wore blue baseball caps, T-shirts, and jeans. The grocery boy looked at me, and I turned away. A lump formed in my throat.

"Hey, Laura!"

I turned around. It was Robert, and Chris was with him.

"Hi," I said. "This is my mom." The three of them exchanged hellos as I explained to her how they were the ones I'd met at registration.

"We just saw *The Dark Lord III*. It was great," Robert said. "What are you here to see?"

"Laura and I don't like the scary ones," Mom said.

"Yeah, we're gonna see *Love Triangle*," I said. From the corner of my eye, I saw the grocery-store boy and his friends move to the theater doors.

"You'll have to let us know how it is," Chris said.

"Yeah, I will."

The line moved. Mom stepped up to the ticket window, but I stayed back, leaving the line.

"Hey," I said to Robert and Chris. "Do you know those three guys over there wearing baseball hats? I've been seeing them around. I think they go to Forest View." I pointed over my shoulder.

"Who?" Robert and Chris said at the same time.

I turned around. The boys were gone. The only people standing there were a group of adults.

"Never mind. They must have already gone inside."

"We know everyone at Forest View," Chris said. "Show them to us at school, and we'll tell you who they are."

"Okay, I will. Thanks."

"Ready, Laura?" Mom said.

Mom and I handed over our tickets and entered the lobby. Like an invisible veil of loathing and animosity, the stale, popcorn scented air overwhelmed my senses, and for a moment, I couldn't breathe.

I scanned the lobby. The three boys stood next to a row of video games. With crossed arms, they turned toward me, their lips rising in weak, menacing smiles. Goosebumps formed on my arms, and my nostrils flared when I took my next breath. The grocery-store boy lowered his head, one thick eyebrow sinking as he winked at me.

"How about popcorn?" Mom asked. "Extra butter?"

"Yeah, I guess," I said. A sick feeling formed in my gut, swirling below my belly button.

We joined the shortest line at the snack bar. The boys took root at the far end of the room, their backs anchored against the wall. My skin crawled and my stomach churned from their presence, something handfuls of popcorn would not be able to settle.

In the theater, I sat with my legs crossed, my free foot bouncing at the ankle as I glanced over my shoulder every few minutes. When the lights dimmed, and the screen flashed with a preview of an upcoming superhero movie, my blood pounded in my ears, and I bit the end of my straw so hard, I could hardly suck soda through it.

I couldn't stand it. It was time to confront them and find out what was up. "I'm going to the bathroom," I whispered to my mom. I handed her the bag of popcorn and scooted through the aisle.

The lobby was practically empty. The smell of sticky candy and roasted hotdogs entered my nose. A teenaged employee by the entrance swept crushed popcorn bits into a dust bin, another emptied a trash can, and two girls behind the snack counter tapped their phones, completely oblivious as I crossed the room.

The three were still against the wall, their heads high and hands on their hips. The boy from the grocery store smirked, and the other two followed, their full lips stretching over unusually white teeth. High cheek bones, perfect skin, and well-defined noses made the three oddly handsome, despite the palpable fear they radiated.

"Hey?" I said as I approached them. "We need to talk."

The boys laughed and turned to leave the theater.

"Wait," I said. "I want to talk to you. Why do you keep giving me dirty looks? You don't even know me."

The door swung closed behind them. An employee emptied a second trash can, shaking a new bag open with a thunderous clap, and one of the girls behind the counter had helped herself to a soda. I went back to my seat.

Enjoying the movie was impossible. Every sound, the crackle of a candy wrapper, the slurp through a straw, and whispers between the couple behind me, kept me on edge. The trio's unfounded animosity toward me plucked at my nerves until the movie's end.

"So what did you think?" Mom asked when the credits rolled and we made our way to the aisle.

"It was okay," I said.

"Just okay? I thought it was great." She rubbed her lower back. "Worth the back ache I'm going to have from sitting for so long."

I remained one stride ahead of my mom as we left, stretching my neck to see into the lobby. So far, so good. The boys were nowhere to be seen.

"My sciatica," Mom groaned as I held the glass door open for her. She hobbled through. "The pain is shooting down my leg."

Wincing, she took a few more steps and stopped. "Maybe you should . . ." She sighed and eyed a group of kids ahead of us. I knew what she was doing—making sure there'd be plenty of people heading to the parking lot, so she could ask me to bring the car around, and I wouldn't be going into a dark place all alone. "Get the car," she continued while rubbing the base of her spine.

"Sure," I said. My lips trembled when I smiled.

Inhaling the warm night air released some of my pent-up anxiety, but I shuddered and quickened my pace to get within a few yards of the couple in front of me.

The Challenger was at the far end of the parking lot, gleaming under a buzzing parking-lot light. I dug in my purse for my keys, looked over my right shoulder, and opened the door. It started with the first crank of the engine. Gripping the steering wheel hard, I took a big breath.

The boys were not to be found. I drove to the front of the theater and picked up Mom.

At least I had something to look forward to the next day—my date with Brell.

# CHAPTER 10

I lay in bed, studying the necklace Brell had given me, tilting it to catch the sunlight breaking through my bedroom window. The charm's colors shifted from copper to silver while the leaf design at its center oddly remained the same hue, a greenish gold. I looked for signs of paint, scraping it with my fingernail, but there wasn't any.

What if Brell did belong to a cult and this leaf design was their secret logo? There was no way a community of people could be living in the woods without the authorities knowing about it. But maybe they didn't actually live there, and the Grove was a state-owned campground the cult used as a front.

My heart beat hard as I ran a bunch of scenarios similar to this in my head, things I'd seen in the movies or on television. By the time I'd worked through as many of them as I could think of, I was doubting whether or not I should go alone on a date with Brell.

What I needed to do was find out more about the cults in this area, and with my crappy internet, there was only one place to go—the library. My date was in four hours. With plenty of time, I dressed and headed out.

The library parking lot was pretty empty, and so was the library. The circulation desk was unattended. A mother with her child was on a couch in the children's section, reading a book together, and an old man sat at one of the eight computers happily tapping away.

I followed the row of computers to nab one at the far end. I was just about to sit down when I noticed a set of pictures hanging on the wall. Some were posters, reprints of famous paintings, and others were original works of art by local artists. A pair of unsigned drawings in oil pastels looked oddly familiar.

There were two figures in the drawings, a boy and a girl dancing on a patch of grass in a clearing wearing billowing shirts and leggings. I pulled my keychain from my purse for a comparison. The faces were the same, and the clothing was identical down to the number of laces on a pair of boots. Their ears were also pointed.

In the second sketch, the couple stood in a circle on an outdoor stage while a third figure played a musical instrument —a strange, boxy-shaped guitar with a protruding curved mouthpiece.

"Hi, Laura."

As I jumped and spun around, my necklace swung and settled back into place against my chest.

"Oh, hi, Phyllis."

"I'm sorry. I didn't mean to startle you." She smiled and shifted her eyes to my neck. "What a beautiful necklace. Can I see it?"

"Sure."

Phyllis lifted the charm from my neckline and cradled it in her hand, titling it back and forth to catch the light. "This is extraordinary, Laura. So unusual. I've never seen anything quite like this before. Where did you get it?"

"A friend gave it to me."

She let go of the charm and winked. "Then that makes it even more special."

"It does. Thank you," I said, smoothing the charm against my chest.

"What do you think of my drawings?" she asked.

"They're beautiful. I had a feeling they were yours. They're identical to the figures on the keychain you gave me. Why aren't they signed?"

"I'm a bit modest when it comes to my artwork."

"You shouldn't be. I'd take credit for them if I was you."

"If people ask, I tell them, but not many people do."

"Probably because they're at the back corner. You should move them up front. Everyone would appreciate your talent." I moved closer to the last drawing and pointed. "The forest looks so real. I love how the sunlight cuts through the trees, making shadows."

"Thank you, Laura. Makes it almost magical, don't you think?"

"Yeah, it does," I said.

"Have you spent a lot of time in the woods around here?" Phyllis asked.

"No, not really. There's a forest in front of our house, that's all."

"You should visit the woods some time. It's such a peaceful retreat. Just don't get lost and find yourself walking in circles." She laughed and flipped her ponytail over her shoulder.

"If I ever decide to explore the woods, I'll take a compass," I joked back.

"'Good idea." She brought her hands together, prayer-like. "So, what can I help you find?"

"I'm actually here to use one of the computers."

"Oh, that's right. Your uncle told me you have trouble getting internet at home."

"Yeah, we do."

"Then I'll leave you to do some exploring on the web."

She headed to the circulation desk, and I sat down at one of the computers, checked my phone to answer any texts or missed calls that finally went through, and got to work.

Thirty minutes later and after entering every key or phrase I could think of, I wasn't any closer to finding information on a cult or commune living in this area. There were a bunch of wacko groups waiting for a spaceship to arrive, including the one Robert mentioned, but the landing strip they'd built was in another state. Just because I didn't find anything, didn't mean Brell didn't belong to a sect with strange beliefs.

There were tons of websites and articles about cults explaining how they were defined by their spiritual or philosophical beliefs, and how their main goal was to recruit new members and brainwash them.

Phyllis walked up with two books in her arms. I quickly closed the browser. She set a book on my table. The cover was scuffed, its pages yellowed, and it had an old-book smell of an ancient tomb. It didn't have a title, but the cover art was reminiscent of Phyllis's drawings. Within an arch of tall trees, two regal figures with pointed ears sat on ornate, high-backed thrones.

"My inspiration," she said, nodding in the direction of her artwork. "I thought you'd like to flip through it."

"Thanks."

"And here's the second book in that series you started. Dean returned book one for you the other day, so I figured you were ready for the next one."

"I am. Thanks."

"I'll hold it at the desk for you." She walked away, her ponytail swinging and her steps as smooth as a ballerina.

Giving up my internet search, I flipped through the book Phyllis left with me, skipping the text and focusing on the photos. The images were beautiful, briefly taking me to imaginary worlds of myth and mystery. But I had too many things on my mind to truly enjoy it. Leaving the book where it was, I headed to the circulation desk.

As I handed Phyllis my library card, a chill rode the length of my spine. I shuddered, looking over my shoulder. The grocery store boy stood on the other side of the glass door. His face crumpled in a ghastly frown.

At this point, I shouldn't be so alarmed. This was a small town after all, and it was summer break. I was actually surprised I hadn't already run into Robert and Chris more than once. I just wanted to know why he continued to mock me the way he did.

"Here you go," Phyllis said and handed me my book.

I snapped my head back around to face her. "Thanks," I said.

Her eyebrows came together as she looked over my shoulder. The reflection of light in her eyes flickered. I heard the door open and close and held my breath, listening to his footsteps. The muscles in my legs tightened as I prepared to turn and confront the grocery-store boy once and for all.

"Wow, what a coincidence—two of my favorite ladies." A hand clamped on my shoulder, and I spun on my heels to find Uncle Dean.

"Whew." I released a big breath. The grocery-store boy was gone. "Hi, Uncle Dean."

My uncle opened his arms for a hug. "I saw your car outside. Do you still like it, or are you ready to hand it off to me?" He chuckled as we hugged.

"Of course I still like it." My heart rate dropped with another deep breath.

"I'm taking Phyllis to lunch. Want to join us?" he asked. "We're going to Bob's Barbecue. Best barbecue in the state. At least I think so." He chuckled again.

"Thanks, but I have a bunch of stuff I need to do today." If I could get outside in time, I might be able to find the boy before he took off.

Phyllis pulled her purse from behind the counter and one of her assistants peered around a bookcase and gave her a wave good-bye.

"That Challenger really is a nice-looking car," Phyllis said as we entered the parking lot. I glanced left and right. No grocery-store boy. "The only thing bad about it was its previous owner."

Uncle Dean laughed. "Yup, he got a stripper from Vegas, but you got the car."

"Dean!"

"Oh, Phyllis, she don't care. Do you, Laura?" He batted the air with his hand.

"No, not at all," I said, as I continued to take note of my surroundings.

"Are you sure you don't want to come?" Phyllis asked.

"Yeah, I'm sure. I have leftover spaghetti waiting for me at home."

Uncle Dean held the door open as I slid inside. He gave the hood a tap as he walked away. I gave them a wave and drove home.

***

The sun was high in the sky. A wisp of wind rippled across the porch, catching a strand of hair to brush against my lips. I unstuck it with a flick of my finger.

A deep howl shot through the forest. I dashed to the edge of the porch, peering deep into the woods. Bay pushed through a stretch of trees, running to meet me as I stepped down from the porch. Brell wasn't with him.

"Good boy," I said. "Where's Brell?" He lifted his nose and licked my wrist as I gave him a pat. "Brell?" I shouted toward the tree line. "Brell?"

Bay tilted his head, catching my hand in his mouth. As I pulled away, he adjusted his jaw, taking it again. Holding my hand loosely between his teeth but firmly enough to keep me at his side, he led me to Molly's stall and let go. Bay barked twice, and Molly whinnied.

"You want me to take Molly? Is that it, Bay?" He barked again. "You are one smart, highly trained wolf," I said. "If that's really what you want me to do."

I gave the trees another thorough scan, shading my eyes with my hand. No Brell.

"Okay, wait here, boy," I ran to the house and got my paddock boots. I'd go as far as the boulders and wait for him there.

Molly cantered through the woods, steady and strong. Bay ran at our side, a model of grace and confidence. With the boulders just ahead, we slowed to a walk, and Molly whinnied as we entered the clearing. Her whinny was immediately followed by another.

"Thank you for coming," Brell said, while mounted on the most beautiful white stallion I'd ever seen. "This is Adiness." He rode up to me, and Molly and Adiness touched noses.

"He's stunning," I said. The stallion sidestepped, and his tail danced. "I didn't know you had a horse."

"Like Bay, he is my companion."

Adiness's bridle, a twisted cord of gold fabric and leather, draped around his nose, up toward the forelock, and across his neck to his withers, where Brell held the reins loosely in his hands. Brell wore something similar to what he'd worn before—a billowing shirt, thick leggings, and boots—but instead of matching the colors of the fallen leaves, his clothes were deep green and interwoven with golden thread.

A leather band wrapped across his forehead, disappearing into his hair, and a thin braid of matching leather ran parallel to his headband, falling behind his half-covered right ear. He was regal not rustic, his clothes spotless, and boots shiny. Against the backdrop of the forest, he looked unreal.

A splash of jewels trimmed his leather saddle, spiraling at the pummel to a mounted cow's horn capped with a ball of gold. The saddle pad's scalloped edge flashed from a weave of golden thread, and gem-encrusted stirrups delicately hung from thin straps.

"Brell, I don't get this," I said, raising my hands in the air. I looked down at my scuffed, manure-stained paddock boots and trendy, faded blue jeans with a hole in one knee.

"You look like you're ready to go to a comic-book convention or attend a renaissance fair. And how did you train Bay to do what he did?"

As he tilted his head with a soft smile on his lips, everything about him exuded a state of calm. He rode Adiness around to Molly's side and set his hand on mine as it rested upon my saddle horn.

"Soon you will understand," he said. "The forest brought me to you, and the forest is never wrong." He swallowed and his eyes focused on mine. "These trees are wise. They know you. They know me."

With those words, something in me softened. My heart rate slowed as my muscles relaxed, putting me at ease. And although I was skeptical, deep inside, I knew I wasn't at risk of being physically hurt by him.

"Let me share the beauty of these woods with you," Brell said.

"Okay," I answered at a half-whisper.

At a canter, we wove between the trees, dodging large stones and jumping over fallen trunks. Graceful yet strong, Brell rode in rhythm with his horse, his back straight and hands level with the bottom of his ribcage, slowing to a trot when we reached the edge of a tiny clearing. With a voice command I didn't recognize, Brell brought Adiness to a halt. Molly stopped next to them.

"This is absolutely amazing," I said. "I had no idea this was here."

A winding creek cut through the thick grass where wildflowers ran the length of the bank, growing in small clusters. A small waterfall fell above a patch of grass, clouding it with a dissipating fog.

We dismounted, and I pulled Molly's reins over her head, ready to tie them to the nearest tree. "There is no need," Brell said. "She will not leave you."

"But—"

"Watch them and you will see."

I let go of Molly's reins, and she and Adiness walked to the closest tree and stood next to one another with heads bowed, ears forward, and tails swishing. Bay crossed the stream to lie in the shade of a large maple tree, but Molly and Adiness remained side by side, their heads lowered to the ground, nibbling grass.

Brell lowered himself to the ground in a motion so smooth, he appeared weightless. I sank to my knees, distributing my weight between my palms and rolling backward onto a patch of thick, spongy moss to sit next to him.

My heartbeat quickened, though I felt at peace. I leaned forward, catching a pleasant smell, something clean and floral, yet spicy and warm. My next breath lured me to fall against his chest, but I resisted, and locked my arms over my knees instead.

Taking a small breath with lips parted, he moved closer and smiled. "Eeliss."

"What?" I asked.

"Your hands smell of garlic," he explained. "Eeliss grows here in the spring."

"Oh, that's the scientific word for it? I ate leftover spaghetti for lunch today and made more garlic bread." I sniffed my fingers but couldn't smell anything.

I sighed. "Okay, Brell, it's time to tell me what's up with you," I said as gently as I could, keeping my voice low. "I've done some research, and from everything I've read, it seems like you must belong to some sort of cult." I took a breath. "And to be completely honest with you, if your plan is to indoctrinate me, then I don't know if we should see each other again because I don't want to be indoctrinated." Even though my feelings for him were just developing, the idea of not seeing him again made my heart sink.

He lifted his chin, and I met him eye to eye. "You seem like a really nice guy and everything," I continued, "but no matter what, I'll never believe in what you believe or want to live the way you do."

"I want you to believe in my people and understand how we live," Brell said. "But it is not in the way that you think it is." He reached for my hand.

I drew away, folding my hands in my lap. "Then in what way is it?"

Brell lowered his head, unfastened the band of leather across his forehead, and set it on his thigh. A piece of hair fell across his eyes. He caught it with his index finger, pushed it behind his ear, and turned so I could see the side of his face.

I gasped, pushing away from him as I traced the delicate curve of his ear with my eyes. Brell's ear rose from the lobe and arched upward, ending with a distinct point. I'd seen plenty of ears that were more pointed than rounded—including my own—but they were nothing like this. The upper half of Brell's ear extended for half an inch before tapering.

"I don't understand," I said. "What does this have to do with how you live?"

"I am not human. My people are not human," he said, his voice wavering and with a sincerity I'd never heard in him before.

The gleam in Brell's blue eyes intensified, and I leaned backward, searching his body for something I might not have noticed before, something besides his clothing, strange accent, and incredible good looks that made him different.

"Brell. You're scaring me," I said, scooting farther away from him. "If this is a joke, you need to stop right now. And if it isn't, you need some serious help."

He jumped from the forest floor in one move, pushing up with one hand and quickly bringing in his feet. Keeping his arm parallel to the ground, he held out his hand and spread his fingers. The fallen leaves stirred beneath his palm, the dead foliage rising as it whirled, gaining momentum. He curled his fingers, and the spinning increased, forming a funnel.

My jaw dropped. "How are you doing that?" I asked at a half-whisper.

"Magic," he said, one eyebrow lifting as he smiled. "It is called 'working the wind'."

I rolled onto my knees and crept closer, bending my elbows to lower my body and examine the twirling leaves from all angles. There was no sleight of hand, invisible wires, or hidden fan. It was real magic, but how could that be?

As fascinated as I was, it frightened me. To have that kind

of power, as small and simple as his demonstration was, also meant there were others who could do that and maybe more. A bolt of panic shot through my chest, and for a moment, I wished I'd never entered the woods alone to find a boy and his wolf.

I scooted further away from him. "What are you? An alien?" I asked.

He made a fist and the forest debris settled to the ground. "No. My people are from this earth. I am a Landaffen," he said and sat down.

"Lan . . . Landaffen?" I stuttered, staring at the pile of leaves.

"Yes, Landaffen," he repeated. The word flowed from his lips, a soft rhythm, a partial hum, strangely warming my soul. My pronunciation was harsh in comparison, lacking his smooth accent.

"But except for your ears, you look human. And you sound human. You have an accent of some kind, but you actually speak English better than most people I know. You use a lot of really big words."

"Landaffens are the keepers of the old language and acquirers of the new. Mastery of the spoken and written word is cherished and revered by my people." He smiled. "Extending one's vocabulary is valued and expected. We take pride in our choice of words and the fluency of our speech. For Landaffens, language learning is not a skill. It is instinctive."

"So you are saying that you're born already knowing how to talk?"

"Yes, the Landaffen language, but the words do not yet have meaning and the tongue and mouth cannot yet voice them until the age of walking."

"Say something to me in your language," I said.

"Lennt baugh naw roo neesh," he said, the words rolling from his tongue like a song.

"What did you say?"

"I said, you are the loveliest female I have ever seen."

He shifted to face me as he sat, bringing his legs closer to his chest. His stretched leggings thinned at the knees when he moved, and the golden threads woven into the thick fabric glimmered. He pushed aside the hair from his forehead.

I couldn't believe it! Was Brell a living example of modern fantasy fiction, a character race from dice contests and video games?

"Are Landaffens elves?" I asked.

"That is a human word," he said. "My race is familiar with human fiction of elven beings with pointed ears, tales passing from human elders to youths, tales evolving with distortions and inconsistencies."

He moved closer. "In the ice region, they are known as huldufolk, the hidden people, mischievous sprites, stealers of human babies. In some myths, they are small magical creatures— toymakers, shoemakers, or the keepers of pots of gold. There are the Ljosalfar and the Dökkalfur, and the winged-ones, faeries and sprites. From the beginning of humankind, the Landaffens have unintentionally inspired and influenced those stories."

A cool breeze washed over the clearing, bringing goosebumps to my arms. My mind raced with questions, and I swallowed a rising lump in my throat.

"Lan, Lan . . ."

"Landaffens," Brell said and smiled.

"Landaffens. I've never heard that word before."

"Only a few from beyond a Grove have," he said.

"How many of you are in the Grove?"

"Our colony is small compared to most. Just over two thousand." He brought his headband to his forehead and tied it back into place.

I drew in my legs, draped my arms over my knees and interlocked my fingers. My head spun, a myriad of thoughts swirling, bringing me to the point of light-headedness. I crossed my bent legs at my ankles and took a deep breath. How could this be real?

"I still don't know if I can believe all of this. I mean, we would know about you. Two thousand people couldn't hide like that," I insisted.

"Two thousand of us do not leave the Grove at the same time," he said. "In the Grove, we are protected. Those who do not belong there, cannot enter, and only scouts are allowed to leave the Grove. I am a scout, and when I do leave, I make myself unseen."

"How?" I picked a blade of grass and twirled it between my fingers.

"With our magic," Brell said, "we can make ourselves invisible when we choose to do so. We have been doing so since the beginning of time."

"How do you do it?"

"Standing motionless like a tree. Walking through the woods with steps unheard and undetected. We hear, see, and sense the presence of humans before they reach a Grove or cross our paths. I am a scout; therefore, I am one of the few permitted to leave the Grove. Your uncle didn't see me yesterday because I did not allow him to."

"But you made yourself visible to me," I said. My cheeks warmed.

His lips curved into a soft smile, and his eyes danced as they caught the light. "Yes, I did," he said and lifted an eyebrow. "Some can escape our magic. See through our charms. Laura, you are one of those people."

"How? Why me?" I asked. The lump in my throat returned.

"Because you intrigue me."

"So you let it happen." I hugged my knees tighter, lowered my head, and blushed. "I have so many more questions for you, Brell. I'm trying to believe everything you're saying, I am. Really! It seems real. Your ears, and the thing you did with the wind, but at the same time, I just can't wrap my head around it. I can't help being skeptical. I need to know more."

"And you will, but now I would like to know more about you."

"What do you want to know? I can't top what you've already told me about you." I laughed. "My life isn't very exciting."

He picked up my hand. "We cannot choose the life we inherit at first breath. It is what you choose to do with that life. Your passions. Your motivations. Your purpose. The person you become. And the people you choose to be with. That is was makes life exciting."

My eyes grew misty. I lowered my head and told Brell about growing up in New Mexico, and while I did so, he played with my hands. I told him about my parents and their bitter divorce, and how sometimes I felt like I didn't belong anywhere. How deep inside, I had an urge to do something with my life completely unexpected. What that was, I didn't know. I was still struggling to find it.

"And that is exactly what intrigues me about you, Laura." He kissed my hand and my body tingled. "You are amazing."

He smiled and stood, bringing me up with him. Bay ran to Brell's side. Adiness whinnied, shaking his head, his ears forward, and neck curved with his chin to his chest. Molly did the same.

"I must go. I was not to leave the Grove. It will be noticed that I am missing," Brell said. "I know there is much more you want me to tell you, but there is also much more for you to see."

"More magic?" I asked.

"Yes, the magic of the Grove."

"You're going to take me to the Grove?" My heart thumped hard, and I sucked in a big breath.

"Yes, meet me in the trees tonight when the moon is highest in the sky, and I will take you there."

"You mean midnight tonight?" I could easily sneak from the house, Mom was a heavy sleeper, but the fear of the unknown pulled at my nerves, twisting them until every nerve seemed to fire at once.

"Yes," Brell said.

"So you really don't have a clock or any way to tell time." My voice shook when I spoke.

"Time is determined by the movement of the sun, the moon, and the stars." He took me by both hands, locking his eyes with mine. "You are afraid," he said. "There is no need to be. We will be together, and everyone else will be asleep." He squeezed my hands. "I promise I will explain more to you when we are in the Grove."

"Okay," I said. "But I can't stay long. If my mom wakes up and realizes that I'm gone, I'll be in a lot of trouble."

"You will not stay long."

He stepped closer, taking me into his arms, and we held each other without saying a word. I listened to the beat of his heart and the soft trickle of water flowing in the brook.

"Thank you for our date," he said when we let go of one another.

Brell jumped onto Adiness's back as effortlessly as if a spring board had been set at his feet. I mounted Molly, pushing myself up from the stirrup. Bay followed as we cantered to the forest edge through the last fringe of maples toward my home.

"Until high moon," Brell said.

"Yes, until high moon."

# CHAPTER 11

The afternoon came slowly; the heat, the loneliness, and the anticipation of seeing Brell again at midnight made the minutes drag by like I was lost in the forest once again walking in circles.

Midnight couldn't come soon enough, and when it did, Mom was still awake. I lay in bed at eleven forty-five, watching the sky from my window and listening to the soft pat of her bare feet against the tiled floor. Glass tapped against stainless steel which meant she'd just set a dish in the sink. The soft clap of wood signaled she'd just closed a kitchen cabinet.

The light from the living room shot down the hall and into my bedroom, casting a thin beam of yellow across the hardwood floor. I pulled my necklace from my shirt and held its charm in my palm. The smooth lithel sparkled iridescently in the moonlight, creating lustrous, rainbow-like colors.

With a soft click, the ray of light disappeared. Mom shuffled passed my room to the bathroom. The water turned on and off with the washing of her face and the brushing her teeth, and I counted the seconds in my head, breathing deeply in a futile attempt to control my impatience.

The dull clack of plastic rang against something ceramic. She'd dropped her toothbrush in its holder. Her footsteps followed, and seconds later, I heard the creak of bedsprings.

On light toes, I crept from my bed and tugged on the clothes I'd conveniently left on my dresser. Using the flashlight on my phone and a tiny mirror, I reapplied my lip gloss, brushed my hair, and wrote a quick note to my mom just in case she woke up before I'd returned home.

She'd be pissed I'd left the house in the middle of the night by myself and without permission, but at least she'd know I hadn't run away from home or been kidnapped. Having a believable excuse ready would have been good, but I couldn't think of one. Hopefully, it wouldn't come to that point. I shoved the folded note in my pocket.

Placing my hand against my bedroom door, I pushed it softly, widening the opening just enough to slip through. The hall was empty, and my mother's bedroom door was closed.

The toe of my right tennis shoe brushed against the door frame as I squeezed into the hall, producing a muffled squeak, but that sound was nothing compared to the noises I expected from the next feat I had to attempt. Creaking unforgivingly underfoot since they day we'd arrived, the section of flooring in the living room was going to be my enemy.

Exhaling through tight lips, I moved forward, lowering each foot slowly, cautiously with each step, distributing my weight evenly between my toes and heels. I expected the grind of plank edge against plank, and I held my breath, cringing, but the sounds never came, and within seconds, I'd slipped undetected to the front door.

I brought my hand to my chest, inhaling deeply through my

nose, and with my other hand, tossed my note on the table next to the door where Mom kept her car keys. The side with the word "MOM" landed face up.

The doorknob had been stubborn since the first day we'd moved in, needing a gentle rattle through the twist, something that had taken me a week to master. I gripped it, rocking the knob while rotating it, clenching my jaw, anticipating the click as the latch released from its plate in the doorframe.

It gave easier than I expected, but I kept my hold tight, bringing the knob back to center as I opened the door and snaked through it to the porch, softly closing the door behind me. The porch light was on, attracting every bug in town, and I ducked, dodging a beetle making a beeline for the bulb. I noticed a mosquito on my arm and smacked it away. My mom's wind chimes stirred, but not enough to make any noise.

I shoved my phone in my back pocket and searched the tree line for Brell, my shadow elongating as I crept down the porch steps. Cutting across the half-dead grass, I avoided the gravel driveway and quickened my pace as I cleared the patch of dirt separating my house from the woods.

"Brell?" I said when I reached the edge of trees. "Brell, are you here?"

Insects buzzed and chirped, their arthropodic song a chorus of intertwining clacks and twitter. I faced home. The roof shone steely gray under the stars, but the windows were dark and non-reflective. Mom had to be asleep by now. A small breeze gave me goose bumps, despite the warm, humid air, and I took a step backward, shivering.

"Brell?" I said again, whispering this time.

Leaves crunched, the sound thin and wiry like it had stretched over some distance to reach my ears. Turning slowly, I faced the direction of the noise.

"Brell? Is that you? Please answer me." Twigs crunched in whispery clicks as if the wave of sound had come from far away.

The chomp of feet and crack of sticks grew closer. My eyes strained to see, my ears struggling to hear more. The hair rose on my arms. Minutes passed. The sound of feet upon the forest bed continued. Closer and closer. I remained mute, breathing slowly, standing as still as the trees, my pulse pounding.

Something touched my shoulder. I flinched, spinning as I jerked away.

"I am sorry, Laura. I did not mean to startle you," Brell said.

"Oh, my god! You scared the crap out of me," I gasped and lowered my fists.

Kissed by moonshine, Brell's hair glistened silver, accenting the thin braid wrapped crown-like above his head band. Shadows at his jaw emphasized his cheekbones, and his eyes, appearing more gray than blue in the dark of night, contrasted sharply against his milky skin.

"I called your name, but you didn't answer," I explained.

"Did you hear me approach before I touched you?" he asked.

"Yeah, footsteps," I said. "Unless it wasn't you." I lifted onto my toes to check the trees behind him.

"No. There is no one else here," he said. His eyes moved to the trees, and he cocked his head.

"Is something wrong?" I asked.

"No. Nothing is wrong. I am sorry. I did not hear you call my name, or I would have called your name in return."

"It's okay. I'm just glad you're here."

"I would not be anywhere else, since it meant seeing you," he said. "I would have waited until the sun's return to see you."

I smiled, warmth rising in my cheeks. A soft breeze swept between us. A strand of hair fell across Brell's eyes, and I was half-tempted to brush it back into its place, to touch his soft hair and skin.

"Come with me," he said, slipping his hand into mine.

On light feet, he trod, missing branches and large stones, while I copied his steps to avoid stubbing my toe on what I could barely see. When the terrain became more uneven, he gripped my hand tighter and pulled me against his side to keep me steady, and on two occasions, I exaggerated my wobble, so he'd have to do it even more.

"Are you okay?" he asked.

"Yeah, I'm fine."

"I will walk slower," he said and interlinked his arm with mine.

We passed the boulders and continued toward a thicket where the trees were extra dense. I squinted, peering deeply into the woods ahead of us as an open patch of sky let in more moonlight.

"Are you still taking me to the Grove?" I asked.

"Yes. It is just ahead."

We pushed through a compact run of trees, leading with our shoulders and stepping sideways between trunks.

"I don't see anything but trees."

"The trees are just an illusion," he said, slyly, letting his elbow unlink with mine and taking one of my hands. "Close your eyes."

"Why?"

"It is the only way you can enter the Grove." I squeezed his hand a little harder, the soft tone of Brell's voice doing little to ease my fear.

A gust of warm air hit my face, a wind with body and substance, unexplainably palpable like I could snatch it from the air and clutch it in my hand. I tried to open my eyes, but couldn't, and when I parted my lips and called Brell's name, another swirl of wind muffled the sound like a candle flame snuffed between two fingers.

My heart pounding, I forced the air from my lungs and drew in a long breath. The wind subsided, whipping into a gentle breeze, and the muscles in my jaw and throat relaxed.

"We are here," Brell announced.

"But how will I get back?" I said, searching for some kind of identifiable opening or door. I pushed a branch aside and then another and couldn't find anything.

"Upon the wind," Brell said, "the same way in which we entered. When you wish to leave, it will unseal. The magic cannot force you to stay against your will."

I let go of his hand and turned around.

"Welcome to the Grove, Laura," Brell said.

I gasped, almost losing my balance.

We stood on a low ridge, overlooking a valley with a winding river and village set within acres and acres of tall trees ablaze with moon beans. Within each tree, ornate, wooden dwellings sat many feet from the ground, each wooden door glistening with gold filigree and jewels. Bridges made from rope and slats of polished stone webbed between some of the smaller homes, intricately connecting them to one another. Fire flickered from tall torches lining pathways, and lighted windows danced with candle flames. From what I could tell, the Grove didn't use electricity.

"It's so beautiful," I said, holding my free hand against my chest and studying a home cradled between two trees.

Ivy decorated the tree's trunk, twisting across its branches to the roof where it spiraled downward, wrapping the handrail of the stairs like the stripes on a candy cane. A flowered bush grew to the left of the steps, its tightly closed buds sparkling with dew.

"I can't believe this. How can this be real?"

My knees buckled as a wave of vertigo shook my senses. Brell caught me by the upper arm. "Are you okay, Laura?" His shoulder bumped against mine, and a pleasing shiver spread through my body.

"Yeah, I just—this is just so much for me to take in. It's beyond comprehension. It's . . ." I sighed, too stunned to explain any more.

"Let us sit," he said.

The grass was thick, rubbery and spongy-like. We sat shoulder to shoulder with bent legs. With a deep breath, my head came back to itself.

"It's different here. The weather. It's cooler." I inhaled slowly. The air was crisp, fresh and sweet, like biting into a chilled apple. "Where do you live?"

"That is my place of living," Brell answered.

He pointed to a small house nestled within the branches of four evenly spaced trees. A leaf pattern identical to the charm he'd given me decorated its carved, arched door, and golden, cone-shaped spires set at each corner of the roof, twisted upward, coming to three points reminiscent of fleur-de-lis.

"And what is that just behind it?" I asked.

A large rectangular structure sat within the crooks of four of the largest trees in the Grove. With its slanted roof and trio of simple wooden steps leading to an unadorned door, it was plain and rustic, setting it apart from the others.

"That is the esllus, our school," Brell said.

"What do you learn there?"

"Many, many things." He smiled. "It begins with leaning the symbol for each sound of our language and putting those symbols on paper to make meaning. Then we study numbers—quantity, structure. The relationship between— points, lines, and shapes. Using the stars and the moon to navigate and understand time. Engineering and design. Working with wood. Making metal and weaving cloth. The study of plants for healing and food. The history of the earth and our people."

"Who else knows about this place?"

"You are one of the few humans who have come to this Grove, and the only human to do so during my breath on Earth."

The clouds shifted, exposing more of the moon, and a chill swept up my spine. I took a deep breath, drew up my legs, and cradled my bent knees with one arm.

"I still don't understand; how can this place exist without everyone knowing about it?"

An expansive fringe of tall, closely grouped trees surrounded the Grove, but it wasn't thick enough to obscure a village or prevent people from passing through it. Even if the wind could keep people out, the land would have been surveyed at some point, accounted for, and put on a map.

"When humans come too close, they are tricked by the woods," Brell said. "They lose their sense of direction. It is part of our magic." He smiled. "It happened to you once. I am sorry for that. I did not know it had happened, or I would have come for you sooner."

"The day I was lost and walked in circles?" I asked.

"Yes," he said.

"I was also attacked by birds." I cringed and rubbed my head with the memory of being pecked.

"The birds and the trees are our protectors. I am also sorry about the birds," Brell said. "They will not bother you or Molly again. They understand now."

"Understand what?"

An owl spread its wings and took flight, cutting though the glow of the moon, creating a flash of blue shadow across Brell's forehead.

"The Landaffen's bond with nature is strong. It is what humans would call a sixth sense." His eyes shifted to the sky and back. "You asked how I had trained Bay to guide you to Molly's stall, so you knew to ride her to our date. It is this connection that made it possible."

"Is this the only Grove?" I asked.

"No, there are Groves all over the world."

"So when a person gets lost in the woods and walks in circles, does it mean . . .?"

"Yes, it means there is a Grove nearby."

"But how?" I said, breaking from a whisper. "I still don't understand. This doesn't make any sense."

"Like I said, it is part of our magic."

Brell's words were almost tangible, entering my ears ghost-like in a melodic sweep of breath and sound.

"I've never believed in magic," I said louder than I had intended. I brought my hand to my mouth, eyeing each door and window in the distance expecting to see one or more of them open.

"Do not worry," Brell said. "No one can hear us. Before I left, I summoned a wind to remain here and carry our words away." The sides of his mouth rose into a delicate smile, his eyes penetrating yet comforting, but I slipped my hand from his.

"How many Groves are there in the world?"

"Hundreds. But there were more." He folded his arms across his knees and sighed. "As forests disappear, we have had to combine our populations."

"Disappear because of humans?"

"Yes. As your territory grows, ours shrinks. Humans have taken the land, taken the trees."

Chainsaws cut away at their world. Industrial waste polluted their streams. The Landaffens lived in harmony with the environment while we hindered it.

"I'm sorry," I said.

"It is not your fault. One human is not responsible."

"I know, but it's my people who are taking the land and the trees. If we knew about these Groves then—"

"It would not matter, Laura. Humans know about the animals that live in the woods. They know the effect it has on them, and it does not stop the humans from taking the animals' worlds away."

"But we do a lot to protect the animals, too," I said. "There are animal preserves and national parks."

"And zoos where animals are not free." He paused, rocking forward and letting his arms drop to his sides. "Our abilities, our connection to nature, make us different, and in the human mind, that would make Landaffens a threat. Make us something to restrict and exploit rather than live with in peace." He exhaled softly. "There are more humans than there are Landaffens. My race would not win the battle to live independently and without human laws and human interference. Everything we are, everything we believe in, would be destroyed."

As much as I didn't want to admit it, Brell was right. The minute a human stumbled upon a Grove, the Landaffens' way of life would change forever. And being outnumbered, they'd be forced to live out their lives watched and regulated.

I thought of my mom and every other human I knew. How they didn't know about this place. How ignorant I'd been this whole time in believing humans were the only intelligent beings on this planet.

"Then how come you weren't afraid to take me here? To show all of this to a human?"

"I know you will keep our secret."

"No one can know about this? Not even my mom?" I asked, although I knew if I told her, she wouldn't believe me without proof, something I couldn't give her. She'd end up taking me to counseling. She'd think I was losing my mind. I couldn't put her through all of that just like I couldn't put her through waking up tonight and noticing I was gone. As much as the serenity of the Grove enticed me to stay, it was time for me to leave.

"No one can know," he confirmed.

"I should go," I said. "But I want to come back. Will you bring me here again?"

"Yes," Brell said. He smiled and rose, offering his hand and bringing me up with him. "You are special, Laura. That is why I brought you here."

"Why am I special?"

"Why did you enter the woods in the first place?" he asked. "What made you want to explore?"

"I, I don't know. Curiosity, I guess," I said, though deep inside I knew it was more, as if I were a piece of metal being pulled to a magnet.

"Have you not seen things, heard things, felt things when others could not?"

I had, but I'd never really thought about it before. And I hadn't known my mother thought so, too, until Uncle Dean had mentioned it to me.

"Yeah, I guess."

"Your senses are superior—your sight, hearing, smell, touch, taste. And your connection to the environment, to all living things is deep and unique, giving you the ability to sense the life force in all that lies within the realm of the natural world."

"I know that sometimes I think I can sense things, feel things, but that's just my intuition—a gut feeling I get about people."

The moon hung lower in the sky, dusting the village with blue light as each window in the village sparkled like a distant star. Brell turned his head toward the cluster of homes, and his ear caught the light.

"Yes, and it is stronger in the Grove. Close your eyes," he said and held my hand. "Take a deep breath."

His words were soft and gentle like a ball of cotton grazing my ears. I closed my eyes, drawing in a long breath.

"What do you hear? What do you smell?" he continued.

"Nothing unusual," I said. Tree leaves rustled with the wind, cricket chirps echoed in the trees, and I didn't smell anything.

"Take another deep breath and try again," Brell said. "Concentrate. See the Grove in your mind. See it as you would with opened eyes and in the daylight. The magic of the Grove will help you."

I inhaled, aware of my chest as it expanded and my shoulders when they rose. Exhaling slowly, my posture settling, the Grove appeared in my head. One tree and then another. One home and then another—every detail—doors sparkling with jewels, windows flashing with colored glass, leaves wet with dew.

"I see it," I beamed. "It's beautiful. More so than I thought it was just minutes ago."

"You are seeing it with all of your senses," Brell whispered with happiness. "Now, what do you hear?"

A baby's cry erupted to my right, followed by a string of words I couldn't understand. I jumped, shifting left. "Who's here?" I asked.

"No one," Brell said. "The child and mother are in a dwelling on the other side of the Grove."

The soft scent of jasmine filled my nostrils. "And I smell something now. Flowers."

"Lusmar," Brell said. "They bloom with the setting sun and close with the dropping of the moon."

"I see them," I cried. "White, five petals, pointed like stars. Night-blooming jasmine."

"Yes," he said.

I opened my eyes and looked at Brell. "But I hadn't seen them before. I hadn't even noticed them." I turned back to the village. "But I do now. There they are."

I pointed to the far end of the valley where a tiny plant with dots of white flowers grew next to a stone path. "I, I don't understand," I said.

This had happened to me once before. I saw Brell's face in my mind before I'd met him. At the time, I thought it was just my imagination.

"Blind sight and words as images," Brell said.

"The magic of the Grove is helping me do this?" I asked.

"Yes," he said.

"This is insane," I said, shaking my head. "This whole thing. You. The Grove. Landaffens. Honestly, I'm more confused now than I was before. I still have so many questions."

"And I promise you, I will answer them the next time we meet." His voice was calm, lulling me to relax. I released a pent-up breath.

We turned to face the fringe of trees where we'd entered the Grove. As the reality of Brell's people and his world rattled in my head, not quite sinking in, the light-headedness I'd felt earlier returned. Woozy, I held his hand, and looked over my shoulder to take one last look at the Grove.

"You will feel a wind like you did so before. Do not let go of my hand. And stay by my side."

We stepped forward. A blanket of warm air wrapped our bodies, pulling us from the Grove. The woods we entered were dark and cold, lacking mystery and magic, and as we came closer to my home, a flash of anxiety washed through my chest.

"I hope my mom's still asleep," I whispered. "If she isn't, I'm going to be on restriction for at least a month."

"She is asleep," Brell said.

I knew he was right. I felt it, too—in my gut—but that sensation and gnaw of intuitivism was stronger than it had ever felt before.

We walked through the last row of trees. My car flashed with dew, and my house shone silvery gray in the dimming moonlight. The porch bulb burned yellow, insects bathing in its glow, and inside my house it was dark, and everything was silent.

"I would very much like to see you again tomorrow. Have another date," Brell said.

"I would like that, too. What time?"

"At early sun. I will wait for you in the woods."

"That means the morning?"

"Yes," he said.

"That's a pretty big window of time. How about nine o'clock?"

"Yes. Head to the boulders. I will hear you and come for you."

"I know what I'm getting you for Christmas," I said even though he might not have known about human holidays.

"What?" he asked.

"A watch."

He embraced me, crossing his arms at his wrists, holding me tightly at the waist. As I drew closer, he kissed the top of my head. I put my arms around his neck, turning until the top of my head nuzzled under his chin.

"I promise I won't tell anyone about Landaffens or the Grove."

"I know you won't. I trust you, Laura."

Yearning for his lips to meet mine, I raised my head. His

lips slid to my mouth. His kiss was soft. Tender. I drew him against me, the ardor of passion bubbling through my body, inflating my being with something I had never felt before.

I pushed my tongue between his teeth, into his mouth, cupping the back of his head firmly while the fingers of my other hand pressed into his back. He jerked away, stunned, as if I'd bitten his tongue.

"What's wrong?" I asked, pushing away from him.

"Nothing, I, I just." He stared at the ground. "You are the first girl I have ever kissed. The first girl I have ever touched this way."

"The first? Really?"

"Yes," he said. "I am inexperienced. Inept."

"You're not inept." I smiled and took one of his hands. "It was nice—really nice. I couldn't tell you hadn't done it before."

"Thank you," he said, squeezing my hands. Brell's words and the airy, whisper-like tone of his voice lulled me into a state of wanting to kiss him even more. "I will see you at the next early sun."

"Yes, at the early sun," I said.

On light feet, I cut through the dead grass to the driveway and tiptoed up the porch steps. When I reached the front door, I lifted my necklace from my shirt and held it tightly in my hand. When I opened my palm, it twinkled like a star. I turned, giving Brell a final wave. The doorknob twisted without much of a rattle, and I crept through the kitchen and down the hall to my room.

I undressed and lay in bed, turning onto my side, closing my eyes, and imagining the Grove. It formed in my mind as clearly as it had done when I was with Brell, and I took a deep breath through my nose, savoring the beauty of the Landaffen village, fresh and vibrant, as if I were still at his side overlooking it.

Brell entered my mind, his warm hands against my skin and

soft lips meeting mine. Another deep breath sent a sweet shiver down my spine. When he'd told me we were brought together by the trees, it didn't make sense, but now I understood. It was why I'd entered the forest in the first place.

I fell asleep imagining each tree was a person anchored to the earth by root-like feet. It was an odd picture but strangely satisfying at the same time.

# CHAPTER 12

As I showered the next morning, I closed my eyes and thought about Brell—again. I couldn't help it. Though we hardly knew each other, reliving his touch brought an aura of peace through my entire soul, leaving me complete and satisfied. He was responsible for the perpetual smile on my face. It was almost time for our date.

The morning sun shone brightly against the clear blue sky, its rays dancing upon the table as the kitchen curtains fluttered from a light breeze. Mom was already at work. A veil of mist lingered in the woods, clinging to the trees like phantom overcoats. I sighed at the forest's beauty, my heart warming as my residual disbelief in what I'd learned the night before dissipated like an early fog.

I reached the edge of the woods and stopped, staring at the rim of trees. Lifting my chin toward the rising sun, I inhaled slowly. The morning air roused goose bumps on my arms and legs, and I shuddered from the contrast between my cold limbs and the heat forming in my chest and cheeks as Brell entered my mind's eye, his face haloed by a backdrop of smooth, green birch and sugar maples leaves.

Opening and closing my hands dissipated the tingles in my arms, but the rhythm of my heart increased. Watching my feet with my arms out to my sides, I walked over a spread of large rocks, keeping my balance as I continued down an otherwise beaten trail carved by the hooves, claws, and paws of woodland creatures.

Brell was in the clearing. "Laura," he said when I was close enough for him to reach for me. He took both my hands and leaned forward, his mouth en route to my forehead. I closed my eyes as his warm lips gently pressed against my skin. My body rippled with excitement. My chest inflated, and I resisted the temptation to lift my chin, so his mouth could slide onto mine.

When he drew away, our eyes locked, and the stirring in my chest increased. As if one's personality was something tangible, and feelings were transmittable via wave lengths, his thoughts seemed to connect with mine, intertwining like a magical song.

*Laura*. His mouth didn't move yet the word pulsed through my head.

*Brell*, I said in my mind.

He dropped my hands, taking a step backward, and I released the air in my lungs. A ray of sunshine shot through the forest, casting a circle of bright light onto the space in which we stood. Three butterflies appeared, fluttering as if summoned by the tranquility of the woods, and a small bird landed on the tree behind Brell. We sat down on one of the boulders.

Brell's emerald shirt, embroidered with tiny trees and minute blades of grass, billowed from shoulder to wrist. An intricate woven sun with rays of gold covered his right shoulder, and a moon of silver masked his left.

A cape of green velvet pinned at his neck with a jeweled brooch hung to his waist. His leggings were of the same material and color, and his fitted boots were slick, shining like black glass.

"Your clothes are different today," I said.

"Yes, I am dressed for a five-day celebration and feast. It begins tonight at the fall of the sun."

"What kind of celebration?"

"It is the turning of the seasons, summer to fall." He lowered his chin. "During this time, no one is allowed to leave the Grove. I will not be able to see you again until the festival's end."

"Oh, that's a bummer," I said. "Why didn't you tell me about this last night?"

"I thought my parents and the council would agree to a brief reprieve each morning during the periods of rest so I could see you, but my request was denied. It would not be fitting for the son of . . ." Brell blinked and turned his head.

"Son of what?"

"My father, he is the ruler of the Grove, the king of our colony."

My heart leaped. "You're a prince?"

"Yes, that is a good translation. I am the next to take the throne. My family holds this birthright. That is why I must not leave the Grove during the feast. I cannot break the rules. Break the tradition."

"Five days is going to feel like five years."

He leaned over and kissed me, a kiss barely touching my lips but leaving my pulse pounding. He lifted my chin and kissed me again.

"I wish I could take you to the Grove for the change of seasons," he said. "I would teach you the traditional Landaffen dance and hold you under the stars. But I cannot bring you into the Grove again," he said. "Not yet, but I promise I will soon."

"I would love to go with you, too," I said. In my mind's eye, the sky darkened. A river of stars appeared above our heads, and Brell held me against his chest as we danced.

I dropped my chin to my chest. Who would he dance with if I wasn't there? The image in my head transformed. The girl Brell held wasn't me. It was a Landaffen girl, tall and lean, under layers of flowing fabric woven with fancy designs.

He brushed his lips against my forehead and smoothed my hair with his hand. "I do not want to be away from you for so long. It is only five more sunrises. On the sixth sunrise, we will be with each other again."

"That's the first day of school. Once school starts, it'll be harder for me to sneak into the woods." I ran my hand down his chest, stopping at an embroidered leaf to trace it with my fingertips.

"As long as I see you, Laura, I am satisfied. As a scout, it will be easy for me to come to your world." Brell dropped his head. "But I am worried," he said.

"Worried about what?"

"That when you begin school, you will choose the roads over the forest, and I will not see you again," he said.

"That's not going to happen. Just because I'm in school doesn't mean I can't come here again. I want to see you."

His smile weakened until he was almost expressionless. "If you stop coming here, you will forget about me."

"I could never forget about you." I set my hands on his shoulders. He closed his eyes and took a deep breath. When he exhaled, his breath was sweet and warm against my arms.

"Tell me more about being a scout," I asked. "I feel like I've stepped into a fairytale, and I still need to keep turning the pages."

"Even though scouts are one of the few who actually get to leave the Grove," he said, "we do so cautiously and only when necessary. It is actually uncommon for the son of the king to be a scout, but I insisted on the opportunity. Hearing tales of humans was not enough. I wanted to see them for myself." He kissed the top of my head. "It was my destiny to venture outside the Grove, or I would not have found you." He put his arm over my shoulder. I lay my head against his chest, listening to his heart beat slow and become steady.

"So your people believe in destiny and fate?"

"Yes, we all have paths to follow, and my path led me to you."

I nuzzled against him. "You've been to town?"

"Yes, as a scout, I need to periodically survey the landscape of this city and its people."

"What do you wear when you go there?" I asked.

"I own human clothing, but I only wear them if there is a possibility I will be seen. Most of the time, I wear Landaffen apparel and travel unnoticed, unheard."

"When do you want to be seen?"

"When it is necessary to interact with a human. At the library, when I learned about computers and used one for the first time."

"You know how to use a computer?" I imagined him at one of the computers with his fingers poised delicately on the keys.

"Yes, and a cellular phone. There is no need for computers or phones in the Grove, but it is important for my people to know about their existence and the way they are accessed and used in the human world. As the Landaffen rely on our ancient knowledge and senses, humans rely on artificial means of acquiring, keeping, and processing knowledge. This is something Landaffens should understand."

"I'd like to see you in human clothes."

"Then you will. On my next travel from the Grove as a scout, you can join me."

I pictured Brell in a T-shirt, the fabric tight at his shoulders as his biceps stretched the sleeves, and jeans worn a little loose at the waist but fitting perfectly at his rear. Skater shoes and a baseball cap completed the look. Damn he was hot!

"How do you buy clothes?"

"I take them. Hide them in a pouch."

"So you steal them?"

"Yes, it is the only way."

"Why do you need to look like one of us if you can make yourself unseen?"

"To conceal oneself requires deep concentration, physical strength, and stamina. Maintaining the mask requires practice through the change of many seasons. As scouts, our endurance to do so is unmatched, but there are still times when we become weak, and can no longer hold the illusion. When that time comes, we are visible, vulnerable, and must *be* human until our power to become invisible are renewed. Because of this, when we leave the Grove, we wear baseball hats to cover our ears."

I let go of Brell's hand to scratch a bite on my upper arm. The red lump was larger than it was the day before.

"You have been a meal for a taulik," Brell said. "A mosquito."

"Yeah, he got me yesterday."

"She," Brell corrected and smiled. "Only females bite."

With his index finger extended, he brought his hand to my arm. I stopped scratching and watched as he placed his fingertip against my bite and closed his eyes. My skin pulsed with fresh heat, its fire penetrating and burning with a bee-like sting.

He removed his finger, and it was gone—the bump, the redness, the itch, and the pain. Everything was back to normal.

"Mr. Miyagi wouldn't have been able to do that." I laughed. "Landaffens can heal. That's how you took the pain away from my hip. I'd thought it was just the heat from your hands."

"I did not heal you. You healed yourself. Magic only accelerated the process."

"Can you heal any wound? Cure any disease?"

"No. All the Landaffen magic in the world could not bring someone from a state close to death. But there are others in the Grove, our healers, whose regenerative skills are superior to mine. As a scout, my training in that area has been limited."

"How many scouts are there?"

"Twelve."

"What else do scouts do?"

"We are required to learn all we can of human ways. Your language. Your traditions. Your weaknesses and your strengths."

"Keep your friends close, and your enemies closer," I said.

Brell tilted his head. "I do not understand."

"It's a proverb, an old saying. It means to be aware of your surroundings. Know where your enemies are at all times, so if or when they strike, you'll be ready for them."

I leaned my head on his shoulder. His shirt was soft, elaborately detailed with twists and turns of silver thread patterned through its green fabric. A set of thin buttons, shaped from smooth river rock, ran its length, but the top two buttons were unfastened, revealing his gold chain and charm.

"I mean, we're your enemy, right?" I half-whispered.

"It is prophesized in the Book of Landaffia. When the ground is artificial stone beneath our feet. When the trees are no longer respected, planted only for human need. When human encroachment puts our world in danger of discovery, and humans find a way to penetrate our magic and destroy our Groves . . ." He shook his head.

"What will happen?" I asked.

"The Landaffens will let go of their magic and their traditions to hide among humans in peace." He swallowed hard, looking up at the sky. "We must always be prepared for that day.

To do so, scouts must leave the protection of their Groves and return with knowledge and truth. As a scout, it is my job to acclimate to human ways and teach all that I have learned."

"Then there are others besides me who you've shown yourself to?"

"No. Scouts do not need to interact with humans in order to learn about them. It is an oath we take. We must not enter their world through their eyes. It is forbidden. Scouts do not communicate with humans."

"Doesn't that mean you were not supposed to interact with me?"

"Yes, but you are different."

"How am I different? Please tell me," I urged. "You've already shown me the Grove and used your magic in front of me. You might as will explain everything."

He leaned closer. His warm, honey-sweet breath hit my ear. "I fear you will not accept what I tell you," he said.

"I've accepted everything else, haven't I?"

"Yes, you have, but this is something that involves you," he sighed.

"Then it is something I need to know now. Please tell me," I said, raising my voice. A pair of birds burst from the foliage above our heads. "I promise I will listen and accept everything you say."

Brell took a deep breath and released it. "At our second meeting, you asked me why I called your name and then waited so long to show myself to you." He set his hand on top of mine. "Calling your name," he said. "Seeing if you could hear me and also see me were part of the test. I had to be sure. Now after last night, I am sure."

"Sure of what?"

"You were lured to these woods because you were close to a Grove, close to my people. You were driven by instinct."

"Why?"

"You can see me. Other humans cannot do so. Your uncle could not see me."

"So anyone who's good at reading people's emotions can?" I asked.

"No," he said. He set his hand on my knee. "Your perception of others is special. Advanced. Beyond ordinary, Laura. You are much different from other humans."

"I still don't understand."

His eyes grew wider as he spoke, and the tone of his voice rang in my ears like something solid rather than a mere sound wave. "This connection and your perceptions are getting stronger. The more time you spend in the woods. The more time you spend with me. Because of this, the birds will not attack you again. Because of this, you can see me and enter the Grove."

He picked up my hand, cradling it in both of his. "Laura, one of your ancestors was of half-race."

"Half-race?"

"Yes. When this world was very new, a small colony of naïve Landaffens befriended a band of beings unlike themselves, beings with blunt ears and unrefined perceptions—humans. Unaware of the humans' need for control over land and sea, the Landaffens entrusted the humans with their only weakness—the want for peace over power—and their greatest strength—communication with the trees and beasts.

"With this knowledge, the humans sought for an unjust advantage over nature's keep. When the Landaffen refused to abide by human demands—to call deer to their slaughter and whale to be slain—the Landaffen colony was destroyed, picked off by the humans one by one as the Landaffens chose death over a life of forced servitude."

My heart dropped.

"But before the last Landaffens were killed," he said, lowering his head, "the strongest, most beautiful human females were taken into Landaffen beds. They mated and bore children—those of half-race."

"So one of my ancestors, a great, great, great, great, great grandmother, or something like that, had a child with a Landaffen?"

"Yes. You are of human blood *and* the blood of my people."

"What? Are you sure? I don't look like . . ." I brushed my fingers across my ear.

"I am positive. Your grace. Your beauty. Your elegance. Everything else about you is very much Landaffen. You saw me in the woods. No human could have done that unless he or she was of half-race."

"You allowed me to see you."

"No. I did not. You saw beyond my magic. Your capacity to sense and connect with those who have a soul is not as powerful as a full-race, but as you learn to understand and recognize your Landaffen skills, they will become greater. You connected with Bay the minute you saw one another."

"Yeah, I guess I did."

"You also have a special bond with Molly. The Landaffens' connection to the equiss is stronger than with any other animal. We can sense their needs, their desires, their pains, and their happiness, and they can sense ours. It is a special, mutual awareness."

The warmth of his hand radiated up my arm, sending a tingle through my chest.

"Every living creature has a soul—even the trees have souls. In Landaffen, it is called a 'laspis'. The laspis lives forever." He held my hands tighter. "And your senses are beyond that of a human's. You have noticed things, felt things, when others around you could not. You think it is human intuition, but it is not. You are a half-race."

"But . . ." I shook my head. I couldn't think of anything that made my mom or my dad Landaffen.

"And you could not have entered the Grove—even with my help—unless Landaffen blood pulsed through your veins."

"If you're right, wouldn't the rest of my family be like me, too?"

"No," Brell said. "Landaffen genes are strong, but they are selective, lying dormant like a seed and eventually taking root. You might be the only one in your line to carry the Landaffen legacy."

"How many people are there like me? There must be half-race people in other families, too."

"Yes, there are many of half-race throughout this land and lands across the seas, but not all of half-race will be discovered by a scout, and of those who are, not all will be given the knowledge of their sacred ancestry and introduced to a Grove."

"Why?"

"Not all of half-race share the same capabilities. A heightened intuition alone is not enough to share our secret. When a scout recognizes someone of half-race, the scout does not acknowledge him or herself. The scout reports it to the council, and the council determines whether or not the half-race is worthy. If that is the case, the scout will bring the half-race to the Grove."

"But a heightened intuition is all I have," I said.

Brell laughed. "No, Laura. There is more. Your connection to nature is also strong, and like your intuition, it will become stronger now that you know the truth. You are aware of your surroundings and your perception of those around you is sharp. Your ability to make magic will come."

An awkward chill spread though my chest, and I gasped.

"I've . . . I've never done anything remotely magical before," I said. "I can't even do a cheesy card trick without messing it up."

"The older the Landaffen, the greater his or her magic. My powers are weak since I have only seen 19 winters, and my training has been minimal. You will hone your Landaffen skills in time."

"Like to control a wind?"

"Yes, the power to work the wind is one."

"Honestly, if this is true, I don't know if it's a blessing or a curse. If you're right, what's going to happen to me now?" My bottom lip trembled. "I have a life as a human. It is the only life I know."

"Yes, that is true, but unlike a Landaffen of whole race," Brell said, "you can be allowed to live in both worlds, while keeping mine a secret. No one can know about my people—not even those who are closest to you."

"I will never tell. I promised I wouldn't, but still, I'm not sure I believe I really am a half-race." I gulped. "This is just too much to take in right now."

He cupped my chin in his palm and brushed my cheek with the back of his other hand.

"I know you won't tell our secrets. I trust you, Laura. Part of your essence, your soul—they are Landaffen. I was drawn not only to this but to your human side as well. I sensed your intelligence, your kindness, your respect for all living things. But," he paused, "if you were whole human, I would still feel the same way about you."

He kissed me, his fingers melting against my back. I brought my arms around his neck, and my chest touched his. A blissful shiver washed over my body. I parted my lips, and he did the same, our tongues meeting. Like a sweet melody, a wave of euphoria filled my chest, vibrating every nerve of my being. I wanted his kiss and his touch to last forever, but I loosened my arm and drew way.

"You said I could live in both worlds *unlike* a Landaffen of whole race. So, you mean you can't be in my world, too? Wear clothes? Make yourself seen by humans, but keep your ears covered, wearing a baseball cap?"

He scooted closer, and I watched the lean muscles in his thighs contract under his dark-blue leggings. "The amount of time I spend outside the Grove is something to be determined by my father. Soon I will take you back to the Grove to be welcomed and accepted by my colony."

"You haven't told anyone there about me?"

"No. But I will during the turn of seasons when there is a reason to celebrate many things."

"Are you sure your people will accept me?"

"Yes, you are half-race," he assured. "And my father is the king."

He kissed my forehead, and I closed my eyes, savoring the brush of his warm lips against my skin, easily believing everything he'd told me. "It is time for me to go," he said, turning his head toward the sky. "The celebration will soon begin. My presence is needed."

As he lifted his hand to stroke my hair, the sleeve of his tunic grazed my cheek. He kissed me lightly on the lips. "I will call for you in five days."

"I have school. I won't be home until two, and that gives me only a few hours before my mom comes home."

"I will send Bay to wait for you. When he sees you are home, he will let me know, and I will come for you."

We walked through the woods and stopped when my house came into view. We hugged, and he gave me a long kiss, leaving my whole body tingling.

"Good-bye, Laura," he said. "I will see you in five days' time."

"Good-bye," I said.

When I reached my porch, I turned toward the woods and watched him slip between the trees. I sat down, staring at the woods, wondering how and if I really wanted to keep something like this a secret from my family.

What was going to happen to me now? How would I balance my life in both places? I couldn't leave my world for the Grove—or could I? No! I'd have too much to lose when it came to the human ways I loved and have always known.

I wasn't sure I could live without a television, a computer, or a cell phone. Could Brell take me to the homecoming dance, winter formal, or even to my prom? What about a high school football game?

I wanted to go to the mall with a boyfriend—to sit next to him at the theater, eating popcorn. I wanted a boyfriend who could bring me flowers on Valentine's Day and spend Christmas day snuggling in front of a fireplace after opening presents.

But at the same time, I didn't have any real plans for my future here. I didn't know what I wanted to do for a career or what I wanted to become. A deep yearning to do something significant with my life burned deeply in my soul. I couldn't remember a time in my life when it hadn't. And the path I needed to take in order to feed that desire was still something I had to figure out.

None of this seemed to matter when I was actually with Brell. When he'd kissed me, my world became a distant place, and I felt ready to give up everything human in order to be with him.

But now, on the porch, facing the forest, I yearned not only to feel his hand in mine, but to bring him into my human life as well. I wanted him to experience being an American teenager with me.

Being a half-race, if I really was one, didn't necessarily mean I had to split my world between here and the Grove. I could forget everything Brell had told me, forget him, and go on with my life as if we'd never met and the word Landaffen meant nothing to me.

I'd finish high school and live at home while attending the local junior college and working twenty-hours a week. And by then, maybe I will have figured out what I want to do with my life. But what if I don't?

There was one problem with the scenario I'd just painted for myself. I knew I'd never be able to forget Brell or the Grove or anything he'd told me. With Brell stuck in the Grove for five days, I certainly had plenty of time to think through everything.

I yawned, rolling onto my back, the reality of being a so-called half-race flooding my mind. I couldn't remember the last time I'd slept so soundly and so late into the morning, but now my heart raced, and for a second, I couldn't catch my breath.

I sat up, forcing myself to inhale deeply and exhale slowly through my nose. Sitting in my bed with a poster of my favorite boy band hanging on the wall and my dresser piled with drugstore makeup and bottles of fingernail polish, none of what Brell had told me seemed real again.

In the Grove, everything had been so much easier to believe and except. But right now, besides my growing emotions toward Brell, I didn't feel any differently than I had when I lived in New Mexico.

There was only one thing I could do at this point—try not to overthink everything and act as normally as I could. Soon I'd be with Brell again, and he'd help me figure all of this out.

I dropped onto my back, imagining myself in the Grove dancing with Brell under the stars, until my alarm went off, spoiling the image. Until now, I'd forgotten all about my morning plans.

Today while Brell celebrated the turning of summer to fall, dancing under the moonlight to who-knows-what kind of music and enjoying a royal feast made up of who-knows-what kind of delicacies, I'd be taking a tour of Forest View with Odd Ninja Todd.

I checked my phone—of course there weren't any notifications—and got ready for what I anticipated to be a boring day. For breakfast, I ate a granola bar, washing it down with a glass of orange juice, and headed out the door with my locker number and class schedule.

Fog shrouded the trees, and whiffs of mist spilled into the field by the road like steam from a witch's brew. I wondered if the Grove was also being shaped by the magic of the mist. The Challenger started easily despite the cool, damp air, the purr of its engine breaking the morning silence. I revved the engine several times, enjoying its power, and drove to school.

Todd was right about it being a teacher work day. When I entered campus, heading toward building two, I passed an adult I assumed was a teacher. She said "good morning" to me when I walked by. The main door to the science building was also propped open.

Building two was a long, two-story brick-clad structure with a door at each end. Both doors were open, revealing the hall. I checked my phone. Todd was five-minutes late. Something inside me told me he wasn't going to make it. A feeling of unease grew in my chest, but I ignored it.

I sat down on a bench next to the building and waited, catching up on all the missed texts and notifications that blew up my phone once I'd had reception again.

A mulberry tree in a cracked cement planter bellowed with bird song. Leaves crackled against the wind, and a bumble bee buzzed to my left, lumbering toward me and flying away with the swipe of my hand.

Two guys walked into the quad, their faces buried in their class schedules, and I could only assume they were freshman doing the same thing I was going to do once Todd got here. I watched them break into a jog toward the ramp, kicking up dust as they cut across a patch of dirt instead of taking the sidewalk. The clomp of their shoes against concrete faded into muffled taps at the top of the ramp as they dashed to the right and disappeared behind another building.

My phone vibrated. It was Todd apologizing for having to cancel. His grandfather had a stroke in the middle of the night, and Todd had been in the hospital at his grandfather's bedside since one in the morning. Todd had fallen asleep in a chair, and just woken up.

I texted there was no need to apologize; I completely understood, and I hoped his grandfather would be okay.

Popping up from the bench, I walked to building two, and entered. I could do this on my own. I didn't need a self-proclaimed ninja to escort me.

Lockers with peeling blue paint lined the walls on both sides of the hall between classroom doors and glass cases displaying high-school memorabilia—trophies, faded pennants, science fair awards, medals with crumpled ribbons in the school's colors, laminated newspaper articles, and yellowed paper certificates curled at the edges with age. A translucent panel ran the length of the center of the ceiling. All but two of its fluorescent tubes were burned out, and those that remained flickered and hummed.

Halfway down the hall on the bottom row, I found my locker, number 236. I lowered to one knee and put in the combination with one hand, holding the pink locker card with the other to read the numbers. The dial was stiff but loosened with several turns. I pulled the latch. The catch lifted, but the door wouldn't budge.

I jerked the handle, and the bang of the metal door against its frame boomed through the hall, rattling with an echo as it sprang open. A layer of dirt lined the bottom of my locker along with an abandoned bookmark that read: "We read to know we are not alone."

Just as I was about to close my locker, the double doors to my right slammed shut, pinching off the beam of sunlight entering the building from the west. The muscles in my legs tightened.

"Laura," someone said in a deep whisper.

In my mind's eye, I saw the boy from the grocery store, mocking me with an evil sneer. I shot up from the floor and kicked my locker closed with my foot. No one was there.

"Who's there? What do you want?" I said as I walked toward the opened doors at the left end of the hall, taking short, controlled breaths.

The lights above flickered and buzzed. My class schedule slipped from my hand. A dull rumble sounded, and cool air shot from the vents overhead. One door to the left swung from its frame and closed, the ray of sunlight on the tile floor collapsing like a silk fan. I quickened my pace. With a heavy creak, the second door joined the first, closing slowly as I broke into a run. It clicked closed before I reached it.

I pushed the metal bar with both hands, but the spring-loaded crash bar locked in place and the door wouldn't budge. Ramming it with my side, I tried again. A band of light whipped across the linoleum at my feet, and I turned.

At the other end of the building, one side of the double door had re-opened. With fingers spread, I held my hand in front of my eyes, filtering the blinding sunlight, but the door re-shut before I could see if someone had entered.

Anchoring my feet on the floor, I butted my hip against the door a second time, hitting the crash bar with my full weight. It remained locked and didn't budge.

"Who are you? What do you want?" I screamed.

The lights went out. I gulped and twisted, pressing my back against the door. From both ends of the hall, a thin line of light bled from beneath the solid, double doors.

The sound of footsteps cut through the corridor, light steps with soft soles. I sidestepped to the wall, fumbling down its length.

I caught a doorknob to a classroom with my hand and gave it a twist. It was locked. I found another knob and another. They, too, refused to turn. Peering down the hall, I squinted against the darkness.

As my eyes adjusted, everything black became gray, and the more I concentrated, the more contrast I saw between the banks of lockers, glass cases, and the floor. A figure appeared, an elongated dark smear against the wall across from me.

"What do you want?" I demanded again, lowering my chin and glaring at an oval shape in the place where a pair of eyes should be.

The line of light under the door at the other end of the hall morphed into a solid beam of brightness as the door re-opened slowly.

The smudge sprung toward me, a weightless blur of gray, and I dashed to my right, pumping my arms as I raced toward the open door. A silhouette took its place in the door frame, piercing the light.

I increased my speed and raised my forearm across my face. The figure stepped to the side as I broke through the doorway and entered a small courtyard outside the gym.

Three trees lined the edge of the quad leading to the front of the school, and underneath one of them stood the grocery-store boy. I looked over my shoulder. The door to building two closed. Two streaks of white whipped toward me and stopped. I scrambled to my left to avoid them.

And now there were three—the grocery-store boy and his two friends from the theater. They stood in a row facing me with their arms crossed and legs shoulder-width apart, their expressions hard and unforgiving. All three wore jeans, white T-shirts, and blue baseball caps.

The two freshmen boys I'd seen earlier entered the quad, heading toward building two.

"Hey," one of them said to me with a lift of his chin.

The guys in baseball caps didn't move, and the freshmen walked by without taking any notice of them. The three were Landaffens! Scouts! They had to be!

"Why aren't you at the feast," I said, drawing my shoulders back.

The grocery-store boy grinned, two dimples pocking his cheeks.

"Does Brell know you're here? Does he know you've been following me?"

According to Brell, scouts weren't supposed to immediately interact with those of half-race. They're required to alert the council first. Brell would have known they'd found me. He would have told me there were others from the Grove who'd recognized me for what I was.

This wasn't right. It wasn't supposed to be this way. There was something unnerving and dangerous about these scouts, and my intuition told me they weren't from Brell's Grove.

"What do you want? I asked.

The three moved forward, taking slow steps. I dashed left, the *pat pat* of their boots behind me. The Landaffens were faster, cutting me off as I rounded the next building.

Spinning on my heels, I ran back the way I came, my purse

banging against my hip. A blur burst to my right, and the grocery-store boy appeared again, matching my pace. Another scout jumped in front of me. I stumbled to a stop, staring him in the face and catching my breath as he approached, the other scouts joining him.

I shuffled backward against the closed door of the building behind me. "What do you want?" I shouted again.

The grocery-boy sneered, lifting one eyebrow. Was he toying with me, testing my abilities?

My hands trembling, I clasped the building's handle, pushed the release, and raced inside. This building was the gym. I pulled the door closed and sprinted through the foyer and across the lacquered floor.

The lights were off, but rows of windows cast beams of dusty light across the retracted bleachers and onto the wooden floor. Half of the hinged windows were propped open. The others appeared nailed or painted shut.

A gymnast's balance beam sat at one end next to a pile of stacked tumbling mats. I could hide there. Wait until the scouts were gone. Lifting the biggest mat, I propped it against the wall in the corner and crouched down behind it, taking deep breaths through my nose as I listened for them.

The gym door clicked open and slammed shut.

"Estuan swalsion esh."

I took an imperceptible breath. The floor vibrated, and the rumble of bouncing wood, the bending of metal joints, and the turning of rusty wheels echoed through the gym as the bleachers began to extend from the walls.

"Lethlo heth signos." The voice came from above, resonating with anger and delight. "Gasherlin emf lef queran!"

My mat was flush to the wall with the exception of a tiny, coin-wide gap where the interior foam was crushed and thinned. Rising to my knees, I peered through it, and gasped.

A Landaffen stood on the basketball hoop above me, the center of his boots balancing upon the orange rim. He looked at me, chuckled, shook his head, and jumped.

Kicking away the mat, I scrambled to my feet as he landed in front of me. Another scout was at my left, and the grocery-store boy guarded the back door.

Sprinting to the bleachers, I raced toward the only place I thought I might escape. I rushed up to the open windows, skipping every other bench as I leapt upward. At the top, I pulled my cell phone from my purse and turned to face my tormentors.

"I'm going to call the front office. People will come for me."

I tapped my phone, bringing up the school's website and its directory. The grocery-store boy jumped, landing atop the third bench from the floor, his movements controlled and graceful. The bleachers barely moved or rattled.

"I'm calling right now," I warned bringing my phone to my ear.

"Thank you for calling Forest View High School," a recorded voice said. "School will resume on . . ."

"Hello, I'm locked in the gym," I said.

"For information regarding late registration, please refer to our website . . ."

"They're on their way," I said.

The grocery-store boy jumped again, clearing four more rows.

I shifted right, pressing my back against the wall just below the row of windows. A gust of warm air hit my face. The grocery-store boy jumped from the floor, light-footed, landing within six rows from me.

In one movement, I grabbed the window ledge, digging my fingers into the hardened putty as I gripped the termite-eaten frame with my hands. Swinging my leg upward and out the window, my purse and upper body followed. With my wrists twisting and fingers fumbling, my other leg cleared the window.

Dangling from the sill, I swayed, readjusting my grip. The muscles in my arms burned. My fingertips numbed. I let go, bracing for the pain I'd feel in my heels and calves when I landed. But the pain never came.

I popped up on my feet and raced to the front of the school, upsetting a flock of pigeons as I crossed the lawn in the upper quad. At the top of the parking-lot stairs, I dug in my purse for my keys and rushed down the steps to my car.

The Challenger roared to a start. I gripped the steering wheel, hit the gas, and knocked it in reverse. As I backed from the parking space, the Challenger jerked backward and rocked. I threw it in drive, and it pitched again.

A shadow shot across my windshield. I followed the smudge of grey. It morphed into the grocery-store boy as he stared at me through the window. His eyes grew wide, and one side of his lip rose into a warped smile.

I increased my speed through the parking lot. The Challenger rumbled. Its engine roared. A car pulled out in front of me, and I was forced to stop and wait. The boy laughed, throwing back its head.

The Challenger creaked, and a soft rattle emanated from the trunk. I twisted to see out the rear window. Another scout stood on the back of my car, his knees bent and arms extended, his upper lip twisting into a mocking grin. The car ahead of me started down the row toward the exit lane. I gritted my teeth, as I followed the car at a snail's pace. The scouts bobbed but remained steady on their feet.

Shifting into first, I jerked the steering wheel left, popped the clutch, and hit the gas. The Challenger lurched forward, its wheels spinning with a screech. Both boys barely moved as they swayed in time with the Challenger's acceleration.

The third boy appeared as I turned onto the street. Snarling under thick brows, he jogged alongside my car. The grocery-store boy disappeared, and I heard him land on the roof. I readjusted my hold of the steering wheel and pressed the gas harder, breaking the speed limit until the light ahead of me turned yellow and then red.

Peering through the driver's side window, the third boy met me eye-to-eye. My face and chest grew hot. He tapped the window and nodded to his right, daring me to open the car door.

*Beep! Beep!* The driver behind me stuck his head from his driver's window, and shouted, "Come on, move it. What are you waiting for?"

I pressed the gas, and the Challenger jumped forward. The grocery boy leaped from the hood, a fuzzy smudge against the sky. The boy on the trunk jumped to the asphalt, his arms flying out to his sides as he landed. The scout to my left took off in a sprint, disappearing with his friends, and I continued down Main Street unable to go over thirty-miles-per-hour due to the traffic.

The next light went from yellow to red. I stopped, and with a flash, the grocery store boy was in the street standing in front of my car. He smirked, his knees bent and arms out to his sides. In a smooth, graceful movement, he jumped, catching the street-light cable with both hands. He pulled himself onto the wire and stood trapeze-like, arms folded and head bowed. The streetlight bobbed and became still.

My pulse pounded in my throat and neck. I gripped the steering wheel hard and readied my foot to hit the gas when the light changed. It turned green, and I pressed the pedal. From my rearview mirror, I saw him on the asphalt behind me, legs apart and arms still folded across his chest. He dashed to the sidewalk as the car behind me came toward him.

At the next intersection, the light changed from yellow to red before I could cross through it. I came to a stop. "Damn it!" I shouted between clamped teeth.

The light changed. I stomped on the gas pedal and released the clutch. The Challenger shot forward.

There he was again, balancing on the next traffic-light cable like he'd done before. I hit the top of my steering wheel with my fist.

Traffic flowed perpendicular across the intersection. Pedestrians occupied the sidewalks on both sides of the street, but no one noticed the ball-capped boy teetering twenty feet above.

When the light changed, I smashed the gas, and the Challenger took me to the next block and through the next light. There was only one more light before I'd turn onto the road leading out of town. From there I could punch the accelerator and lose him.

The light switched to yellow. There was no way I could beat it before it turned red. As I came to a stop, there he was. He tugged the bill of his baseball cap and glared at me with squinted eyes. I revved the engine and he winked.

When the light turned green, I raced forward, the Challenger's muffler rattling. From a side street, a blue truck pulled into the lane next to me. It was Uncle Dean. Phyllis was with him. They waved at me. As I waved back, the grocery-boy scout appeared from out of nowhere at a sprint and jumped onto the roof of my car.

Uncle Dean rolled down his window, gave me a thumbs up, and shouted, "Lookin good, Laura."

Phyllis wasn't smiling, and she didn't look at me. She kept her eyes fixed on my hood and the scout! Did she see him? I flashed a glance at her, trying to catch her eyes, trying to see if she'd give me some kind of hint of recognition, but she wouldn't turn her head.

Was she a half-race like me? It would make sense—the keychain, her paintings, and how she wanted me to look through that book of magical woodland creatures. She knew I was a half-race, too.

Then why wasn't she doing anything to help me? With eyes unblinking and lips slightly parted, her face remained unexpressive, bordering on unconcerned.

The scout continued to ignore her, focusing all of his attention on me. He knew Phyllis, and she knew him. That was the only explanation. And it also made Phyllis my enemy.

When Uncle Dean reached a driveway marked with the sign "Mary's Greasy Spoon," he flipped on his right turn signal. He waved as I passed. Phyllis still hadn't moved. When I looked back at my hood, the scout was gone.

I turned onto the two-lane highway leading toward out of town and punched the gas bringing my speed to sixty-five-miles an hour. A moment later, the Challenger jerked, sputtered, and slowed. I pushed on the gas, but it continued to lose power. I smacked the steering wheel and checked the gauges. The oil pressure was low, but the temperature was high, the orange needle reading between the midpoint and the "H". Steam erupted from under the hood.

This was the last thing I needed. Thankfully there was a two-pump gas station just down the road and in view.

The Challenger chugged on, steam rising, partially obliterating my view, as I pulled into the station. The owner's name was Dick. Uncle Dean had told me Dick preferred to be called Richard, but everyone called him Dick anyway. He was an old man in his sixties with salt and pepper hair, a big belly, and a tanned, wrinkled face. His eyebrows were overgrown, and stray, gray hairs stuck from his ears and nostrils.

I rolled down my window.

"Hi, little lady," Dick said. "Looks like you're having a problem." He pointed to the steam coming out from under the hood.

He wore overalls without an undershirt, exposing the leathery aged skin of his arms, shoulders, and a good portion of his chest, which was also covered in salt and pepper spindly hair.

"Yeah, it's not running right. I pulled over, so I could call my uncle. It seemed to just lose power for no reason."

"I haven't seen you or your mother here in quite a while."

"Yeah, we haven't been going into town that much lately."

He ran his hand across the roof of my car and patted it like a dog. "Yep, I heard you were the one who bought this car. You're going to have every motor head in town jealous of you. That librarian," he continued, "she's a stitch, that sweet gal. She refused to sell this baby, and after a while, most of us assumed she'd auctioned it off. But I figured she had it hidden, and I was right." His laugh turned into a cough, and his cough turned into a gag. He spit in the dirt.

Dick circled my car, stopping at the trunk. "Oh, boy," he said, wiping his brow and shaking his head. "Here's your problem."

I got out of the Challenger and joined him behind my car. He bent down and pulled a wad of something from each tail pipe. He shook the material in his hands, and the wads un-crumpled and fluttered like crimson flags.

"What are these?" he asked. "Scarves?"

"I have no idea," I answered, furious that someone had tampered with my car. He handed them to me. They were soft and sheer, and on closer inspection, I saw the material was hemmed with metallic thread.

"Now, who would have done that?" Dick asked.

I stared at the glistening fabric. It had to have been one of the scouts. "I'm not sure," I answered, although I had a feeling who the culprit was. The pulse in my neck throbbed, as I scanned my surroundings. There was no sign of a scout.

"You couldn't have gotten far with your exhaust all plugged up like that."

"I came from Forest View."

"Must be one them high school boys pulling a prank. Jealous you got this car." He snickered and coughed for the umpteenth time.

He walked to the front of the Challenger and popped the hood, waving his hand as a cloud of water vapor hit his face. "And the culprit didn't stop there," he said. "Stuffed this in front of the radiator. Restricted the air flow. Made it heat up." He held up a piece of oil-soaked white fabric.

Something brushed against my leg. "Huh?" I stiffened and held a gag as the grocery-store boy crawled from beneath my car.

"You ok, little lady?" The old man leaned closer to me.

"Yeah, I'm fine." From the corner of my eye, I glared at the jerk-of-a-Landaffen.

"Now, don't you worry about whoever did this. These local boys are harmless. Just givin' you a scare. I'm sure nothing will happen again." I took the square of fabric from Dick, and he brushed his hands together.

The grocery-store boy dashed to the other side of my car, and I noticed he was missing one of his shirt sleeves. The material matched the square of fabric I held.

"I hope so," I said, crumpling the cloth in my fist and chucking it into the trash can by the pump.

"Now get in and start her up," Dick said.

The scout crept slyly to the back of my car. Leaving my door open, I sat down and started my car, revving the engine.

"You're good to go," the old man said, patting the hood.

"Actually, I might as well top it off while I'm here." I dug in my purse, found a ten-dollar bill, and scooted from the seat to hand him the money. "I'll take five dollars' worth," I said, pulling the fuel nozzle from the nearest pump.

"I'll get your change." He hobbled back into the station.

The grocery boy moved closer, peering at me from behind the pump. "Leave me alone," I warned and squeezed the pump's trigger, releasing a stream of gas onto his head and chest. He gagged, springing away from my vehicle.

I shoved the nozzle in the pump, jumped into my car, started the engine, and drove away, my tires spinning. Dick rush from the station, waving my change in the air. Shifting into second, third, and fourth, I reached the posted speed limit in a matter of seconds.

From my rearview mirror, I watched a head pop up from the trunk. "What the hell?" I muttered and thrust the pistol grip back into third, pressing the gas pedal to the floor. The Challenger came alive, accelerating toward redline with a jerk that forced me to lock my elbows and squeeze the steering wheel as hard as I could.

From my mirrors, I saw the boy's eyes strain to remain open. His red lips pursed. His ball cap flew from his head, exposing the points of his ears poking through his cream-colored hair as thin strands undulated wildly with the wind.

I shifted back into fourth. As my speed increased, the skin on his cheeks wrinkled toward his ears, and the tips of his fingers paled as he tightened his grip at the base of the hood.

With miles of straight, empty road ahead of me, I maintained my speed, the tires squealing, grasping for traction, pressing me deeper into the seat as the car vibrated and roared. The speedometer needle rose: 110, 115, 120 miles per hour.

A blur shot backward as the boy flew from the trunk and

rolled onto the side of the road, generating a rock-loaded cloud of dirt.

I slowed to a stop, and when the dust cleared, I saw him lying lifeless, his body curled in a fetal position. He looked dead. I didn't want him to die. I just wanted him to leave me alone. It didn't need to be like this.

I put my car in park and opened the door. As I twisted from my seat, his legs twitched, and he stretched his arms toward the sky. Rolling onto his stomach, he lifted his head and curled his lips into an evil sneer. I slammed the door and drove off, hitting sixty miles per hour in a matter of seconds. The grocery-boy got to his feet, jogged to the middle of the road, and stood. I shifted gears, driving home as fast as I could.

# CHAPTER 14

The trio of Landaffens had become more than mischievous stalkers. They were bold and intrusive, their boyish faces indifferent, cold, and evil. I didn't want to find out what they had planned for me. Whatever it was, it wasn't good. I could feel it.

I had to tell Brell what happened. I had to find out who those scouts were, why they were terrorizing me, and how Phyllis fit in to all of this. Unfortunately, I couldn't do much of anything until the feast ended or until I confronted Phyllis.

My heartbeat quickened and my knees and hands trembled to the point of spilling my mug of chamomile tea. I sat at the kitchen table hoping it would calm my nerves as I peeked through the crack in the curtains and listened for any foreign sounds.

It was just past ten o'clock in the morning. Mom wouldn't be home until about five-thirty. I'd made sure both doors and every window in the house were locked, but nothing made me feel safe. The grocery-store boy didn't seem to be able to run fast enough to follow me, but for all I knew, he'd secretly trailed me once before and already knew where I lived.

Molly whinnied. I set down my cup. It wasn't her "I'm hungry" kind a whinny, and she'd already been fed. It came in short bursts like an alarm or warning. I rushed to the other side of the house and peered out the window.

The sun was just below its highest point, casting short shadows on the ground. The wind rumbled and whipped, and a deep humming sound rode the breeze. A pair of trees next to the house swayed, their topmost branches nodding, and the hum, now a controlled noise, grew louder, reverberating through the house in a coordinated rhythm of whines and buzzes.

The windowpanes shook in their frames. The front door thumped in its casing. I dashed to the living room window and moved the curtain aside to view the porch. In a chaotic swirl of noise and color, my mother's wind chimes pitched and stirred, their movements becoming more erratic, their clang growing louder as strands of beads and strips of metal twirled and tossed independently from one another.

The frenzied clanking increased, and a simple melody broke from the madness, a distinctive eerie rhythm of flat notes and sharp tones sending chills up my spine and through my chest.

There was only one explanation. A Landaffen worked the wind, weaving the wind chime's dance into a taunting Landaffen song!

The house hitched, vibrations shooting from wall to wall. A soft thud on the roof cut through the gale's violent rasp, and like a distant drum, something beat against the side of the house. A myriad of taps followed from one exterior wall to the next.

There was more than one!

I couldn't call my mom, Uncle Dean, or the police. Once they arrived, the Landaffens would either flee or simply not be seen, and I'd be stuck, having wasted everyone's time. I'd have to say that I'd mistook the weather for a trespasser in order to cover up the unbelievable truth.

A series of thumps rumbled across the roof, and a thud hit the porch floor. The front doorknob rattled, and the dead bolt twisted with a click even though it had been locked. I drew a big breath and backed away from the door and toward the kitchen. My car keys were on the counter, the etched charm sparkling in a ray of light sneaking from between the curtains.

The clatter of wind chimes ceased, the last of its mocking Landaffen tune fading into the afternoon like a gentle breeze, and all was still and quiet, except for the beating of my heart echoing in my ears.

I held my breath. The doorknob turned. I snatched my keys from the counter. The door opened. The ripe, oily smell of gasoline hit my nose.

"Laura." It was the grocery-store boy.

He crossed his arms, and his shoulders lifted and settled. His clothes were tattered, plastered with dust. The side of his nose and his left cheek bore scratches and purple bruises. His hair, a tangled mess of blond, was clumsily smoothed against his ears. A drop of dried blood hung from his swollen bottom lip.

"What do you want?" I asked.

Another boy appeared in the doorway behind him. The grocery-store boy unlocked his arms, bringing one hand to his waist where the handle of a knife protruded from a tan, leather sheath that hung from his belt.

I shifted left, spun, and ran to the other side of the house. Menacing laughter rose behind me as I unlocked and opened the back door. The third Landaffen was on the back patio, grinning, one eyebrow sharply arched like he'd been expecting me.

Dodging to the left, I burst past him, but his fingers caught my sleeve. Yanking from his grip, I pushed forward to the front yard. The Challenger was only a few yards away, its white hood glistening like a mirror in the afternoon sun.

Something tugged my arm and traveled to my hand—the suction of air twisting and pulling my fingers as I reached the driver's door. The grocery-store boy was on the porch, working the wind, his fingers plucking the air. I resisted, fighting to keep my keys tight in my grip. Currents of air rippled, tugging my fingers, draining my strength. Against my might, my index finger peeled from the keychain, my muscles weakening.

My keys dropped to the ground, upsetting the dusty earth. With a flick of his wrist, the wind subsided, my tensed muscles relaxed, and I dropped to my knees. The ground beneath my keys twirled, a tornado of dusts and leaves. Caught in its suction, the two keys lifted a few inches in the air, but the charm acted as if glued to the ground.

The grocery-boy Landaffen spoke to the wind, gesturing frantically with his hand and scowling, but my charm didn't move. I reached for my keys. A blast of wind knocked my arm aside, and I fell forward.

Dust burned my eyes and coated my damp lips in a grainy film. I coughed and gagged. Rising to my palms and kicking off with my feet, I lunged forward. But abruptly, the wind died, and I fell flat on my stomach, scraping my chin on the ground. A boot-clad foot came down on my keys, barely missing my fingers. I looked up to find the grocery boy glaring down at me.

I pushed away from him, rising to my feet. Another Landaffen appeared to my left, and from the corner of my eye, I saw the third, a thick blur of brown, dashing toward my right.

The grocery-store boy tapped his sheath with his hand menacingly.

Taking a step backward, I spun and sprinted to the back of the house toward Molly's stall. I threw open the gate, grabbed a handful of Molly's mane at the whither, and pulled myself onto her bare back.

Molly's head jerked and ears dropped as the trio of Landaffens stopped outside her stall. She snorted, pawing the ground with her hoof. I gave her a kick and made a clicking sound, and she bolted from her stall. The dodging Landaffens futilely reached for her as we blew passed them.

Moving my body in rhythm with hers, I shifted my weight. She was especially receptive to my commands, responding with the squeeze of my legs and movement of my upper body.

Guiding her toward the woods, I looked over my shoulder. Two Landaffens used the trees, swinging and leaping from branch-to-branch, rapidly catching up to us. The grocery-store boy racing on foot was the only one of the three coming close enough to mount Molly.

"Come on, girl," I screamed and gave her another click and kick. Molly's legs burst with power, but the Landaffen met us at her flank, and in an instant, I felt the boy's chest against my back. The smell of gasoline was thick as his hot breath bathed my neck.

His hands fumbled to my waist, trying to get his grip around me. I threw my free arm behind me, jabbing my elbow into his side. A sharp gasp escaped his lips and he lost his hold and slipped from Molly's rear. Looking back, I saw the grocery-store boy leap to his feet and disappear into the trees.

Suddenly Molly gave a loud huff. She lowered her haunches and stiffened her forelegs, skidding to a stop. I jerked forward, squeezing my legs just in time to stay mounted.

"Come on, girl," I gasped. "We can't stop now. They'll catch up to us."

I kicked her sides and made clicking sounds with my mouth, but she wouldn't move. "Molly, go!" I desperately screamed. Twigs snapped. Leaves crunched. "They're coming," I said, giving her another kick. She didn't move. "Damn it, Molly!"

I slid from her back, grabbed the nearest branch from the ground, and held it above my head. Ready to fight, looking to both sides, listening for footsteps.

We were in a small clearing within a ring of trees. The tree closest to me was marked with an "X," meaning the Grove was just ahead.

I lowered my arm and dropped the branch. No wonder Molly stopped. Doomed by the magic of the Grove, if we'd kept going, we would have lost our sense of direction to become easy prey. There was only one thing we could do.

"Trust me, girl," I told Molly, lovingly stroking her neck. With a gentle tug to her reins, she hesitantly inched forward. "Good girl," I said and gave her another pat. She planted her hoof and took another step. "We can do this," I reassured her, brushing her forelock with my fingers.

A branch snapped, and at the far end of the clearing, a Landaffen dropped from a tree and rushed toward us.

"Let's go, Molly. This is it!" I said, jumping onto her back. If I really was someone of half-race, this should work.

We plowed forward, breaking through the circle of trees. A thick blanket of wind engulfed our bodies, warm and sweet, as it pulled and twisted, draining the stiffness from my limbs. Abruptly, the wind settled, and I opened my eyes.

"We did it. We're in the Grove!" I said under my breath. The Landaffen hadn't followed me. But why?

"Ledian bain!"

I gasped, and Molly arched her neck.

Two Landaffen males stood before us at the top of a ridge with arrows notched and bows drawn. They wore flowing fabrics of green, restricted at their chests and shoulders by thick leather plates.

I looked past them at the valley below. The Grove's rolling hills, river, and charming village were as magical and captivating in the daylight as they had been in the dead of night.

# CHAPTER 15

"Please, don't hurt me. My name is Laura, and this is Molly," I said, raising my hands in the air. "Brell is a friend of mine. Please take me to him," I said quickly.

I glanced over my shoulder. The trees were still. Molly pinned back her ears, and her muscles tensed beneath me. I dared to slowly lower one hand to pet her on the side of the neck.

"It'll be fine, girl," I whispered.

The men exchanged glances and lowered their bows. Both Landaffens had brown hair to their shoulders, blue eyes, and delicately sculpted faces. One wore his hair drawn behind his ears. A silver cuff wrapped across his forehead.

"The one called Laura will come with me. Gwent will take your horse," the man with the headband said. His accent was thicker than Brell's.

I dismounted Molly and hugged her neck. "You'll be okay, girl," I said and ran my fingers down her forehead to her nose.

Gwent held out his hand, and she touched it with her

muzzle. He took her chin in his palm and led her from the ridge.

"I am called Parolin," the other Landaffen said. His headband sparkled, reflecting the trees.

He was slightly taller than Brell. His wide chest expanded gently with each breath, his leather armor rising and falling in unison. Strapped onto his left calf just above his ankle, a sheath and dagger hung, its wooden handle exposed, displaying intricately carved images of leaves surrounding a mighty horse head with flared nostrils. His eyes rode the length of my body.

My jeans, boots, and shirt were blotched with patches of dirt, and my hair felt heavy and smelled like dust. I brushed a film of dirt from my chin and found a scratched patch of skin. It stung when I daubed it dry with my fingertips.

"The one called Laura, how were you able to enter this Grove?"

I swallowed hard. "I'm, um, half-Landaffen," I said.

He brought his hand to the right side of my face and pulled my hair from my ear. His eyebrows furrowed. "Come with me," he said.

From the valley below, the sounds of trickling water, bird song, and the low hum of music hit my ears, but the Grove itself appeared empty.

"Where is everyone?" I asked.

"It is the time of Silent Appreciation. It will be over soon, and then the next feast will begin."

An elaborately carved staircase of polished wood took us from the top of the ridge to the bottom of the valley. With each step, the partially exposed blade of Parolin's dagger flashed in the sun. In his left hand, he held his bow, and a quiver full of arrows fletched with red feathers, hung across his back. Brell hadn't carried any weapons.

"Are you a soldier?" I asked. I had a million more questions, but they would have to wait.

"I do not know that word. Is it the same as a protector?"

"Yeah, it is about the same. Are there a lot of protectors?"

"Yes."

"Where are we going? Are you taking me to Brell?" I asked when we reached the bottom of the stairs.

"No. I am taking you to see our queen. She is the overseer of Grove security."

"Brell's mother?"

"Yes."

I didn't want to tell her about the scouts. My racing heart beat even faster. I rubbed the palms of my hands against my jeans.

"In honor of our time of Silent Appreciation, from this point forward, we are to walk without speaking," Parolin said.

"Okay." I took a deep breath.

A tiny waterfall trickled rhythmically from the top of the ridge, spilling into the thin, winding river. The protector nodded and walked ahead of me as I followed him along the riverbank, stepping to my left to avoid a cluster of mushrooms.

We passed Brell's house, the school behind it, and a series of Landaffen homes poised within the trees. As the harsh midday sun poked through the canopy, the trim of each dwelling, bedecked with colored jewels and smooth polished stones, twinkled, sending glints of light in all directions.

I dared stepping from the trail to another path leading toward Brell's, my mind half-scheming to make a run for his door. Parolin reached for his sword, his eyes narrowing, and I stumbled back to his side like I'd tripped and hadn't meant to move in that direction.

At the far end of the tree colony, one dwelling stood apart from the rest in both its size and distance from the others.

Seeming to defy gravity, its palatial three stories balanced within the tree limbs while a narrow staircase gently curved down to meet the forest floor. Arched windows were stained-glassed in geometrical shapes of deep reds, blues, purples, and greens, and at the home's highest point, a sharp-peaked roof pierced the sky.

With shoulders back and rounded chests, two Landaffen, one male, one female, with sheathed broadswords strapped to their waists and dressed similar to the protector, stood at the bottom of the stairs. Another Landaffen male dressed in royal blue, kept post at the entrance of a filigreed double door inlaid with the golden leaf pattern identical to Brell's front door design and the one on my charm.

The protector nodded, and with one eyebrow lifted and eyeing me suspiciously, he motioned for us to climb the staircase. When we reached the landing, the male in blue paused, squinting questionably before opening the doors.

We entered a wide corridor with white marble floors and ivory walls. Ivy hung from the ceiling, draped in decorative patterns, their vines twisted into abstract configurations, while below, more ivy growing from stone vessels trailed up the walls to meet and intertwine their tendrils with one another. A rectangular pool of clear water was at the room's center, brimming with lily pads in bloom. I closed my eyes and inhaled, taking in the wonder and beauty of the room.

The protector led me to a corridor, then down one of four hallways, and into a room partially exposed to the sky. One of the home's supporting tree trunks extended from a square opening in the floor and jutted upward, spiraling to a skylight where its branches opened out into a parasol of cool, green leaves.

As we passed, I slowed to watch a sparrow flutter down from above, making a gentle dive through the floor's opening where it landed on the lip of a small fountain at the tree's base. The protector glanced over his shoulder and I picked up my pace, following him to a rope and wood-slat bridge that barely bounced nor swayed when we crossed it.

A hall with ceiling-to-floor windows emptied at the base of a staircase that coiled upward into a creamy pink hollow of burnished stone. The protector nodded for me to take the lead, and the rubber soles of my paddock boots make a dull clack against the polished rock.

A Landaffen woman stood on a small landing ahead. She placed one hand on the hilt of her dagger as we approached. A door behind her was unlike the others, its narrow arch of frosted glass and gold glimmering as if under a magical spell.

My protector emerged from the staircase, raised a hand, and gave a small headshake. The woman dropped her hand from her weapon but stepped forward to whisper in his ear. I heard my name twice during their exchange, their pronunciations of the word "Laura" harsh and obtrusive, each syllable breaking the rhythmical flow and cadence of the elegant Landaffen language.

The woman turned, opened the door, slipped inside, and closed it behind her before I could see inside it. She returned a minute later, and while she whispered once again to the protector, I closed my eyes, savoring the almost hypnotic tones of the Landaffen tongue, yearning to understand it. When I opened my eyes, the protector was gone.

"The one called Laura," the female said softly, "Sennille will break her silence to see you."

"Thank you," I said, matching her low volume as she moved aside and opened the door.

Inhaling deeply, I entered, my pulse pounding as the door clicked closed behind me. The room was large but its furniture sparse. A round bed, cupped with a headboard of carved wood, sat against the side wall with a matching cabinet to its right and a full-length, framed mirror to its left. Another fountain on a raised pedestal of marble marked the center of the room where two white rabbits nibbled at a patch of grass growing from a planter built into the marble floor.

A pair of paned, double doors stood open at the far end, their doorframe flanked with sheer white curtains that fluttered softly from a gentle breeze. Beyond the doors, a tall, thin figure stood against the railing of a wooden balcony. A wolf, its coat darker than Bay's, lay at her feet.

The figure turned, lifting her chin as she folded her hands. "Come forward." The wolf raised its head.

I crossed the room in slow, controlled steps, breathing through my nose, and wiping the palms of my hands on my jeans. When I reached the balcony, she turned toward the sky, and with a few more steps, I joined her.

With eyes closed, she placed her hands on the railing and tilted her head upward. Her long, brown hair glistened, the loose strands at her cheeks dancing in the wind. A thick, golden ribbon looped through her hair at the top of her head like a crown, and her white dress hung limply, puddling at her feet while its neckline scooped, revealing a large portion of her upper chest.

She turned, opening her eyes. "I am Sennille. I am the queen of this Grove." She smiled, and her creamy skin caught the light, glistening from a dusting of gold powder. She looked too young to be the mother of a nineteen-year-old boy. "I have been made aware of you by my son. It is something he spoke of one half-day before the last horn sounded, marking our day of silence. His timing was rather calculated, leaving his father and me little opportunity to verbally react to this indiscretion." She lowered her head. "Nonetheless, Brell has taken an odd interest in you, and I assume you feel the same way about him."

My hands shook, and I swallowed the lump forming in my throat. "Odd?" I asked.

"Is that not the word in your language?" She lifted her hand, and her sleeve slipped to her elbow, exposing a trio of thin, gold bracelets. "To be unusual, abnormal?" she continued.

"Unusual—maybe—but not abnormal," I said. "At least I don't think so. Is it wrong for him to like me, a half race?"

"It is rare, and it is discouraged," she said, twisting once again to face the sky.

I did the same, placing my hands on the railing. The sun was at its peak, sending rays to delicately cut through the trees and illuminate the pasture below where hundreds of horses roamed—white horses, black horses, chestnuts, palominos, appaloosas, and paints. A light wind stirred the branches above our heads, and shadows rippled across the balcony.

"Brell does not behave like the son of a king," the queen said. "He never has, and he never will. My husband and I have learned to accept that. Like his father and his father before him, Brell was never supposed to leave the Grove, but he was full of curiosity and eager to explore the world beyond, the world of dangers, the world of uncertainties. A world where we would not be able to protect him."

She lowered her head, and with her right hand, brushed the railing under her hand, tracing a carved flower with her fingertips.

"In order to fulfill these desires," she continued, "Brell requested the assignment of 'scout'. His father and I reluctantly agreed and now he lives apart from the royal manor—something unheard of for a prince. After his training, he became part of 'the three'—the scouts who leave the Grove at each whole moon. As such, he has contributed to the Grove in many ways with the knowledge he has acquired. Until recently, we did not regret our decision."

She gripped the railing hard, a dull tap resounding as her fingernails met the wood. "We are proud of Brell, but when he told us about you, we were disappointed. He broke a very important rule. It is the first rule every scout learns. Do not interact with humans."

My bottom lip trembled. I crossed one arm over my chest and took a long breath through my nose. "But he didn't. Since I'm a half—"

"It is not because he feels no pride for his legacy and his future as king of this Grove," the queen interrupted, raising her voice. "He just does not like being treated as such. He is a prince who does not want to live the life of a prince. I am sure you have seen that in him." She blinked and wiped her eyes with the back of her hand.

"Yes," I said.

"And it is more than that," she said, facing me. "Brell's interest in you has turned to love. He said that when he's with you, he feels your souls combine and become one. This is how it is for Landaffens."

I sucked in a quick breath. He was in love with me? Did I feel the same way about him? No! It was infatuation. It had to be. I thought about him all the time and longed to spend every minute of my life with him. But love? We'd barely spent any time together.

She shook her head. "You are too human," she announced. "Of all emotions, love is the most powerful, especially for Landaffens. It taints one's judgment. The ability to think rationally. The future is neglected and consequences ignored."

"We've only known each other for a short time," I said.

The queen released the railing and drew back her shoulders. "As I suspected. You do not love my son. Fear, mistrust, jealously, greed—in humans, those emotions are strong and unforgiving. Emotions hindering a human's ability to love easily and unselfishly." She crossed her arms. "Human love is tainted. Unlike my people, human love cannot be trusted and does not always last."

"That's not completely true," I said, though I pictured my mother and father arguing about money and the fact that my father went on so many trips without her and me.

"Yes, it is," she snapped. "But it is not true of Landaffens." She inhaled and lowered her voice, gracefully folding her hands at her waist. "We read each other's senses. We are a sensual and sensitive race, lacking the pre-judgement and doubt of humans. There is no need for suspicion and loathing among my people. Without the interference of negative emotions, we love quickly, easily, and for eternity. That was Brell's mistake in regards to you."

I leaned forward, resting my forearms on the railing, watching the horses below toss their heads and swish their tails.

"But you have done something we could never expect a human to do, even one of half-race," Sennille admitted. She took both of my hands in hers, and the heat of her palms radiated warmth up my forearms. "You were able to enter the Grove without a Landaffen at your side. Your abilities are strong for a half race. That is one of two reasons why I agreed to see you rather than send you away. I also sensed you care deeply for Brell, despite not loving him. That is the other reason."

"I do. I care about him more than I have for any other boy. I might not be in love with him yet, but I *am* falling in love with him. It's just too soon to be real."

"Landaffens mate for life," she said. "And upon the celebratory union of a male and female, it is customary for the couple to remain in their bedchamber together for many days, loving one another, taking each other's bodies. It is not rushed.

It is not spontaneous, and it is a pleasure reserved for only after marriage and not before."

I shifted my eyes from hers and looked at the floor.

"Brell loves you," the queen said, "and he will love only you. But I am wiser than Brell when it comes to human love. Your kind uses the word 'love' loosely and you mate loosely. This I know is true, is it not?"

I lifted my head. "Yes, for some it is, but not for all."

"Humans can love, and have more than one mate, enjoying each other's bodies before marriage even when they are not in love."

"That's true, but that doesn't mean humans can't find true love. It just might take longer to develop. And after they get married, they can also be faithful."

"The colony is anxious to see their prince joined, married. They do not know about you, but they know he is in love and has found his mate. They have sensed it in him over the last half-day. It was an emotion he could not keep hidden after speaking of it to his father and me. They also sense this love extends beyond the trees and assume he will join with a female from another Grove." She tapped her fingers on the railing. "But since you do not yet love, you are not ready to be joined."

"No, I'm not. And I'm not sure when I will be." Did I even want that person to be Brell?

"When the colony is told you are half-human, they will understand your hesitation and need for more time. They have been schooled in your people's foolish human ways. Waiting will be difficult, especially for my son. You must not link your bodies, be a victim of your physical desires. Doing so would break one of our most important codes."

I lowered my head again. "We won't," I said. My face grew hot; I exhaled slowly through my teeth.

"I fear for my son. I fear that when you are away from the

Grove, you will find another to satisfy your needs. Or when you are alone, you will tempt him into doing so with you."

"I won't do either one of those things," I said sharply. "I care about him too much. And I respect your rules."

Sennille lifted her head. She placed a hand on either side of my face and took a step forward. Her eyes, fathomless and full of passion, leveled with mine.

"I believe you, the one called Laura."

"Thank you," I said.

In my mind's eye, the grocery-store boy appeared, chasing me, mocking me, and though I felt safe in the Grove, I parted my lips, ready to tell the queen all that had happened.

She gently removed her hands. "But unlike Brell, who is in love and his senses are now muddled, I sense you *have* taken a male. Is that correct?"

"Yes," I said, "but don't judge or belittle me for that. I don't regret what I did. He was my first. I didn't love him. I just . . . I just wanted to . . . I just . . ." With my elbows poised on the railing, I held my face in my hands, shaking my head, imagining the night in the back seat of Nathan's car.

"There is no need to explain your primal, human urges to me," the queen said. "Your past actions are expected and not a surprise, though Brell will be unwilling to hear about it."

"Just because I've . . ." I turned to Sennille, straightening my back. She continued to look at the sky. "It doesn't mean I can't love someone else. Brell doesn't even need to know about it because it doesn't matter now."

She spun toward me and slid her hands from the balcony. "To keep secrets is also a very human thing to do. I told Brell your blood line does not matter. You have lived with humans for too long. You will always be more human than Landaffen."

For a moment, the thought of being Landaffen sent another twinge of fear and doubt through my chest, and the same gnawing questions resurfaced. Did I really want this? To lead a dual life? To be a part of something my family couldn't know about?

My mother's face entered my thoughts. Tiny lines formed at the corner of her eyes as she smiled, her cheeks rosy, and eyes sparkling. Brell's face replaced hers, handsome and majestic, making my heart beat in my throat.

A distant horse whinnied, and I shifted my gaze to the pasture below. Like a cloud caught by a rush of wind, in my mind's eye, Brell's face morphed, and the grocery boy replaced it, glaring, his jaw tight and lips curled mockingly.

I could run from the Grove. Leave their world. But then what would I do? The Landaffen trio waited for me on the other side, and I needed Brell's help to understand why. I needed Brell to tell them to leave me alone.

"But the king," Sennille began again, "is not as unyielding and perceptive as I am. Like his son, he is naïve and more forgiving than he should be, a dreamer and what you humans call a 'hopeless romantic,'" the queen snickered. "He would not send you away. Therefore, neither will I."

Raising her head, she continued, "The council will meet to consider your status," she said. "Until then, the one called Laura, you are welcome in the Grove. That is what my son would want." She sighed and relaxed her arms at her sides. "The time of Silent Appreciation will be ending soon, and then we will feast."

I looked down at my clunky boots, exposed legs still sticky with dust, and dingy clothes. "Thank you," I said.

"Come," she said. "I will send for Thriss. She will take you to a guest chamber and supply you with the proper attire for the festival. She is a scout like Brell. She is familiar with your world, and she, too, speaks your language without difficulty."

I followed her through her quarters to the door, where the

female Landaffen kept guard. They exchanged words in their language, the queen eyeing me while they spoke. The guard nodded and retreated to the stairs.

"You are to wait here," the queen said, closing the door, leaving me alone in the landing.

I sighed, straightened my shoulders, and walked to the window across from me. Facing in other direction, the view was different from the balcony in Sennille's room, though part of the pasture was visible as it wrapped toward a stream that cut snake-like through a patch of trees.

Sunlight broke through each section of the window, covering the floor in geometrical patterns. With my index finger, I traced the run of gold solder delicately yet solidly holding each section of glass in place.

Footsteps echoed up the staircase, and a girl of my height and approximate age appeared. The corners of her plump, plum-colored lips lifted when she saw me. With her delicate, tiny, pointed nose, rounded cheek bones, and blue, wide-set eyes, her features were fine yet distinct.

A strange feathered creature the size of a crow sat on her shoulder. A long neck met its lizard-like head. Its hind legs, thick with muscles, ended with clawed feet. Its front legs were more like arms, bent at the elbows, while its hands consisted of three reptilian fingers, curled and also clawed.

A spread of folded wings ran the length of each appendage, its tail coming to a blunt point of feathers. It was basically a miniature velociraptor with wings.

"I am called Thriss," the girl said at a whisper so soft, I had to read her lips.

"What's that?" I whispered back and leaned closer.

"A lontee. Her name is Mheek. You can touch her. She is tame."

"I've never seen something like this before." I stroked her

head and she tucked it under my palm. "It reminds me of a dinosaur."

"I do not know that word," Thriss said. "Lontees were one of the first animals to roam this world. They survived the Fonson Rui and—"

"Fonson Rui?"

"Yes. Before the Laramiss. Before the humans. When the skin of the earth crumbled and life renewed. Now they can only be found in a Grove."

A low, mournful hum rumbled through the hall becoming louder, its pitch rising into a rich melodic tone pleasant to my ears.

"The call of the horn," she said when the sound ended. "The time of Silent Appreciation is over. "We can speak normally now." She leaned toward me with eyes squinted, breaking my personal space. "I have never seen a half-race. Can I see your ears?" she asked in a semi-snotty tone.

"Sure," I said and lifted my hair away.

"A long but rounded tip," she smirked. "Interesting. And now I am to take you to a guest chamber and provide you with garments fit for the feast."

I let my hair fall back into place. "Thank you," I said, and followed her down the stairs.

She wore baby-pink leggings sheer enough to see the creamy peach of her skin beneath, and a long tunic of a darker hue that narrowed at the waist and extended over her hips to the tops of her knees. With each step, her glossy brown hair swung.

She stopped at a door at the end of the hall, opened it, and waited for me to enter first. "This will be your chamber," she said.

The room was furnished in the same minimalistic manner as Sennille's, with its round bed, white linens, wooden cabinet, and a long mirror propped next to a chair, but it was much smaller. "And this is the dressing area."

She pointed to another room extending from the first, its floor a series of large boulders. One boulder was scooped at its center to form a large bathtub. Two at waist level were erected into a counter with a small sink-like basin. Above it hung a mirror, and next to it sat an oval bar of cream-colored soap and glass bottles containing liquid of the same color.

"Landaffen plumbing," she said. She lifted a metal bar above the basin and water trickled from a wooded tube. "It is stream temperature." She wiggled her fingers below the flow of water. "Warm for this time of year." She reset the metal bar.

"I'm sure it will be fine," I said.

"What happened here?" she asked, making a face and pointing to my chin.

"I fell. In the woods on my way here."

She walked back into the larger chamber and returned with a long, white gown draped over her arm. "I believe this will fit you." She laid the dress across the counter. "Your shoes will be fitted and made when Sennille's attendants come to prepare your hair and face."

"Prepare my hair and face?"

"Yes, it is the last day of the festival. It is the coming of fall. We wear leaves in our hair and gold powder on our faces."

"Oh, okay," I said.

"They will be here shortly. You must bathe quickly and dress."

"Thank you. Will I see you at the festival?"

"Yes, I will be there." Thriss lifted a lever above the bath and water flowed into the tub. "This is for your body. And these are for your hair," she said, tapping the cork caps of three bottles next to the tub.

"And Brell will be there?" I asked.

"Of course. Everyone attends the festival."

"Does he know I'm here?" I asked.

"That I do not know," she snipped. "I was only told you are of half-race and a much-welcomed guest of the prince." She bowed and left the room.

Three thick towels folded lengthwise hung neatly from wooden pegs, capped with colored jewels. Two brushes, one for hair and the other for teeth, were positioned side by side on a wooden tray. I undressed and slowly lowered into the basin. Goose bumps covered my arms and legs as the lukewarm water hit my skin.

The liquid soap and shampoo left my body soft and my hair slick and shiny. I wrapped a towel around my torso and combed my damp hair, letting the sun dry it naturally as its rays penetrated the frosted window in the dressing chamber.

I sighed, shaking my head as I sat at a dressing table, looking at myself in the mirror. Here I was, trapped between Brell's world and mine. It had to be about 1 o'clock. I only had about five hours until my mom came home from work.

According to Sennille, Brell loved me. I could easily fall in love with him. I was falling in love with him! Or maybe I already had. My heart swelled when I pictured him, a sweet sensation rippling through my chest, but my head told me I was too young, and it was too soon.

Either way, I could never abandon my family. Choosing one world over the other would be impossible. I could spend most of my time in the Grove, but I wouldn't be happy unless I could divide my time between the two places, and these arrangements couldn't take place until after I graduated from high school. I couldn't just run away from my mom at age seventeen to abandon high school and my plans for college. Or could I? I just didn't know.

I slipped the satin-like gown over my head, and as it

slithered down my body, there was a knock at the door. "Please, come in," I said, rushing to answer it.

Three ladies were at my door, two in their teens, one younger than me, maybe thirteen or fourteen, and the other about my age. The third was probably in her late thirties. Each carried a leather bag. The oldest lady bowed her head and spoke.

"The one called Laura. We are here to prepare you for the festival."

"Yes, thank you," I said and moved from the door as they filed inside.

"I am the one called Allete," the oldest one said. She pointed to the two girls. "Dari and Keena."

"Nice to meet you," I said.

"Your ennvah," Keena said. "I will repair." She tugged the hem of my dress, adjusting the slip of fabric beneath the first.

"Oh, does it have a tear?" I asked, inspecting my gown as I smoothed it with my hand.

"Keena is just learning English," Allete said. "I believe she meant 'straighten.'" Keena pulled my dress sleeves and repositioned the neckline so it draped evenly across my shoulders. "I was a scout in my youth. I know your language well and am teaching it to my daughters."

With their pointed chins, chestnut hair, and green, almond-shaped eyes with long, thick lashes, I should have guessed they were all related. "Please sit," she added.

The ladies unloaded their bags onto the dresser, and I carefully lowered onto the only chair in the room. Allete stood behind me, brushing my hair, decorating it with a weave of ribbon and gold leaves, while Dari, the older daughter, smoothed cream across my cheeks and chin. Using a fluffy white feather, she dusted gold power across my eye lids, and using black balm from a metal jar, darkened my eyelashes with a tiny comb. Pink cream from another jar was used to gloss my lips.

"Shows," Keena said, holding up a pair of white shoes laced with ribbon.

"It is 'shoes'," her mother corrected.

Keena lowered to her knees and pulled the ballerina-type shoes onto my feet, drawing up the shiny fabric, pulling it tightly, and wrapping them over the top of each foot until they fit snuggly in both length and width. They were dainty little shoes, elegant but comfortable, with one-inch heels and thin, soft soles.

When they were done, I stood in front of the mirror and gasped. The gown fit snuggly at my waist and chest, making my athletic figure more feminine. Two sections of hair near my face were braided, twisting to the back of my head, making my neck appear longer and extra thin. My makeup, light and dewy, accentuated my cheekbones in a shimmer of gold. And with the top of my ears hidden by hair, I could be taken for one of them.

"You beautiful, the one called Laura," Keena said. "Your looks will please the first son of the Grove."

"Thank you," I said.

"Our prince is also very handysome." She blushed and covered her mouth with her hand, hiding a smile.

"Yes, he is handsome," I corrected. My cheeks also filled with heat. "And you can just call me Laura. All of you can."

The daughters turned to their mother. Keena's eyes widened.

"For my people," Allete said, "using one's name alone is a sign of friendship, closeness, trust. Until that type of relationship is established among us, 'sha laush epshaw,' 'the one called' is used to address each other. It is a sign of respect."

"Oh, okay," I said. "It just sounds very formal, and I'm not used to that." Brell had only ever called me just by my name.

"The one called Laura," Keena said, "your joining comes soon?"

Her mother's forehead wrinkled, and her brows came together as she whispered something to Keena in Landaffen.

"I apologize for Keena." She patted Keena's head. "We heard Brell pledged his love to you, so they assume you are here to prepare and make plans for your joining with the prince."

"I am sorry, the one called, Laura," Keena said. "That is not a questions for me to ask. I am only to say answers."

"It's okay," I said. "I don't mind if you ask me questions."

Music rang through the halls, filling our room with a magical melody, something with flutes and some kind of stringed instrument.

Allete nodded. "The one called Laura, the festival has resumed. Come. We must go to the Great Hall. Dari and I will pack up our things, and Keena will escort you to the feast."

"Thank you." I followed Keena out the door.

"You must be much excited, the one called Laura. I want to be in love," she said when we were halfway down the hall.

"The thought of being in love scares me." I hugged myself as the cold tile sent a chill from my feet to my chest.

"Scares you, why?"

"Because love can lead to marriage, a joining, and if that doesn't work out . . ." I shook my head. "The thought of divorce scares me even more. At least that's what can happen outside a Grove and in my world."

"What is divorce?"

"It's when a couple ends their marriage," I explained. "And if they have children, it makes splitting up even more difficult."

"Marriage ending?" Keena's jaw dropped. "Joinings are forevertime. Love is forevertime. Humans do not love right if it ends."

"You're right," I said.

We reached the entrance to a large hall opening into a deep courtyard. At one end, a long cloth-covered table was topped with plates, platters, serving dishes, and glass cups. Beyond, a trio of musicians with stringed instruments and flutes stood atop a stage draped in ivy, and at its center, Landaffens danced with arms gracefully poised, soft steps, and gowns flowing.

"We do know how to love," I added. "The human world is just more complicated, that's all."

# CHAPTER 16

In the distance, at a table on a raised platform under a gazebo, I saw Brell. Below the platform lay Bay. To Brell's right, sat an exquisitely handsome man; his distinct cheek bones and sharp jaw framed a thin nose and large eyes hooded by thinly arched brows. He sat casually at the table in a high-back chair, one elbow poised on the arm rest, and in his hand, he held a glass goblet filled with a deep red liquid.

As if charisma was a palpable thing, his presence alone told he was a man of power. This had to be the king, and though Sennille's description of him had led me to believe he was an open-minded dreamer, I shuddered at the thought of looking at him eye to eye.

Keena pointed to the gazebo, her eyes brightening as she smiled. "The one called Laura, he there is. Go."

Sennille was next to her husband. She leaned across him and said something to Brell. He laughed, raising a cup to his lips. As he tipped his head forward, a cluster of silver leaves tucked in his hair caught the light. My hands trembled and a sweet warmth shot through my chest.

"Can I just walk over there?" I asked. Maybe, I thought, there was some kind of proper etiquette I was supposed to follow when meeting the king.

"Can you not walk?" she asked. "Are you hurt?"

"No," I said, and laughed. "I mean, it is okay to interrupt them while they are enjoying the festival?"

"Interrupt?" She tilted her head, her eyes shifting toward the sky before looking back at me.

"It means to disturb, to bother, to um—"

"Go," she urged. "The first son will be joyful to see you." Her lips curved sweetly in a soft smile.

"He's never seen me like this before," I said, bringing back my shoulders and smoothing my neckline.

"Beautiful," she said. "He will be happy to see you."

I took a deep breath, but it did little to settle my heart rate. "Can you, um, go get him for me? Tell him I'm here and bring him to this hall? Then he can introduce me to his parents, and I won't feel so awkward."

"Bother the prince?" She placed her hand against her chest. "I cannot do. I cannot make first words." She set her hand on my shoulder. "The one called Laura, do not be afraid. You bring joyful to the first son."

"Okay." I sighed as she stepped backward, motioning with her hand for me to enter the dining hall.

I entered slowly, my eyes fixed on Brell and his parents, and as I moved toward them, from the corner of my eyes, I saw Landaffens staring at me and whispering to one another. Interlocking my trembling hands, I continued on, holding my head high and parting my lips to hide my heavy breathing.

Bay caught sight of me and trotted over to greet me, and Brell turned.

"Hello, boy," I said to Bay and gave him a pet on the head. He licked my hand.

Brell looked up from his goblet and rose from his chair, unblinking, the edges of his lips rising. His cup slipped from his hand, and as two Landaffens rushed to collect his cup and wipe the spill, his eyes never left mine.

"Laura," he said. Though the music was loud, I heard the word clearly, just like the other day when he said my name without moving his mouth.

As he walked to meet me, he looked over his shoulder at his parents. They nodded, a soft smile on his father's lips, while Sennille appeared indifferent with a faint twinkle in her eye.

I stepped onto the platform, and Brell took my hands.

"Laura, I have missed you," he said. "You are so beautiful, sessena, in my language."

"Thank you," I replied softly.

"And now you are here in my world, to join me at the feast. But how?" He glanced at his parents. "It is obvious my parents knew you were here. I do not understand."

"I have so much to tell you," I said. The evil sneer of the grocery-store boy flickered in my mind.

"Your hands," Brell said. "They are cold, and they tremble."

"I can only stay here for a few hours. My mom's off at five. I need to be home by then," I said. "But I don't have my phone, so I can't keep track of the time."

"Do not worry. I know this turn of the season well. I can read the sun and match it with human hours. I will take you home before your mother arrives."

"Thank you," I said. My hands warmed, but I cringed at the thought of telling him about the Landaffen trio.

I took a deep breath, and he pulled me against his chest. The music stopped, and everyone looked in our direction. Brell and I broke our embrace and turned to his parents.

"The one called Laura. It is time to introduce you to my people," the king said in an accent sharper than either Brell's or the queen's. He stood and spoke to the crowd, lifting and lowering his goblet with each gesture. Brell set his lips against my ear and translated. I watched his people, trying to gauge their approval of me by the expressions on their faces, and a pang of unease developed in my chest.

"She is from the world of humans, a half-race whose abilities were strong enough to see a scout and enter our Grove," Brell translated. "Do not fear her unique capabilities. Chance did not bring her to us. It was fated to happen. I do not know why, for what reason this may be, but as your king, you need to trust my judgment and the judgment of your prince as he wishes for her to be his amorlee."

Brell dropped his head. A rumbling of voices rose from the crowd and settled as the king lifted his hand, and I sensed his people were approving yet skeptical.

"Brell!" I said, partially breaking from a whisper. "Did he say what I think he just said?"

"It is something we have not yet discussed," he said.

"I discussed it with your mother. She knows I'm not ready to be joined. You know human ways, so you should know that, too."

"I do. It is my father. He said what he knew the colony would want to hear. He did not lie. I do wish for you to be my amorlee, my wife."

The king readdressed the crowd. Brell's lips brushed my ear. "My father said your presence in the Grove is sanctioned. You are to be accepted by all and treated as one of us."

His father lifted his cup, and the Landaffens clapped, tapping the closed fingers of one hand against the palm of the other. Unlike Brell, who nodded warmly to his people, radiating confidence, my lips trembled as I smiled and took in a small breath to calm my nerves.

"Welcome to the Grove, Laura," the king said as he

approached. He cupped my chin with his hand, kissed the top of my head, then walked back to his chair.

"A kiss to the head is customary," Brell whispered to me.

"He called me Laura, just Laura," I whispered back. "I know what that means. It was explained to me."

"Then you know my father is now comfortable with your presence."

Brell took one of my hands. "Please, join us."

"Wait. There's something I need to tell you. Why I ended up here. I didn't plan for it to happen."

"Come sit with us, Laura," the king called. "And then you two will dance," he said from his place at the table.

Brell gave my hand a light squeeze. "Can this conversation wait?" he asked.

"Yeah, I guess," I sighed. "For a little bit."

The music and dancing resumed, but many of the Landaffens remained below the gazebo, watching me and the prince.

Still holding my hand, Brell led me to the table, and we sat down on the other side of his father. A woman with a long-necked pitcher filled an empty goblet and handed it to me. It smelled like ripened fruit. The next whiff slightly stung the inside of my nose. "What is it?" I asked Brell.

"Take a drink. You will like it. I am having the same. It is made from berries that grow only during this late time of the sun."

I took a small sip. It was wine-like, acidic but sweet. I took another drink. A man and woman dancing below us stopped to stare at me.

"They have never seen a human before or one of half-race," Brell said. "They have never left the Grove."

"The only real difference is our ears."

"Innate psychological differences cannot be seen with the

eyes, only felt by the heart." He leaned closer, our shoulders meeting. Pleasant heat washed through my chest.

"They know my father would never put them in danger. He accepts you, so they do, too. But it goes beyond any approval the king could give. They can read beyond the shell of your soul. Feel your integrity. Sense your passion to do only what is good and just."

"They fear humans?" I asked.

Brell looked toward the sky. "I would not call it fear. I would call it . . . apprehension. They are wary of humans, and do not trust them."

I eased away from him. My shoulders dropped.

"Humans cut trees and move mountains, working against the earth rather than with it. To Landaffens, this planet is a living, breathing being—a mass of water, soil, and rock for blood, skin, and bones."

"I understand," I said. "I would feel the same way."

"I do not feel these emotions toward you, but it will take time for some members of my colony to feel the same way."

Yet, in the outside world, hate, deception, and the disregard for people and the environment existed, but there was also love, honesty, and the respect for one another and the earth. Maybe we took our conveniences for granted, and at a cost, in the form of pollution and the consumption of land. But the Landaffen life of harmony and balance was also tainted. The trio of boys had already proven that.

"Maybe I don't belong here," I snapped. "Maybe your mother's right, and I've lived in the human world for too long." I took a long sip of wine.

"My mother said that to you?" Brell twisted to face me, his eyebrows coming together.

"It's not anything she hadn't already told you," I said.

"It was meant for only my ears. It was wrong for her to repeat it." He flashed a glance over his shoulder at his mother.

"She might be right."

"Dance! Dance!" the king pronounced, motioning for us to stand.

"It is expected of us. A special song will be played," Brell said, and rose from his seat. "Please, may I have the next dance?" He bent at the waist, offering his hand, reminding me of something I'd read in a Jane Austin novel. It was enough to temporarily snuff my frustration.

"You just want to change the subject," I teased.

"Maybe?" he jested back, taking my hand. We stepped from the gazebo and entered the crowd.

The festival was at its peak. Children danced in the center of the main courtyard, spinning in opposite directions, shuffling their feet with heads high and hands clasped loosely behind their backs, their steps light and movements graceful.

A pair of wolf pups playfully nipped the children's heels. A lontee perched on a little girl's shoulder, spread it wings, took flight, and landed on a boy's head.

The song finally ended, and one of the musicians stepped to the front of the stage. He held a small, stringed box where a long neck thinned to a hollow tube with a mouthpiece at the end. I squinted against the afternoon sun for a better look.

I'd seen that instrument before. At the library! In Phyllis's painting!

The musician brought it to his lips, blew, and strummed, its whimsical melody in deep contrast to the boxy hollow in which the sound originated.

"Follow my lead," Brell said, bringing his right hand to my waist. "And this hand goes here," he said and set my right hand on his shoulder.

"And what do we do with our free hands?"

"They stay relaxed at our sides."

We stepped in rhythm, moving in slow circles. Many couples joined us.

"It is a very . . . I will find the word . . . dignified dance," Brell explained. "Touching is minimal. For my family, public affection is limited." His plump lips thinned with a smile. "I did not keep to that rule when I first saw you here, and I will not keep to it now."

He kissed my forehead, and I closed my eyes, savoring the warmth of his lips against my skin.

"Yes. I have broken it again."

His smile melted my soul, and I caught myself before one of my knees buckled.

"I counted the stars and watched the moons fall, waiting for the day I could send Bay to call you to me. And now, you are here." He kissed me again, pressing his lips lightly and holding them there until his next warmth breath swept against my brow. "How did you enter the Grove?" he asked.

"The same way we entered when we were together."

"The wind did not stop you. That is a good sign." He nodded.

"Two protectors found me and brought me to your mother's chamber."

I continued my story with minimal details, answering his questions to fill in the gaps he was most curious about. He smiled with embarrassment when I told him about Keena thinking he was handsome.

"But I haven't told you why I came here in the first place," I said, increasing my grip on his shoulder.

"It is not because you missed me?"

Behind Brell, a girl spun, hitting his shoulder. She raised her goblet, spun again, and stopped to face Brell. It was Thriss.

She'd exchanged her pink tunic for a long, lime-green gown with a scalloped V-neck.

"Hello, the one called Thriss," Brell said. "I see you are having a good time."

"Rellis heemlock jenuw—"

"In English. You need the practice anyway."

"You jest by saying 'the one called,'" she said. "You are the prince, but you are also my college."

"Colleague," Brell corrected. "And it is not a joke."

"Then I will also call you a dud. You have not danced with me at all this festival. Last year, I could not keep you from the dance floor. You danced my feet sore."

"This year things are different. I have found my only dance." Brell drew his arm around my back.

"But you are not yet joined. Surely you have one dance left for me." She pulled Brell's sleeve. "Your human will not mind."

Brell jerked his arm from her grip. "And surely, the one called Thriss, I will excuse your ill manners. It is obvious your goblet has been refilled with summer-berry wine one too many times this festival." The song ended while we stood there. "Now excuse us. My parents are waiting."

She grabbed at his arm again as we passed, whispering in Landaffen, and though her words left her tongue in an almost magical cadence, her tone was ugly.

"She is a scout with much to learn," Brell said. "I prefer to work with others. She lacks respect, especially for humans and the good they have contributed despite their ignorance."

"What did she say?"

"What she says is of no matter."

"Was it about me?"

"I will never lie to you, Laura. I will only keep a truth if there is no reason to give it." He sighed. "But, I, myself am curious. I am concerned about you, Laura."

"What did she say?" I asked again.

"She said that you were the dirtiest and bloodiest human she had ever seen."

"She's exaggerating about the blood." I lifted my chin, revealing the pink raw patch of skin. "But I was dirty. That's what I need to tell you about."

"Are you okay?" he asked. He brushed a strand of hair from my face.

"Yeah, I'm fine, but I'm scared."

"Come with me to a place where we can talk freely."

We crossed to the main chamber of the palace.

"Nithalahsh a nu remalee. Gee les neev hasnalah, satahneem?" a man said to Brell as we passed. The man bowed, and Brell nodded with the reply, "Losh lahn. Bels vas nee, lesch."

"What did he say?" I asked when we'd reached a small courtyard and were alone.

"He—"

"I've heard the word remalee before. I know what it means. Do not keep this truth from me."

We sat down on an ornate, wooden bench leveled atop two carved stones. A stone path from the bench led to a manicured patch of grass with a marble fountain at its center. The sun shone brightly, but the air was cool and crisp, reminding me that fall and school were just around the corner.

"He congratulated us on our remalee and asked if at the next complete moon our—"

"If our joining would take place?"

"Yes." He sighed. "The remalee is equivalent to what you'd call an engagement. It is the period of time between the sinahneigh and the joining. For us, the remalee is short, lasting only until the next complete moon, but I know for humans it can last much longer."

"So the sinah, um, whatever is?"

"The sinahneigh is the proposal of joining."

"Why do people think we are going to be joined?" I asked. I held my head in my hands, the points of my elbows on my knees.

"Because at the first sun of the feast, I came before my parents and the court and pledged my love to you." He set his hand on my thigh. "I love you, Laura."

"Brell, this is going way too fast." I looked up, shaking my head. "I care about you, I do, but . . ."

"You love me, too. I sense it. Your feelings are strong. Even though you are of half race, I can read you better than I can my own people—even those who are older, those whose senses have ripened. That is the connection we have." He slipped his hand into mine.

Maybe I did love him. We locked eyes, and my chest stirred and pulse spiked. But I didn't believe in love at first sight! We hadn't known each other long enough, and I was too young to make any kind of commitment to a boy!

"I understand how it is for humans," Brell went on. "Needing a place to live together. Making enough currency to buy goods and food and having enough of it to provide for offspring." His eyes shifted to the treetops. "It is not like that in the Grove. We are . . . I do not know the right word. Everyone contributes. Everyone works hard, and in doing so, all of our needs our met in the Grove."

"I'm sorry," I said, "but I can't think about that right now. About us. It's too much." A twinge of fear rekindled in my chest, making me gasp. "I still need to tell you why I'm here. How I didn't have a choice."

"I do not understand. You did not have a choice?"

Taking a deep breath and folding my hands in my lap, I began my story, starting at registration where I saw the grocery-store boy for the first time. "But he wasn't the only one. There were two more," I said, and I told him about the Landaffen trio terrorizing me at the high school, following me home, and chasing me to the Grove.

Through most of my story, Brell listened intently, his chin in his palm while he leaned forward; but as I continued my tale, his lips thinned, jaw clenched, and hands curled into fists. By the time I was done, my head hurt, a dull ache in the center of my forehead, the kind I always get when I cry or study too hard. I pressed the pad of my index finger against the skin between my eyebrows.

"What color was their hair?" Brell asked.

"Blond. But what does that matter?"

"Then it is true," he said.

"What?" The pain in my head doubled. "Please tell me everything." I grabbed his forearm, my fingers catching the soft folds of his sleeve.

He faced me, his back straight and shoulders square. "You eluded three Laramiss abductors, and you were able to enter the Grove on your own."

"I thought they were Landaffens?"

"They are," Brell said. "They are of the same race, but they are from a different colony, a different Grove, the Laramiss Grove. They are known for their light-colored hair. All Groves are named. We are the Wventorin, we are of dark hair," Brell said.

"The Laramiss tried to suppress your Landaffen abilities by causing you fear. An anxious mind is a weakened mind, unfocused, and unable to perform. It takes confidence and concentration to keep one's senses strong. Even for a full race this can be difficult. But you honed your senses and stayed in control. Your ability to see and hear them under extreme circumstances remained intact." He lovingly held my jaw with his hand. "You are strong which means your Landaffen ancestors were strong—the strongest."

"Why do they want to capture me?" Pressure built behind my eyes, and I blinked to stop a tear.

"It is part of our history, the Legend of Tena, the end of days. It is a legend most colonies consider myth, but there are some that still believe—the Laramiss are one of them."

He slowly closed and opened his eyes with his next breath, the gold thread in his shirt gleaming as his chest rose and fell.

"Believe what?" I asked.

"That a . . ." He swallowed and shifted in his seat. "that a half-race will be responsible for our obliteration, our Armageddon."

"And they think that's me?"

Brell nodded.

"How did they even know about me?" I asked. "How did they find me?"

"The same way I found you. Scouts from their Grove. But unlike me, who came upon you quite by accident . . ." he smiled, "the Laramiss have been sending scouts far and wide with the sole purpose of finding the half-race of the myth. At the last blahshen, a yearly meeting held among all kings, they had announced their decision to do so."

I brought my hand against my chest. "So, they think I'm going to destroy their worlds?"

"Not by yourself," he said gently and patted my knee. "With the aid of all humanity as detailed in the legend. It claims human lust, gluttony, greed, sloth, wrath, envy, and pride will cause you to expose our world, and in doing so, the human race will end our period of occupation on this earth."

"You just named the seven deadly sins, the cardinal sins. They are part of Roman Catholic Theology—Christian teachings. How did they end up in a Landaffen legend?"

"The Landaffens have been on this planet since the beginning of time. Our legends were written long before human existence. The Legend of Tena is a supplemental text added much later and meant to replace the original version. My colony, as do many others, believe the addendum was only made to protect our Groves from mankind, to make us wary of humans, to keep us separate; so we honor the first text, disregarding the newer, bleaker myth." Brell raised an eyebrow. "But the Laramiss colony, they believe it all."

"So they think the human race will completely wipe out the Landaffens?"

"Yes, but in the original legend, this does not happen. Instead of destroying us, when the Landaffens can no longer prosper in isolation and survive without human intervention, we unite with them instead to live cooperatively and peacefully side by side."

"And that's what you believe?"

"Yes, this Grove and many more. But . . ." He took both of my hands in his. The light in his eyes intensified. ". . . both versions of this legend have one thing in common, a female of half race." He tightened his grip and swallowed. "The Laramiss believe this female will lead the humans in war, but we believe she is the mediator who will bring our worlds together. I think that half-race girl is you."

My hands grew hot and slick. As I slipped them from Brell's, heat shot up my arms into my chest and face, and for a moment, I thought I was going to throw up.

"No! I can't be. I don't know anything about diplomacy. How could I be an agent of devastation or an ambassador of peace?" A tear rolled to my upper lip, and I licked it away. "Why me?"

"In both texts, the half-Landaffen is described, and you fit that profile. I tested your abilities when I watched you in the woods—how long it would take for you to hear and see me. You did so before that of a usual half-race. And now I know the wind did not stop you from coming here by yourself." He stroked my hair with his hand and held my face.

"Is that why you'd said that was a good sign?"

"Yes, being able to do so is in the legend."

"But it can't be me. It can't!"

"There is also something else in both legends. The half-race is fated to marry a prince."

Brell brought his arms around my waist, holding me tightly. I pressed my head against his shoulder. A myriad of emotions pumped through my mind, amplifying my headache.

"You are the one, Laura. It is something you must understand and accept."

"No. No," I said.

But as much as I pushed the possibility aside, shredding the thought with excuses and doubt, something deep in my being told me it could be true—that specific destiny and purpose hidden deep inside me that I'd been seeking and needed had come to fruition.

"Whether you believe you are the half-race of legend or not," Brell said, "the Laramiss do, and because of that, they are trying to stop you from leading the humans into battle against them."

"If they catch me, what will they do? Kill me?"

"Yes, or confine you to their Grove, keeping you from reentering your world and bringing knowledge of the Landaffens to the humans. In doing that, the prophecy in which they hold truth could not be fulfilled."

"So what am I going to do?" I asked, pushing away from him. "I can't stay here. I have to go home. If I don't, my mom will think I've been kidnapped or murdered. I can't put her through that!"

"They cannot take you from our Grove. Our combined magic, what keeps us protected, would prevent them from entering. But we would not keep you here against your will. I am not sure how far the Laramiss will go when it comes to your capture, so your presence here could endanger the entire colony. We will tell my father about the Laramiss. He will know what to do." Brell eyed a patch of blue sky. "There is time before your mother returns."

"There's something else. The librarian in town. She's also of half race," I said. I told Brell everything about Phyllis that made me think so.

"Do you think she's with the Laramiss?" I asked, finally.

"That I do not know. During my nineteen winters of breath, I have not heard her name mentioned in the Grove, but that does not mean she is not known by my people. Be wary of her until we know for sure whether or not she is involved."

He rose and pulled me into his arms, holding me as I sniffled and took big breaths to compose myself. The warmth of his body penetrated his soft shirt, sending a wave of euphoria through me. He ran his fingers through my hair, massaging my scalp gently, and I pressed the side of my face against his strong chest. He smelled like lime and fresh-cut wood.

"I will not let them take you," he said.

The Landaffens near the gazebo parted as we stepped up the platform to join the king and queen at the table.

"The one called Laura, I sense fear, apprehension, and disbelief," the queen said. She turned to Brell. "You have told her what you have suspected."

"Yes," Brell said.

"I find it odd she does not feel honored and privileged." She set her goblet on the table.

"You will not find it odd once you hear what she has told me."

Brell scanned the crowd below us, and put his hand on his dad's shoulder. "We will speak in Laura's language. There is no one close enough who can hear and comprehend it."

"Serious talk during our time of merriment?" Sennille whined and delicately crossed her legs at the ankles.

"Yes, it needs to be told now," Brell said.

Sennille shot me a disapproving look, her eyes in a partial roll as she gripped the arm rests of her chair.

"I'm sorry," I said. "I didn't wish for any of this to happen."

"It is not your fault," Brell said. "Fate needs no apology."

A lady crossed the platform with a tray of food and set it on the table. Tiny cakes, glazed and covered with fruit, glistened, a sweet, flora scent perfuming the air. Steam rose from a collection of hand pies leaking with a savory-looking broth.

Another attendant filled our goblets. "Drink," the queen said. "It will ease your anxiety. Eat, and it will suppress your hunger for answers." She handed me a goblet. "But I am full of questions," she said.

"Yes, Mother," Brell said. "You need to hear this, too. Your support and guidance are also needed."

While Brell retold my story, I sipped my wine and watched the Landaffens dance. I'd always be more human than Landaffen. The Grove was beautiful and majestic. Life here was simple. But all of my needs could never be met in a Grove. My dependence and desire for the modern conveniences and modes of entertainment in the human world were too strong. Moving forward, I would have to live as both Landaffen and human. I couldn't choose one over the other. But if I was the half-race of their legends, maybe that's what it would take in order to bring both worlds together.

"She will be assigned the three," the king said, breaking my reverie.

"They will keep you safe," Brell told me. "Three against

three. An even pairing, but we have the advantage. Our protectors have the strength and skills of ten scouts."

"What if there are more than the three I saw?" I asked, "or they replace them with some of their own protectors?"

"Then we will do whatever is needed to keep you safe," the king said, "even if it means breaking a code."

Brell eyed the sky, squinting against the sun. "Five o clock human time," he said. "Laura needs to return to her home."

"To the courtyard," the king said, rising. "I will make the preparations. Our feast ends tonight."

# CHAPTER 17

The king entered the courtyard followed by three men, their metal headbands glinting in the afternoon sun. They were dressed alike, leather chest plates over dark green shirts, deep brown leggings, and boots. At their backs hung bows with arrows, and at their waists, slung sheathed swords.

"Your protectors, Laura," the king said. "They were scouts in their youth and understand your language well. They will be the three for as long as needed."

"What's 'the three?'" I'd been told before, but I felt the need to ask again.

"At any given time, only three are to leave the Grove and enter your world if need be," Brell explained. "This code applies to every colony. In your world, a dead Landaffen is a visible Landaffen. With three, the death toll outside a Grove is limited and colony size is undeterminable."

"That means you can't come with me?"

"No. I cannot. The protectors' skills with the bow and sword are much more advanced than mine."

"We won't be able to see each other then?"

"We will not. My parents will not allow me to leave the Grove, but when it is deemed safe to do so, I will exchange places with one of the three and come see you."

The king placed his hands on my shoulders. "I plan to meet with Tosh to resolve this matter. Finding you is one thing, but trying to stop the one is something they agreed not to do."

"Tosh is the Laramiss king," Brell added.

"I will send a messenger to their Grove with my request to do so, and I will also send word to Glacion."

"Glacion is the leader of all Groves," Brell said. "He will know what to do. How to stop the Laramiss."

"I understand there is another living in your home," the king said.

"Yes, my mother. She works, so she'll be gone from eight until five or six every day during the week, but she'll be home on weekends."

He nodded. "Until this matter is resolved," the king said, "you need to stay inside your home. The three will be watching you. They will be invisible to human eyes. They will keep you safe. If you are the half-race of the old texts, it will be your duty to bring our worlds together."

The king pointed to each protector. "Gressim, Farnaway, and Parolin. My best men. They will take you home."

"Thank you," I said. "But when school starts, I'll have to leave my house."

A wrinkle formed between the king's eyebrows.

"That is something she is expected to do," Brell said to his father. "Something she must do."

"This matter will be discussed, but for now, we must proceed with our original plan."

Keena walked into the courtyard on light feet, her hands

behind her back. Her cheeks reddened when she smiled at Brell.

"This attendant will take you to your guest chamber, so you can change into your human clothes," the king said. "The three will wait for you in the hall."

"And I will also meet you there," Brell said.

"He is so . . . Is handsome the correct word?" Keena said when we rounded the hall. "Meaning attractive, good-looking, and well-formed." She put her hand over her mouth and giggled.

"Yeah, that is definitely the right word this time." I opened the chamber door.

My T-shirt, jeans, and socks sat folded in a pile on the bench next to the bath, and my boots were beneath them neatly placed side by side.

"They have been laundered," Keena said.

I picked up my shirt, and the sweet scent of something crisp and floral filled the room. "Thank you, Keena."

"I look forward to seeing you again." She blushed and left my room.

I pulled the flowers from my hair, wiped the gold dust from my cheeks, and dressed quickly, leaving the gown and ballerina-type shoes on the bench where my human clothes had been. Entering the cold hall in a V-neck T-shirt brought goose bumps to my arms.

"Brell and the three are ready," Keena said.

A chill curdled in my core. Somewhere beyond the Grove, three Laramiss waited for me, and although I had been given protection, I was still scared. "Thank you," I said and walked toward them, rubbing my arms.

Brell reached for my hand. "Can't you please come?" I asked him. "Your father's sending out messengers, too. That's more than three."

"Messengers are the exception. They do not count as the three. They are not trained in combat and can only travel within the trees."

"Be a messenger," I coaxed.

"I have orders to stay here tonight." He squeezed my hand.

"What about Molly?" I asked.

"A messenger will bring her to you."

We slipped through the palace, and I tried to divert my thoughts of fear and doubt by concentrating on the warmth of Brell's hand and counting my steps across the Grove to the far ridge. But it was of little use.

What if three protectors couldn't stop the Laramiss? Would the Laramiss hurt Mom if it meant capturing me? How would I explain things to her if it went that far?

My heart pounded in my throat, and when we reached the edge of the Grove, I was out of breath when I shouldn't have been. At the top of the ridge, Brell embraced me and kissed my forehead, the light touch of his lips as intoxicating as summer-berry wine.

"This is where I must leave you," he said. "But I *will* change places with one of the three. And I will be with you the day you begin school."

I pictured Brell sneaking down the science building hallway, blending into his surroundings in the inexplicable way Landaffens do, while I saw him as clear as day, a hot, renaissance-looking knight from a story book.

"Okay," I said.

He brushed a strand of hair from my forehead, brought his hands around my jaw and chin, and kissed me on the lips. A tingle rustled through my torso.

"You will be safe. Our protectors will not let the Laramiss three take you."

"What about Molly? She's not here yet."

"The messenger will be leaving soon. He and Molly will not be far behind you." He looked at Parolin. "It is time to go," Brell said.

I followed my protectors from the Grove, giving Brell a look over my shoulder as I stepped through the last row of trees. The wind swirled around my head and enveloped my body, pulling me from a world of magic and into a world of menace.

# CHAPTER 18

Goosebumps rose on my arms and legs. The crisp evening air, laced with the scent of dusty leaves, filled my lungs as the wind settled, and I teetered backward, catching the tree behind me.

My fingers raked across its bark, hitting a tacky bead of sap. I'd found one of my marks I'd left in a panic, a crudely cut "X", now an oxidized, brown scar thick with tree blood.

"The one called Laura," Parolin said, "We will take you to the edge of the woods, and from there we will begin our patrol."

"Okay, thank you," I said, eyeing the "X", remembering the day I'd walked in circles, afraid and alone, a victim of the Grove's spell. My shoulders shook as I shuddered.

"Is there something wrong?" Parolin asked, coming next to me.

"This place. It . . ."

He scanned the row of trees. "This tree is marked by a human hand."

"My hand," I said.

He inhaled deeply, his nostrils flaring. "I sense desperation and fear in this clearing. The emotions are strong. Emotions so powerful that they are now part of the trees."

"They're my emotions. I was lost, but then Brell found me."

He tilted his head. "Yes. Happiness and relief. Those emotions are here, too."

With my next breath, my shoulders relaxed, and a sense of calm rode through my chest. "I can feel them," I said, closing my eyes, savoring the sweet memory of seeing Brell for the first time.

We walked toward the edge of the forest, Parolin in the lead, Gressim to my right, and Farnaway at the rear. As we approached the last set of trees, the three stopped simultaneously as if they'd read each other's minds.

"What's wrong?" I whispered.

"I am not sure," Parolin said. "Heosh."

Each protector drew an arrow, raised his bow, set the nock, and pulled back its strings in a single movement, their arms a blur of white fabric as they took an archer's stance, knees bent with one leg in front of the other. I held my breath, my pulse pounding in my throat as I focused on the sounds of the forest and heard the rustling of leaves by a gentle breeze and a cheery melody of bird song. Nothing unusual.

"Tesse," Parolin said.

They lowered their bows. "What was it," I whispered.

"I am not sure. Whatever it was, it is now gone."

With the sun at our backs, we cut through the last fringe of forest, our thin shadows matching those cast by the trees. My house appeared between the trunks, a pickup truck in the driveway. Molly whinnied. A messenger cut through the trees, leading her to me. Molly had been fitted with an unadorned leather bridle and saddle.

"My uncle is there. He's going to wonder where I've been. I hope he didn't call my mom to tell her I'm M.I.A," I said.

"Return your horse and go to your uncle," Parolin said. "We will take our posts. Stay inside your home. Do not come into the trees for any reason. Landaffen powers are strongest in the woods. Strongest when both feet are touching the earth, but they are weak among human wares."

With strong facial features and a lean but muscular body, Parolin was a handsome man, a knight from another world. His head band blinked in the fading afternoon sun, and as his eyes met mine, my face, an oblong reflection, flashed back at me.

"Go now while the forest is at peace," he said.

I nodded and took Molly's reins.

"Thank you," I told the messenger.

A long, dark-green cape concealed the messenger's body, and its deep hood hid his face. He touched my hand when I reached for the saddle horn. The light caught his eyes and forehead when he moved closer.

"Brell?" I gasped.

"Did you really think I would leave you at the Grove and not see you home?" he asked. Brell smiled and stroked my cheek with his fingers.

"Prince Brell?" Parolin said. "You have intercepted our messenger."

"Yes. I sent him back to the Grove. It was my plan from the beginning."

"And the king?"

"I will explain that one goodbye was not enough. You may take your posts," Brell said. Parolin nodded and the three continued through the rim of trees.

I tossed the reins over Molly's saddle. "I wish you could stay. Be one of the three," I said, pushing his hood away from his face. The fabric folded onto itself and dropped to his shoulders.

He took my hand, brought my fingers to his lips, and kissed them. I closed my eyes, and he guided me against him. Our parted lips hit, my hands hard against his back, his breathing heavy.

"I have to go," I said, breaking our kiss. "I have to beat my mother home."

"I know," he said and caressed my shoulders. "I also need to return. Soon I will be one of the three. I will convince my father."

"I hope so." I gave Brell one more kiss and jumped onto Molly's back.

"I will make it happen." He patted Molly's neck.

"Ready, girl?" With a gentle squeeze of my legs, she broke into a cantor and we entered the open field between the forest and my driveway.

Someone was on the front porch. I blinked my eyes and the fuzzy image focused. It was Phyllis. She put her hands on her hips and stared back at me.

"There you are," she said as I came to a stop. I glanced behind me at the trees.

"Where's my uncle?" I asked, trying to control my nerves.

"He's around the back side of the house trying to peek into the windows. We thought maybe you were taking a nap, but when Dean's heavy knocking didn't bring you to the door, we got worried, especially because your car is still here."

"Did he call my mom?"

"Not yet."

"Good," I said, exhaling a tiny bit of relief. "I wouldn't want her worrying for no reason." I dismounted, wiped the dust from my rear, and scanned the yard. There was no trace of the Laramiss or my protectors.

Phyllis dug into her pocket. "I found these next to your car."

"My car keys!" I said, trying to sound surprised.

She dangled them in front of me.

"I, um, must have dropped them."

Phyllis leaned toward me, her eyes twinkling as her mouth rose in a sly smile.

"I, um, need to put Molly away," I said, tightening the slack of rein in my hand.

"There you are, Laura! I've been worried sick about you. I was just about to call your mom." Uncle Dean brushed his hands on his jeans.

"I just went for a quick ride down the road."

He scratched the top of his head. "I could have sworn I once heard your mother say something about how you're not supposed to take Molly out when she's not home."

"You did. I'm not," I admitted, hanging my head. "I'm sorry. I promise I won't do it again. Please don't tell her."

"Okay, I won't." He shook his head. "I sure am a sucker when it comes to my niece." He chuckled and opened his arms for a hug. His big bear arms enclosed around me, and though I felt safe at that moment, I knew that even a human as strong as my uncle wouldn't be able to protect me from the Laramiss Three.

"You better put Molly away before your mother gets home," he said as he let me go.

As Phyllis and Uncle Dean followed me to the stable, I noticed Uncle Dean limping.

"What happened?" I asked him.

"Oh, I was standing on an old stump out back to get a better look into one of the windows, and damn gummite, I fell and hurt my knee. But don't worry. I'll tell your mom I hurt it at work," he said and winked.

"I'm sorry," I said, and led Molly into her stall.

"It's not your fault. I'm just a klutz."

I un-cinched Molly's saddle and slid it and the pad from her back. "I'll get you an ice pack after I put—"

"No, no. I'm fine. I just need to walk it off. Here, let me

take that," he said, grabbing onto the saddle. "But," he said, slowing his speech, "there is something else we need to talk about." Phyllis and I followed him into the tack room.

"What?"

"About your car."

"Oh, um, what about my car?"

"Remember how I told you that I was working at the elementary school up the street from your high school?"

"Yeah."

He put the saddle on a hay bale and crossed his arms. "Well, right around quittin' time, one of the other fellows on the job says, 'Hey, did anyone see that cool white Challenger street racin' this morning? A chick was drivin' it.'

"And I asked him, 'Are you sure it was a Challenger?' and he said, 'it was no mistake; a white Challenger took off when the light turned green and peeled down the road past the school well above the speed limit.'"

I look down at my feet.

"Now, Laura, I would love to give you the benefit of the doubt, but there is only one white Challenger that I know of in this town, and my buddy, well, he's a bit of a drinker, and if it was after working hours, I'd say he was seeing things, but he's stone sober when he's on the job, so I kinda have to believe him."

My shoulders slumped, my brain ticking to come up with a good excuse.

"When I told Phyllis," Uncle Dean continued, "she got worried and wanted to come with me to check on you and see what was going on."

"Uncle Dean, I don't know what to say. I, I . . ."

Phyllis put her arm over my shoulder. "Look, Dean. Laura and I already talked about this before you walked over here. You know Laura is a responsible girl. I was only worried because I thought something was wrong. I didn't think for one minute that Laura was intentionally breaking the law."

"Well, I'm only concerned because there's a lot of power under that hood—power that's easy to abuse." He crossed his arms. "Now I'm not saying I've never street raced before. I have, but I was young, and stupid, and I was lucky that I never got hurt, and now I know how dangerous and wrong it was. One of the guys I grew up with wasn't so lucky, and now he's pushing up daisies in the local cemetery. I don't want Laura to make the same mistake."

"Dean, do you think Laura would actually street race?" Phyllis let go of me and stepped in front of my uncle. "I think your friend is exaggerating quite a bit. Laura just put her foot on the gas a little too hard, and the car jumped and the tires squealed, and it was all completely accidental. She's still getting used to the feel of the brakes. Right, Laura?"

"Yeah, that's exactly what happened. I have no desire to street race. I'm not into that, and I'd never let anyone talk me into it either."

She put one hand on my uncle's cheeks and lowered her chin while keeping eye contact with him. "You're not going to tell Margie about this, are you? You'll just worry her for no reason. Laura didn't mean to do anything wrong."

Uncle Dean dropped his head and shuffled one of his feet in the dirt. "No, I guess I'm not. I'm not trying to be mean. I just don't want Laura to get hurt. I feel responsible for her safety because I bought that car for her."

"Then you have to trust her."

"I know. I trust you, Laura," he said.

"Thank you, and I'm sorry you hurt your knee looking for me. I didn't mean to worry anyone." I gave him another hug.

"I know. It's okay. I'm tough. I'll be as good as new by tomorrow."

I unbridled Molly, and Phyllis gave her a quick brushing while I picked her hooves. From the corner of my eye, I saw a blur of movement within the distant row of trees. My protectors stood at the edge of the woods, strong and mighty, refined and majestic. Phyllis looked in the same direction, smiled, and winked at me.

Uncle Dean looked at his watch. "Your mom will be home any minute. Mind if we stay and visit for a while?"

I took a deep breath, looking left and right.

"Laura," my uncle prompted.

"No, of course not."

When Molly was settled, we walked to the house, and at the top of the porch, I turned toward the woods and the blurry images of my protectors solidified.

Gressim stood, a broadsword unsheathed at his side, its gleaming blade reflecting the dimming sunlight. Farnaway and Parolin had their bows positioned at their hips, as a solid mass of arrows butted from the quivers on their backs in an explosion of bright-red feathers.

My heart sank. The three would have to stay awake and alert through the entire night without any comforts or company.

I walked into the house, my hands shaking as I locked the door behind me. Phyllis sat at the kitchen table, and as I pour us iced teas, Uncle Dean found a bag of potato chips in one of the cabinets.

"So, how did your registration go? Did you get the classes you wanted?" Uncle Dean asked through a mouth full of chips.

"Yeah. It was fine. They don't offer as many advanced classes as my old school, but I took the ones they had." I sat down across from him.

"Well, that sounds good. Did you make any new friends?"

From within the hall leading from the kitchen's doorframe,

a shadow on the hardwood floor elongated. I held my breath and glanced out the window. The sun had set behind the trees.

Uncle Dean set both elbows on the table and leaned forward. "Did you make any new friends?"

*Squeak!*

I placed my palms on the table and abruptly stood, my eyes darting from one side of the room to the other.

Uncle Dean chuckled. "That was just my chair, Laura. Look." He shifted his weight, and the same rhythmic *creak* matched his movements.

"Oh." I lowered back to my seat.

"You sure seem on edge tonight and a bit distracted. Did something happen today?"

"No, of course not. I met some guys at registration," I added to change the subject.

"Guys, huh. Remember what I told you about boys and their raging hormones. If anyone gets fresh with you, you just let me know."

"I will, but I'm sure that's not going to happen."

"Alright missy, but don't forget, you're not invincible and you're not immortal. Teenagers just think they are."

"I'll be careful. Don't worry."

The headlights of my mother's SUV cut across the kitchen window and flickered off as the car drew to a stop. "It's a good thing I ordered an extra-large," Mom said as she entered the kitchen, her purse slung over her shoulder and a box of pizza in her hands.

"Let me get that, Margie," Uncle Dean said. He took the pizza box and set it in the middle of the table.

"Glad to have you join us. What brings you two out here?"

"We were going for an evening drive and decided to stop by," my uncle said.

Mom grabbed a stack of paper plates from the cupboard. "Well, I'm sure glad you did. Dig in, guys."

While we ate our pizza, my mother talked about how tired she was and how much she hated her work, and my uncle explained how grueling his job was on his aging body and how he'd tripped over a bucket of epoxy and hurt his knee, giving him a limp. From under the table, his lie was accompanied by a gentle tap of his foot against mine.

Phyllis complained about her ex-husband. She hardly looked at me and when she did, she smiled instead of sneering like the Laramiss did when they looked at me. Still, she had to know something.

My mother griped about my dad, Uncle Dean jumping in to validate her claims about him being a cold-hearted, selfish son-of-a-bitch, and at that point, I decided to excuse myself to get some fresh air and try to relax a little. I flashed a glance at Phyllis, hoping she'd take the hint that I wanted her to join me because we needed to talk.

I went to my room, threw on a thin sweatshirt, and took my iced tea with me, figuring it would be safe enough to sit on the porch. A few minutes later, Phyllis came outside with a half-eaten piece of pizza. She sat down next to me on the wicker loveseat and stared out into the woods, the paper plate poised delicately in her hand.

"Mind if I join you?" Phyllis asked.

"Not at all. My dad is their favorite subject. My uncle's a great guy, but my mom has him all wound up. It'll be a while before he realizes he's been ignoring his date for too long. Besides, I want to ask you about—"

"Does it bother you when they talk about your dad like that?"

"Not as much as it used to. My dad was a jerk to my mom. I'd be mad too if I was her, but I still don't like to be in the middle of it. Besides," I groaned, "I've got other things to worry about."

"Like being of half race, of course." She lifted an eyebrow. "Why do you think I sold you the Challenger? And the key chain," she said, "holds its own magic. It's made from a special sap produced from trees that only grow within a Grove. I wanted a fellow half-race to have both."

"How long have you known?"

"It was something I felt in you the first time we met, but I wasn't one-hundred percent sure until I saw a scout watching you when you were in the library. I'm of half race, too." Phyllis sniffed the air, closing and opening her eyes. "Summer-berry wine," she announced. "It's been a long time, but I will never forget that smell." She set her plate on the floor.

"You saw him that day?"

"No. Not exactly. I saw something I hadn't seen since I was about your age—a fuzzy, flicker of color, and I immediately knew what it was. My heart sunk, and for a moment, I thought my past was coming back to haunt me." She took a sharp breath. "There's a letter opener in the top drawer of the circulation desk, and I was ready to use it if I had to." She laughed. "But then to my relief, the Landaffin smiled at me, so I knew he was from Wventorin."

Pressure built behind my eyes. I blinked and inhaled, rolling my eyes upward, but a tear escaped anyway. "Phyllis, that scout was not from Wventorin," I cried.

"Not from Wventorin?" Her eyes were wide and unblinking.

"He's from Laramiss, and he wasn't just following me. He and two others have been chasing me."

"Oh my god!" She slapped her hand against her chest.

"Didn't you see him the other day on the hood of my car and hanging from the streetlights when you and Uncle Dean were on your way to get breakfast? He wasn't smiling then."

"Now that you mention it, I did notice something, but I couldn't tell what it was. I thought my eyes were playing tricks on me. I can't believe I couldn't see him. The longer I'm away from the Grove, the harder it gets." She shook her head. "I'm so sorry, Laura. When I saw him at the library, he was just observing you—doing what all scouts do. I never imagined he was there to do you harm." She dropped her head.

"It's okay. I know you would have said something if you thought I was in trouble."

"If they were chasing you, that can only mean one thing. They think you're the one." She sighed. "I wish I hadn't waited this long for us to talk about this, but I had no idea you were in danger." She set her hand on my knee. "The same thing had happened to me and for the same reason, but it wasn't supposed to happen again. The Laramiss promised."

"When?"

"When I was your age. I didn't own a car. Didn't even have a license. I walked everywhere I went. It was midday. July. Hot. Humid. Sticky. I was on my way to my best friend's house. I was almost there, too, when her coonhound came running down the dirt road, barking, growling, dust flying, and showing his teeth." She inhaled through her nose, and her plump lips thinned. "I was confused. I'd known Buster since he was a pup."

She lowered her chin to her chest. "And then I understood. Buster wasn't barking at me. He was barking at someone I couldn't see." Phyllis's eyes filled with fire, the tiny lines at the corners exaggerating as she squinted, staring straight ahead. "He pressed his hand against my face, forcing me to inhale a sleep-inducing pollen. My body became limp. I dropped to my knees and everything went black. When I woke up, I was a prisoner in the Laramiss Grove."

"The Laramiss are always watching, their scouts on the lookout for those of half-race, and, yes, just like you, they thought I was the one fated to bring our worlds together. But I wasn't the one."

"How did they know it wasn't you?"

"Their texts claim that the 'one' will eventually become more Landaffen than human, and after five years of captivity, my Landaffen capabilities had hardly improved. My intuition is strong, but other than that, I am as human as they come." She crossed her arms. "The Laramiss are consumed by power and pride. As a half-race with weak abilities, I was eventually ignored, shunned, and not only forbidden, but unwilling to assimilate to their world."

"So they let you go?"

She nodded. "Only after the Laramiss bragged about harboring a misfit half-race for sport. When the high council found out, they ordered my release. They didn't have to worry about me exposing their world because my magic is not strong enough to enter a Grove."

"The Wventorins kindly offered me refuge, promising to foster what abilities I had while accepting my presence unconditionally, but I wanted to go home; to let my family know and see I was still alive. I'd never had a chance to say good-bye to my family or friends. They didn't know where I was. They thought I was dead."

"That's awful. I would have gone home, too."

"I will admit that life with the Wventorins was tempting, but being a prisoner among the Laramiss had left a bad taste in my mouth. I will never return to a Grove—any Grove—not even for a visit. It would bring back too many bad memories. The few good memories I have are immortalized in my art, and that's all I need."

"I'm so sorry all of that happened to you. When you returned, what did you tell your family?"

"If I'd told them the truth, they would have thought I was

crazy, so I told them I simply ran away. As happy as they were to have me home safe and sound, I'm not sure they ever forgave me. They believed I'd let them mourn for five years, thinking I was dead, something only someone who was selfish and apathetic would do."

Phyllis sighed before continuing. "The whole experience left me bitter, unable to trust, unable to love, and in the end, I ended up marrying Joe, my first crush, simply because he was an escape. He gave me what I needed at the time to feel safe, but in the long run, all I got was a man with superficial values and a taste for gambling and womanizing. When he left, I was mentally worse off than I was before, but then I met your Uncle Dean, Mr. True Blue. He's a little rough around the edges, but that's one of the things I like about him. He's honest. He's real. With Dean, what you see is what you get. He's a good man. I finally have the life I want."

"I'm not sure this is the life I want. I met a boy from the Wventorin Grove named Brell. I care about him a lot, but still!" I swallowed hard, my heart beating in my throat. "The Laramiss thought you were the one and you weren't. The same thing could happen to me."

"Can you enter the Wventorin Grove without an escort?"

"Yeah, I did it today."

"Then your Landaffen powers are incredibly strong for a half-race. I can understand why the Laramiss think you are the half-race of legend. If caught, you will never be allowed to leave their Grove."

"Oh, my god, Phyllis! What am I going to do? I've been assigned three protectors, but what if that's not enough?"

Phyllis put her arm around my shoulder. "You are going to do what you're doing now—let the Wventorins protect you. Are they here now?"

"Yeah, under the tallest tree." I pointed.

Squinting her eyes, Phyllis scooted forward in her chair. "They're in the woods, so they don't have to try as hard to not be seen. So maybe, just maybe, I will be able to . . . I see them!"

One eyebrow rose, and she smiled wryly. "Boy, those men are beautiful, aren't they? It's been a long time since I've seen a Wventorin Landaffen in battle gear. I forgot what a turn-on that was."

I wiped my tears with the back of my hand. She was right about that. I just wished all Landaffens were good.

"I'm here for you, Laura. And so are they. In the meantime, I'm sure your case will go before the Landaffen High Council, and the Laramiss will be ordered to leave you alone. If you are the one, you'll be able to fulfill your destiny as stated in the old texts."

The screen door popped open with a squeak. "So here's where my favorite gals ran off to." Uncle Dean smiled broadly, his hands in his pockets. "Did you ladies get enough to eat? There's plenty of pizza left."

"Yeah, I'm full," I said.

Phyllis picked up her plate of cold pizza. "Me, too."

"Come on inside. Margie's getting the cards and chips. We're gonna play us a game of poker."

As Phyllis and I rose from the bench, I whispered "goodnight" to my protectors, and locked the door.

# CHAPTER 19

"I fold," Uncle Dean said, laying down his cards. "And I'm out of chips. Good thing that was our last hand for the night. Geez, little lady! When did you become such a card shark?"

"I don't know," I said, scooping up my winnings and taking a glance for the umpteenth time out the window.

"What's out there? Someone with a telescope reading my hand, counting cards, and feeding you information?" Uncle Dean chuckled. "You've been looking out there all night. Let's check her for a wireless headphone!"

"No headphone. It's just my lucky day," I said.

My mom had a terrible poker face, and not being a risk taker by nature, she folded almost every hand. My uncle was good at hiding his emotions. So was Phyllis, but I was *still* able to call their bluffs, which made me believe my developing Landaffen intuition had something to do with it.

"Or maybe you can see the reflection of my cards," Uncle Dean joked, shifting in his seat toward the window. "Nope. Window's too high. You can only see the top of my fat head."

"She's not a cheater, Dean," Mom said.

"It's a beautiful night. Who wouldn't want to look out the window?" Phyllis added.

"I know. I'm just joshing my niece." He slapped his knee. "Ready to call it a night, Phyllis?"

"I am," she said.

We put the cards and chips in their wooden caddy, and my mother and I walked Uncle Dean and Phyllis to the porch.

"Don't worry," Phyllis whispered as she hugged me good-bye. "Your three won't let anything happen to you." She got into the passenger seat.

As Uncle Dean backed up and pulled around, his headlights lit the distant band of trees with an arch of bright light, illuminating my protectors. Their weapons twinkled like stars, and cat-like, their eyes glowed orange like hot coals.

"I'm going to bed," my mom said.

I blinked, fanning the dust from the porch as Uncle Dean finished his turn and headed down the driveway. My heart beat hard, my shoulders tightening as I searched the trees.

The forest was empty. My protectors were suddenly gone.

"Um, actually. I'm going to stay up for a while and watch TV."

"Okay, sweetie."

I locked the door behind us. Mom went to bed, and I walked to the kitchen to get a glass of water, peering out the window each time I passed it. The three hadn't returned. I closed the curtains, turned off the lights, and sat on the couch with the TV on but the volume low.

A good sitcom wasn't enough to cut my anxiety, especially with the picture flickering every few minutes when the HD antennae readjusted. I pulled my legs onto the couch and crossed my arms. Maybe they'd returned, and I was worrying for no reason.

I pushed up from the couch and crept to the kitchen on my tiptoes. From between the curtains, a silver ray of moonlight set the kitchen sink aglow, turning its dull stainless-steel basin into a greasy mirror of dull light.

Reaching a trembling hand, I held my breath and parted the curtains. Two eyes peered into mine. I stumbled backward, catching the counter behind me with both hands, my fingers fumbling for the knife block I knew was there. The cold handle of a butcher knife hit my palm. I closed my hand, pulled it from the block, and raised it in front of me.

A muffled whisper filled my ears. "The one called Laura." I leaned forward and the glint of Parolin's metal hand band shot through the curtains. With light footsteps, I rushed to the door, twisted the deadbolt, and opened it just wide enough to see his face.

"What happened?" I whispered.

"A Laramiss scout was on your roof."

"Just one?"

"Yes. The presence of others I do not feel." His eyes shifted to the right, and he looked up. "But the emotions of three linger. I believe that they are making an exchange, leaving one as a spy, so he can test us—bring us in the open, so he can determine our rank."

"So when they come back, we won't be dealing with scouts anymore?"

"No. They will send three of their best *lemdents*, soldiers, fighters, warriors." I shuddered and tightened my hold on the knife handle. "But not tonight. Their Grove is too far for them to return before the drop of the moon."

I pressed my free hand against my chest and exhaled.

"Your weapon," Parolin said, peeking through the crack in the door. "It is unsatisfactory. Your stance and your grip are also inadequate."

"I'm not surprised." I smiled ashamedly.

One side of his mouth lifted. "What you need now is sleep. Do not let worry keep you awake."

The morning fog was heavy on Saturday, sticking to the ground in thick layers while thin tendrils swirled in the breeze, like steam from a witch's caldron, curling at the waists of my protectors.

"You're up early," Mom said through a yawn when she entered the kitchen. "But you'll be up even earlier when school starts."

I closed the curtain and dropped into a chair at the kitchen table.

"Are you excited, scared, or both?" she asked.

"I don't know," I said. School was the last thing on my mind.

She made a pot of coffee and set two bowls, a carton of milk, and a box of cereal in the middle of the table. "Banana?" she asked, snapping one from a bunch.

"Sure." I poured the cereal and milk, and my mother sliced the banana over our bowls.

The telephone rang. She tossed the banana peel in the trash and answered it. I took slow bites and tried to read the cereal box, but the face of the grocery-store boy Landaffen kept entering my mind, making my heart pound and my breathing quick yet heavy.

Mom hung up the phone. "Phyllis asked me to join her book, wine, and lunch club."

"At the library?"

"No, it's at her home. Can't drink wine in a public library. I'm surprised she didn't ask if you wanted to join, too."

"Mom, honestly, do you think I'd want to?"

"You love to read."

"When school starts, I won't have time to read a book on top of all the other stuff I'll be assigned. Besides, I don't think I'd fit in with a bunch of women drinking wine."

"Are you saying we're too old for you?" she smirked.

"Maybe," I snickered.

"Well, I guess I'll get ready. I told her I'd bring a pinot, so I'll have to stop at the store."

I straightened my back. "You mean it's today?"

"Yep, first Saturday of the month."

I dressed, put in a load of laundry, and watched from the window as my mom turned down the driveway. As she drove past our mailbox, Parolin stepped from the line of trees, and I jogged from the house to meet him. Gressim and Farnaway remained at their posts, barely moving a muscle.

"Did anything else happen last night?" I asked.

"No. As it was the day before."

"Did you guys take turns keeping watch, so you'd get a chance to sleep?"

"No."

The whites of his eyes were as clear and smooth as milk, accentuating his blue irises. His complexion, fresh and flawless, showed no signs of lacking sleep, but the tight waves of hair brushing the sides of his face were loose, victims of the mist.

"I'm sorry," I said.

"Do not be. You would do the same for those you needed to protect. And you would adapt and do it well. It is the way of the Landaffen."

"Do you believe I'm the half-race from the old texts?"

"I do."

"And what if I'm not?"

"Then you are not."

"But then all of this would have been for nothing."

"There is a reason for everything." He lowered his head to bring his eyes level with mine. "Even if you are not the 'one' of myth, you are a half-race with ancestral ties to a Grove. We would never let the Laramiss take you against your will. Your fate has already taken root. It is wrong to manipulate another's destiny."

"Are you hungry? I can bring you guys some food."

"We do not require nourishment at this time. When it is necessary, we will begin our rotations in and out from the Grove. During that time, we will rest and eat."

"When it does, I will be able to see Brell. He told me—"

"No. I do not think so. His safety is also in jeopardy when he is not in the Grove. I do not believe his father will allow him to exchange places with one of us until the high council has met concerning this matter."

"What do you think the high council will do?"

"They would order the Laramiss to let fate unfold on its own. But I am not sure the Laramiss would abide by Glacion's ruling. They see humans not only as the ultimate enemy, but as the inferior race. The Laramiss do not want to join with the humans. They want to rule over them. If you are prevented from uniting both worlds civilly, without war, using your influence to link our worlds, the Laramiss will force the future foreseen in the new texts. They will pick up bow and sword, use their stealth and intuition as arms. Deception and acts of sabotage to compensate for their small numbers and inequivalent weapons. It is no secret that the Laramiss have been building an army in preparation for this day."

"One Grove against the whole human race?"

"In the beginning, yes, but loyalty is the life force of my people. Once Landaffen lives are lost through human hands and hope of diplomacy has faded, my people will have no choice than to fight alongside our kind."

"Do you think you'll win?"

"I am not sure. But I do know many lives will be lost on both sides. That is why you are so important to us."

What did I know about peacekeeping and negotiations? Nothing! The world powers wouldn't listen to me. Heck. I didn't even know if the mayor of this tiny town would answer an email from me if I sent him one.

"I don't want anyone to die. But I'm not sure I'm the one to bring our worlds together. And if the Laramiss start a war, I'm not sure I can stop it." I folded my arms. "Don't your people value life as much as mine do?"

"Yes. But unlike the Landaffens in other Groves, the Laramiss also value power, especially over a race they consider inferior." He dropped his head, and I leaned against the tree to my right, its smooth bark cool against my shoulders.

"The average lifespan for a human is about eighty years. What is it for a Landaffen?"

"I do not know the number in human years, but there are many in our colony who were alive when humans created artificial light. But soon they will die and join the woods."

"That was about a hundred and fifty years ago!" He nodded. "What about someone like me, a half-race? How long can I live?"

"I am not sure. Our time is recorded by events not numbers."

"Where are your people buried? I didn't see a cemetery in the Grove."

"That is not what I meant by joining the woods."

"Then what did you mean?"

"When we die, we join the woods by becoming a tree."

I stood upright. "These trees?" I touched the one beside us.

"Yes. Many of these trees were not given life by humans. They did not begin as seeds. They are our ancestors."

"How?"

"At death, the ground opens. The body is taken. Its lapis, its life force, is reclaimed by the earth, binding with the soil to take root and grow to become again." He brushed the tree's trunk with his hand, and I did the same, eyeing a patch of fresh, green bark where a dry piece had peeled and fallen away.

"To feed the air and give us breath," he continued. "To give, so we can take. Shelter, food, heat, and beauty."

"And if it gives too much? Wood to make a fire? To make a home? What happens when a tree dies?"

"A lansk is never without a purpose. There is no life without death." He bent down on one knee and scooped up a handful of soil. "Here," he said.

He stood and poured the dirt in my palm and folded my fingers closed. "Close your eyes, and tell me what you feel."

I closed my eyes, concentrating on the soil in my hand—its damp coolness, the piece of leaf debris biting against my skin, the sharp end of a twig pushing between two fingers. Heat pulsed in my palm, and a silent vibration like a static-electric shock emanated through my fist.

I opened my eyes and inhaled slowly to decelerate my racing heart. "What was it?" I asked.

"The essence of life. It begins here, and it ends here." His tone was soft, almost a whisper, and his blue eyes grew misty.

"Ashes to ashes. Dust to dust," I muttered.

Tears threatened, and I sniffled, wiping my chin, but it was too late. A fat, warm tear ran down my cheek.

"Did I upset you?" Parolin asked.

"No. It's just . . ." A renegade tear joined the other. "I'm worried about what's going to happen and what I'll be expected to do. What if—"

"Yes. I sense this fear," Parolin said. He leaned closer. "When it is time for you to act, you will know what to do. It is in your lansk, the Landaffen and the human."

"Thank you," I said.

"When will your mother return?"

"I have a of couple hours."

"I will use that time to teach you how to fight."

"You're kidding, right?"

He slung the bow from his back. "Prince Brell made the suggestion. Scouts are the most skilled when it comes to stealth and the magic of concealment," Parolin said, "But when it comes to the bow—"

Bay's howl cut the air.

"Brell must be here," I said, scanning the foliage in front of me.

Bay burst through the trees, and Brell followed. "Today I am a messenger," he announced, "though I have no message from the king."

"I did not expect your father to allow this," Parolin said, eyeing Brell's bow and sword.

"Neither did I." Brell smiled.

Like the other protectors, Brell wore chest armor clad with metal plates, but the leather shined like it had been freshly oiled and the plates were unmarred. The fitted sleeves of his dark green tunic gently enveloped his arms, silhouetting his biceps, and his matching leggings ended with brown boots, rising mid-calf. A sheathed sword hung from a belt at his waist, and a thin wrap of leather held a dagger against his thigh.

"You're not dressed like a messenger," I said. My pulse pounded. Phillis was right when she said it was a turn-on to see a Landaffen in battle gear.

"I am not. Today you are going to school with me—Landaffen School."

"You're taking me back to the Grove?" I asked.

"I do not mean to question you, Prince Brell," Parolin interrupted, "but I do not understand. You have permission to do so from the king?"

"I do. My father was more easily swayed then I had expected."

"I will be your escort," Parolin said.

We passed through the trees, Parolin and Brell on light feet. I followed between them, copying Brell's stride, solidly landing my steps toe-to-heel, each punch into the forest floor making twice as much sound as theirs.

"I'm ready," I said as we approached the secret entrance to the Grove.

Parolin nodded good-bye, backing away, and the warm wind of the Grove wrapped Brell's body and mine. I closed my eyes, savoring the sweet scent of flowers carried with the wind. When I opened them, we were inside, standing on the ridge.

Brell took me in his arms and kissed me, his lips starting at my collar bone, light kisses moving up my throat to my chin. I threw back my head, my pelvis pressing against his armor as I gripped the muscles in his shoulder blades.

We kissed long and hard, heat building in my chest. I stepped backward, and he pushed forward, bringing my back against the trunk of a tree. His hands worked their way up from my waist to my ribcage. As his hands rounded to cup my breasts, he stopped, letting his hands slip to my hips.

"You are stunning," he said, lifting away from me.

Sennille was wrong. We would not be a victim of our physical desires and break a Landaffen code.

The fire in my chest rose to my cheeks. "Thank you." I placed my hands on the sides of his face. "And you are so hot."

"You do not mean temperature. I can assume this is a compliment?"

"Yes." I laughed. "It means you are very handsome."

He took my hand. "I do not want anything to happen to you, Laura. That is why you must learn to use the sword."

"At your school? Is that why you're taking me there?"

"Yes."

"But even if you teach me, I don't think I'll . . ." I shook my head. "I don't want to hurt anyone. I can't. I won't be able to do it."

"You may not want to, but you will if you have to. When there are only two options, life or death, you will know what to do."

Brell led me to the school, taking the "backpath" so we were only stopped by a handful of people who greeted us instead of practically everyone in the village. We climbed the steps and entered a narrow hall lined with doors on either side.

"Classrooms," Brell explained. "Our training center is the last room."

Two doors to our right were open, and as we passed each one, I slowed to sneak peeks inside, and Brell matched my pace. In the first room, children sat in rows at long tables, wearing matching, green Peter-Pan-type hats, minus the red feather. Following the teacher as he demonstrated, the students used small, club-shaped stones to grind leaves placed in stone bowls.

In the next room, the children stood in circles holding small animals—mice, rabbits, squirrels, snakes, and lontees. But there were a few creatures I didn't recognize. A goat-like animal with bulbous horns bayed like a donkey until the child set it down. Something the size and shape of a cat with a row of erect feathers down its back cooed, wagging its tail. And an orange long-necked turtle squirmed in the arms of a little girl who laughed while patting its head with her free hand. I stopped to get a better look.

"Nichone Brell," the little girl said. I figured out that "nichone" meant "prince." Her lizard flicked its head, and with his mouth, caught one of two braids at the girl's ear. She laughed, pulling away, and the lizard let go.

"Goven jahn ablie," Brell said, stepping closer to the doorway. The students greeted Brell in return, and the teacher, a woman dressed in blue, smiled and waved.

"They are learning to connect with all living things," Brell told me.

As we walked closer to the end of the hall, grunts, groans, and the clang of metal upon metal rang out. Brell opened the door, and we entered a large, three-walled room overlooking a grass field. At the room's center, two Landaffens engaged in battle, clashing swords. A collection of exposed swords, daggers, spears, and bows hung on the wall by the door.

"What about when it rains?" I asked when I noticed the ceiling was made from wood slats spaced several feet apart from one another.

"The magic here is strong," Brell said.

The Landaffens lowered their swords and turned in our direction. One of them was Thriss. I lowered my head and turned away from her.

"Here," Brell said to me.

He lifted a sheathed broadsword from the wall and held the belt open at both ends.

I stepped forward, and he wrapped it around my waist, bringing our lips inches apart. As he secured the buckle and straightened my scabbard, our eyes remained fixed on one another. His chest brushed mine with his next breath, and when he licked his lips, I knew his impulse to kiss me was as strong as mine was to kiss him.

"Thank you," I said, my words soft and breathy.

My body rocked as he drew the sword from my sheath. He held it perpendicular to his body, the flat side of the blade in one palm, the handle in the other. As the rising sun burned through the lingering mist, the sword's slender, mirror-smooth blade reflected a ray of light. In contrast to the dull, black, leather wrapped grip, the delicately etched guard and pommel shone brightly with a spiral trail of plum-colored gems.

"From the royal arsenal," he said, raising his hands to bring the sword closer to me.

"It's beautiful," I said. "But it's dangerous and scares me," I whispered.

"Do not fear what can save your life. Take it."

"It looks heavy."

"It is lighter than it looks."

"Meresim?" I asked. The word rose up in my mind and escaped my lips effortlessly, without conscious thought. I clamped my hand over my mouth.

"Yes," he said, and smiled. "Meresim is a metal found and forge only in a Grove. It is beginning to happen, and earlier than I had expected. Soon you will be fluent in our language just as you will become proficient in our ways of weaponry."

"How would I know something I haven't learned?"

"The same way a spider knows how to spin a web, a bird to make a nest, and for all creatures to care for their young. You are born with the ability, but like fruit on a tree, it needs to ripen." He leaned toward me, his lips meant for my forehead. I closed my eyes, anticipating his sweet touch.

"Brell!" Thriss snapped. "Thiy nesto lahn kheen hanh," she said.

"And whose permission does she need other than mine?" Brell returned.

Thriss pursed her lips.

"Maybe we should practice somewhere else," I said.

"She will not bother us," Brell said, offering me the sword.

I wrapped my fingers around its hilt, keeping my grip strong, and lifted the sword from his palms. He pulled his broadsword from the scabbard at his waist and we walked to the far end of the room.

"Copy my stance and follow my lead," Brell said.

He held up his sword, his right hand below the guard, the pommel level with his belly button. "Think like a Landaffen. Move like a Landaffen. It is in your laspis. You will not find your abilities. They will find you."

He stabbed and struck, slicing the air, and I followed, keeping most of my weight on my forward right foot, while keeping my left, bent leg behind me, rising to the ball of my foot with each blow.

With vertical, horizontal, and diagonal strokes, slaying invisible enemies, Brell was amazing, a perfect dance of man and sword, while I struggled, my arms shaking and shoulders aching.

When exhaustion affected my stance, the weight of the sword caused me to lean to one side and lose my balance. Brell came behind me, grasping my hands as they held the sword, and brought me into a coordinated combat of lunging and attacking. Cheek to cheek, his chest stiff against mine, it was hard to remain focused, and twice I lost my concentration as I inhaled the sweet musky scent on his collar.

"You are doing well," Brell said. He kissed me just above my ear, and a happy shiver made me lift my shoulders. My insides lit with flame. I lowered my arms, resting the point of my sword against the ground.

"No, I'm not. I can't do this. It's too heavy." The blade winked, but I was too exhausted to smile at its deadly beauty.

"Yes, you can," Brell said and rotated in my arms to face me.

He kissed my forehead, backed away from me, and drew his sword. "You are thinking like a human. Let your Landaffen instincts pump hard through your veins."

"No, I can't," I scoffed. From the corner of my eye, I caught Thriss smirking as she watched us. "I mean. Yeah, I can." I raised my sword, ignoring my trembling muscles.

"Ready?" I asked as a splinter of jealousy struck my nerves.

We continued our banter, Brell overcoming me every time, forcing me to drop my weapon. We fought until my pounding heart needed a break and my sweating hands refused to keep their grip. A trail of sweat ran from my forehead and stung my eyes. My arms shook and my biceps burned. Brell looked as fresh as he did when I first saw him that morning.

"Nichone Brell," came a voice at the door. It was the teacher from the classroom full of animals. A large, brown bird sat on her shoulder. She spoke and Brell answered, smiling and nodding.

He turned to me. "The children are going to dance with their animals. They wish for me to watch."

"Okay," I said.

"And you will join me?" he asked. His eyes shifted to someone behind me, and with her next footstep, I knew it was Thriss.

"There is a technique I want to show you," Thriss said. "You go, Prince Brell, and she will stay here with me."

"Laura?" Brell asked.

"Yeah, that's fine. Go ahead." I regretted it after I said it, but Thriss had me by the hand, pulling me closer to the open end of the room, and Brell left with the teacher.

"Draw," Thriss said, brandishing her broadsword.

The school was at least twenty feet from the ground, and Thriss's practice area of choice took us just a few feet from the edge of the room. Horses pranced in the field below with riders either seated or standing. I took a deep breath, drawing back my shoulders.

"What did you want to show me?" I asked.

"Draw," she said again.

I drew my sword, holding it and planting my feet the way Brell had taught me.

Thriss lunged toward me, slicing her sword toward my head. I blocked the blow, bringing my sword down against her blade. She spun and struck again. On the defense, I stepped backward, keeping my blade parallel to hers, but with her next hit, my weak arms withered like rubber bands, and I dashed to my left to avoid being hit.

I didn't realize I'd overstepped my bounds until the wind caught my hair and pulled at my T-shirt. I landed on the field on both feet but stumbled onto my back with a thud. I closed my eyes against the sun and let go of my sword.

"Where is Laura?" I heard Brell ask, the tone of his voice elevated and full of worry.

Thriss answered in Landaffen, so I couldn't understand.

A cloud of dust hit my face, and I opened my eyes to see a Landaffen boy hovering above me, holding a beautiful appaloosa by the reins. Brell jumped from the platform, landing next to me, followed by Thriss.

"Are you okay?" he asked.

"I guess," I said, pushing up with my palms until I was sitting.

"Please leave us," Brell said to Thriss.

"I was showing her how to counter a surprise attack," Thriss said and then continued with a string of words in Landaffen.

"Leave!" Brell shouted.

"What did she say?"

"That you took a defensive position when it should have

been offensive. That you lost your confidence and let your guard down."

"What confidence? I don't have any. I'm not right for this," I whimpered when Thriss and the Landaffen boy were gone. "I can't be the one. This proves it." I wasn't anything special in either world.

He pulled me to my feet, picked up my sword, and we walked up a small ramp leading back to the school. "You are right for this," Brell said. "You need to encourage yourself like I keep encouraging you. Believe in yourself."

The training room was empty. We sat down on a small bench near the equipment. I inhaled, and the muscles along my ribcage twinged with pain.

"Is everyone in the Grove trained for battle?" I groaned.

"Not everyone. Only those who leave the Grove or *might* need to leave the Grove. Protectors are given the most instruction. Scouts, the least, though there are exceptions."

"Why the least?"

"Our invisibility is our weapon. We take a defensive position. It is our job to explore, learn, and bring knowledge to the Grove, avoiding confrontation and discovery at all cost. The deeper we enter the world of humans, the weaker our magic becomes. Concealing a weapon would be too difficult and tiring. We cannot take them with us."

"But you're one of the exceptions?"

"Yes. There are currently two in our unit of scouts. Thriss is the other. Parolin was in charge of our tutelage."

"Being a prince, I understand why you should learn, but why Thriss if she's just a scout?"

"She plans to become a protector when she is ready to do so."

I rubbed my aching right bicep and sighed.

"You did well today, Laura. As I predicted, you are a fast learner."

"As fast as Thriss?" Thriss—the sound a tire makes when it's losing air.

"Yes, as fast as Thriss, but there is always more to learn. She has her struggles. Not letting go of unnecessary thoughts. Letting her subconscious abilities flow into her conscious. She prefers not to work hard, and she is not receptive to criticism."

"She sounds like a high maintenance know-it-all."

"High maintenance know-it-all?" Brell asked. "That is an expression I am not familiar with."

"It means she'd rather just sit around like a princess and not have to do anything because she thinks she already knows how to do everything and doesn't need anyone's help."

He laughed under his breath. "That would be an accurate description."

"A lot of human girls are like that, too, and I don't like any of them."

"And I would guess that they do not like you," Brell teased, a twinkle in his eye.

"Why do you say that?"

"Because they do not like seeing in others what they wish for in themselves. They are envious of you."

"No. They aren't. Believe me. They have nothing to be jealous of."

"Yes, they do." He came to me eye-to-eye. "You are an amazing girl, Laura, and I love you."

My chest fluttered, and for a moment, I forgot my arms were tight and sore and the muscles in my legs felt like Jell-O. The whinny of a horse drew my attention, and I walked back to the outer edge of the room, taking Brell's hand to bring him with me.

"This place is so beautiful," I said, squinting against the

afternoon sun. A light breeze rustled the surrounding trees, and the soft scent of something floral filled my nose.

"This. All of this is still so hard to believe." Anxiety replaced my pleasant thoughts. My heart beat hard in my chest, and my right knee buckled.

"I can't do this. It's not me. I can't cut it. You saw what happened today."

Brell took me in his arms. "Yes, I saw what happened today. I saw a half-race learn as quickly as one of full blood. I saw legs that would be broken from a fall, stand tall and strong. You are becoming more Landaffen than human."

"But what if I don't want . . ."

"You cannot change what is meant to be. It is fated. You can do this, Laura."

We took our time taking the backpath to the ridge. "I don't know if I'll ever get used to this," I said, anticipating the whirl of wind when we'd made it to the top.

"I want you to take my sword with you."

"No. I can't. I mean, what if my mom finds it? She's a total pacifist. She'd have a fit. Besides I have the three to protect me. And I won't use it anyway. I told you I'm not ready. Please," I urged.

"Okay," he said. "I understand." He stood behind me and wrapped his arms around my waist.

"What are those?" I asked.

A row of identical buildings lined one end of the Grove. They sat upon raised platforms rather than being nestled in the trees. Carrying baskets, Landaffens exited and entered what appeared to be tiny stores.

"Our stations of trade," Brell said. "The buying and selling of goods produced in the Grove."

"I didn't notice them before."

Brell kissed the top of my head. "Like I said, you are

becoming more Landaffen each day. As your senses sharpen, you will continue to see more of our hidden world."

With Brell stopping many times to hold and kiss me, our trek back through the forest took longer than usual. Brell looked at the sky announcing it was almost one o'clock in human time.

"Do you hear that?" I whispered.

"Yes. It is a car. The one that was here before."

"My mom. I have to go." We walked to the edge of the woods. Raising their weapons, Parolin, Gressem, and Farnaway turned when they heard us, nodded, and lowered their swords.

"Do not leave your home," Brell ordered. "Do not return to these woods unless one of us calls for you. I will come for you tomorrow when I can. And then you will learn the bow."

"Will Thriss be there?" I asked.

"I will make sure no one is there except us."

We kissed, Brell stroking my hair as I ran my fingers down his back. I pulled away and broke into a jog toward my house, and when I reached the porch, I waited and skipped down the steps to greet mom.

"How was it?" I asked.

"Fun. A great group of ladies. And guess what? Dean decided to have an end-of-summer barbeque tomorrow."

I followed her inside to the kitchen. She took two glasses from the cupboard and set them in front of me. I studied the way Mom moved, the way she took the pitcher of iced tea from the fridge and poured it into the glasses. Nothing about her was Landaffen.

Brell had said those genes could lie dormant for generations, but I couldn't see any sign of it. I wouldn't call her graceful and the word "elegant" definitely couldn't be used to describe my mother. Her stiff back, something that she said she's had practically her whole life, forced her to bend slowly, and she was almost as clueless as my dad when it came to being observant and in tune with her surroundings.

"Should be fun, right?" she asked, breaking me out of my thoughts.

"Great," I said and tried to think of an excuse not to go.

# CHAPTER 20

"I have a headache. Maybe I'm getting a sinus infection," I rolled onto my back, and my mother leaned over my bed.

A deep wrinkle formed between her eyebrows, and her lips curved into a frown. She pressed her hand against my forehead. "You don't feel hot, but you should probably stay home today and rest, especially with school starting tomorrow. It's a shame to miss the barbeque, but you certainly won't want to miss your first day."

"Yeah, I probably should rest."

"I'll make us some breakfast."

She left my room, and I stayed in bed to authenticate that I was not feeling well enough to leave the house. I looked out my window. The woods dripped with morning dew and the ghostly fingers of a dense fog hugged the ankles of my protectors. Brell hadn't returned.

I imagined him standing with Parolin, waiting for me, a quiver of arrows on his back and a broadsword strapped to his hip, his hair, damp with mist, spread limply across his forehead.

I blinked, and for a moment, the scene before me wasn't real. It was something from a fairy tale, and I was Laura Brooks, high-school senior, a human of full race, confusing reality with a world I'd made up in my head.

"Laura," Mom shouted down the hall. "I made you some scrambled eggs."

Parolin broke his stance at the sound of her voice, shifting his weight between his feet, and Gressim turned his head toward my window.

It was real—too real.

I walked into the kitchen, stretching my sore arms. Mom picked up a glass of orange juice and handed it to me.

"How are you feeling now?" she asked.

"The same."

"If you don't mind, I'm going to leave a little early, so I can help Phyllis make some coleslaw and potato salad."

"No, I don't mind."

"And I'll probably stay a little later and help them clean up. Are you sure you'll be okay here, all by yourself? I don't have to go."

"I'll be fine. Go and have a good time."

I plopped down on the couch with my plate of eggs and turned on the TV, flipping through the only three channels we had until I found something semi-decent, a silly cartoon geared toward teenagers.

"If you start to feel worse, call me, and I'll come home," Mom said. She picked up her purse and snatched her keys from the trinket basket we keep on a small table by the front door.

"Okay, thanks Mom."

As my mom's car turned from the driveway to the road, Parolin motioned for me to join him, with a subtle nod of his chin. A plum-colored shirt billowed from beneath his chest plate, and his once-dusty boots were slick, shining like liquid glass. Farnaway was still at his post toward the back of the house, but Gressim had been replaced by a protector I'd never seen before.

"You went back to the Grove with Brell," I said.

"Yes. We are in rotation. Meiley is here in Gressim's place."

"Do you know when Brell's going to return?"

"I do not. The queen believes her son should not leave the Grove until the Laramiss end their pursuit. To come here for you yesterday was wrong."

"I understand," I said. "I miss him, but I don't want him to upset his parents."

The soft pat of feet echoed through the trees ahead of us. Parolin pushed me behind him and drew his sword.

"It is me," Brell said, cutting through a moss-covered path.

"Prince Brell," Parolin said. "Your father told me—"

"It is all right, Parolin," Brell said with a nod.

As soon as Parolin resumed his post, Brell turned to me. "For you, Laura." He handed me a bow.

Grasping it at its center, I gently plucked its taut string and studied the intricate carving of leaves running along its length. "It's lovely—I guess. I mean for a bow it is." I brought the bow forward with my left hand, my right hand poised to pull the string again.

"Let me show you," Brell said.

"Are we going back to the Grove?" I asked.

"No. Today the woods will be our training ground."

He lined his body up with mine and adjusted my stance by nudging my arms and legs into the correct position. Gripping the string with my thumb and forefinger, I pulled. The bow arched and my arms shook. When I released the string, its reverberation rattled up through my arm.

"That's harder than I thought it would be," I said.

Brell unstrapped the quiver from his back. "Like yesterday, you will learn quickly."

"If you call that learning quickly." I shrugged.

"It is in your blood." He slipped the quiver up my arm and kissed my cheek. "We will be just beyond these trees," he told Parolin.

Holding hands, we walked into the woods. He brought me in for a hug that turned into several minutes of kissing.

"I missed you," he said, brushing hair from my eyes.

"I missed you, too. You're all I thought about last night."

Under Brell's instruction, I pulled an arrow from the quiver, nocked it, and drew the string. I aimed at the tree we had designated as our target, and released, my eyes wide and my left arm straight and still. He stood next to me, correcting my technique, the smooth leather across his chest emphasizing his broad shoulders. Between shots, we stole kisses, sighing each time we let go.

"Your turn," I said when the muscles in my right arm wouldn't stop shaking. "Show me what my hot—"

I stopped just before calling him my boyfriend. We hadn't really talked about it, making it official that we were a couple. But he was the person I wanted to spend time with and the person I thought about when I wasn't with him. And I knew he felt the same way about me.

"Show you what?" Brell asked innocently.

A flush spread across my cheeks. "What my hot boyfriend can do," I said.

"No problem," Brell replied with a sexy half-smile. "Anything for my girlfriend."

His arm a blur of brown fabric, he emptied the quiver, each arrowhead meeting its mark to form a tightly packed circle of red quills. When I looked closer, I realized they'd formed a heart.

"Awe, Brell! That's amazing," I gushed.

"Our protectors are capable of doing that and more." He put his arms over my shoulder and kissed my forehead.

I imagined Thriss holding a bow, but with her small frame, I couldn't picture her as a protector. "Can anyone become a protector?" I asked.

"Yes, anyone who is willing to fight and die fighting if need be." In one motion, he pulled the clump of arrows from the tree. "Even though I am not a protector, like the three, I will also defend you to the death."

"I don't want anyone to die for me." I squeezed the grip of my bow until it hurt.

"It is their duty to give their life if it means saving yours. They took an oath to sacrifice themselves for the good of the Grove if need be, and they will not break it." He restocked his quiver, slung his bow over his shoulder, and we continued practicing.

An hour later, my arms were too sore to continue, especially after wielding a sword the day before. I set down my weapon. "I can barely lift my arms." I held up my trembling hands as proof.

What was the point? Cutting someone with a sword or shooting someone with an arrow was something I would never have the nerve or the guts to do.

"I have something that will help."

Using both hands, Brell worked the wind, his fingers extended toward a "V" in a tree where a thick limb extended from the trunk. The leaves stirred in a clockwise swirl, building at the base of the branch, forcing the bough to shake. A leather pouch dropped from a dense clot of leaves. He snatched it from the air with one hand.

"These trees are full of our supplies," he explained. "They were stocked by a messenger before I exchanged places with him."

Shading my eyes with my hands, I examined the treetops. "I don't see anything."

"You will," he said. "Your eyes will adjust."

From within a spray of twigs, something shiny appeared. I squinted and the metallic thing became the head of a spear. Next to it were shields, swords, daggers, and large leather pouches. A bow and quiver hung at the highest branch. I stood in awe, a half-race in the middle of all this magic.

Brell produced a wooden jar from the pouch, unscrewed the lid, and dipped his first two fingers in a thick, green salve.

"Flaxien?" I asked. The word slipped between my lips like an automatic gesture.

"Yes," he said and smiled. "It will draw away the pain."

I winced as he took my upper arm in his hands and massaged my sore bicep and triceps, working up to my deltoid and across my shoulder blades. He fitted his hand through the arm hole of my shirt and palpitated my muscles in a rhythm and pressure I had never experienced before.

He switched arms, and the warm, tingly salve did its work, leaving my skin slightly numb but my muscles pain free.

"It worked!" I said, bending my arms and opening and closing my hands.

"And the pain should not return—at least not until after our next practice." He winked.

The branches parted, and Parolin joined us in the clearing. "Two people are approaching," Parolin said.

Brell half-pulled his broadsword from its sheath, cocked his head to one side, and listened. "It is only Gressim," Brell said. "And Meiley. They are changing places."

"Yes," Parolin said, closing his eyes. "I see them now."

"See them? How?" I didn't see anything, not even a blur.

"Through their footsteps and more," Brell answered. "You

try, Laura. Hear them. See them." He touched my temple with his index finger. "Here in your mind."

I held my breath and closed my eyes. The soft crunch of leaves entered my ears in a steady rhythm, and in my head, the forest floor appeared, a carpet of leaf debris pressed by two pairs of phantom feet. "Yes! I hear it. I see it. But how?" I asked.

"The vision is not real. It is your mind's interpretation of the sound, turning it into something you know and can understand," Brell explained.

I squeezed my eyes tighter. Another sound came, the brushing of fabric. Swinging arms materialized above four ghostly boots. "But I don't see their faces."

"Parolin and I have known Gressim and Meiley since first breath," Brell said. "We can distinguish their walk from others. The cadence of their gaits. The amount of weight placed upon each foot. The rotation of their hips. The combination of these factors is specific to the individual. You have not spent enough time with Gressim for his face to appear. And you have not yet met Meiley."

"But it happened to me once before! I did see a face. The second time you called my name in the woods." I paused to catch my breath. "That night, I thought about the voice calling my name. I heard it over and over again in my head, and a face appeared—your face. I saw you in my mind before I met you."

"That is not possible," Brell said. "Landaffen instincts alone could not form a face never seen or known. It must have happened after I found you lost in the woods."

Gressim pushed through the trees. He was a little shorter than Parolin, but the thick, loosely curled hair at the top of his head made up for the difference in height. In the afternoon shade, his blue eyes shone gray, matching the tunic beneath his leather armor.

Meiley came from the other side. He and Gressim exchanged nods as they passed one another, and Parolin left us to go and talk to Meiley. I listened hard to hear what the two said, something about a message from the king.

"Prince Brell," Parolin said, returning. "Today Meiley is a protector and a messenger."

"Yes, I heard. And what does my father have to say?" Brell sighed.

"These were his words: 'I understand his devotion to the half-race, but it does not excuse his disobedience. His familiarity with the town and his human education makes his presence there understandable, but it also puts him in danger. He was not supposed to leave yesterday, not even to bring the girl here, and he was not to leave for any reason today'," Meiley said. "'He must return to the Grove immediately.'"

"You aren't supposed to be here?" I asked Brell. "Or come for me yesterday?"

He dropped his head. "No, but your safety is more important than obeying the king. And I will not let him stop me from being with you tomorrow at school. I need to be there. I want to be there."

"We will keep her safe," Parolin said to Brell. "You cannot go against the king's wishes. Gressim will accompany Laura onto the grounds of her school. Farnaway and I will take our posts on the perimeter of the property. And Prince Brell, you must remain in the Grove."

Brell's posture stiffened, and he crossed his arms.

I placed my hand on his shoulder. "I want you at school with me, too, but at the same time, I don't. I'd rather know you were in a place where you can't get hurt."

"I will obey my father and leave for the Grove," Brell said. "But I *will* convince him to allow the exchange, so I can be with you tomorrow. I promise I will make it happen."

A familiar sound drew my attention. I looked toward my home. "I hear a car down the road. My mom's."

"Yes, it is her," Brell said.

"We will leave you to say your good-byes," Parolin said. My protectors marched through a thick row of trees and disappeared.

"Your senses are improving," Brell said once we were alone. "The more time you spend with us, the more Landaffen you become. It is another sign you are the half-race of legend."

"A sign, but it still doesn't mean I am." I shrugged.

"To make magic, you must believe in yourself. Believe in your abilities. Please do that for me. Have confidence. Stay strong. Let the Landaffen in you dictate your every move. Do not question it. Let it flow freely. It is in your blood." He kissed my forehead.

"Okay, I'll try."

"You have exceeded my expectations today. A Landaffen of full race could not have accomplished what you did with the bow and sword."

"Really?"

"Yes." He nodded.

"I wish I could go back to the Grove with you," I groaned. "And I wish I didn't have school tomorrow."

"If only Landaffens could grant wishes," Brell said. "I would give you both and many more. I do not expect you to ignore the only life you have known until now. You will be leaving at first light?" he asked.

"Yeah, about seven fifteen. I need to be in my first class by eight."

"Then I will see you at the next sun." He kissed me, and my weak legs practically buckled.

"But your father ordered you to—" He closed his arms

around me, and I snuggled my head under his chin. "Please stay in the Grove," I said. "The three will take care of me."

"I will comply with my father's wishes, and return to the Grove today, but tomorrow I will do what I think is best."

"Staying in the Grove is best. I couldn't bear it if something happened to you."

"And I could not bear it if something happened to you."

He kissed me, and my insides danced and stirred like a flickering flame. His hands worked their way down my back and below my waist. I caught the back of his thigh with my hand and drew him closer.

"My mom! She's close. I'd better go."

"I love you," Brell said.

I dropped my head. "You know I'm not ready to say it back." I sighed.

"I know," he said. The sparkle in his eyes faded, and his shoulders rounded.

"I'm sorry, Brell."

I threw my arms around his neck. We *were* brought together by the trees. I felt it so strongly at that moment. There was something powerful, almost instinctual about how deeply I cared for him. He would do anything to protect me and keep me safe.

"Don't leave the Grove," I said, and I gave him a last, quick kiss.

We let go of one another, and I dashed out through the trees, making it back into the house and changing into my pajamas as my mother turned up the driveway. She walked into the kitchen, holding a paper plate wrapped in tin foil.

"You're home early," I said.

"I didn't want you to miss out on this terrific lunch. Barbeque chicken, coleslaw, potato salad, and Phyllis's homemade corn bread. Do you feel like eating?"

"Yeah, I do. I feel a little better. Thanks."

She put her hand against my forehead. "Still no fever. Phyllis thought you might be feeling sick because you were nervous about starting a new school."

"Yeah. Maybe. I don't know. I guess I'm a little nervous."

"Well, you didn't miss much except . . ." she smiled, "for a nice boy who was there. His name was Todd, um, I don't remember his last name. He said he met you at registration. His mom is a friend of Phyllis's."

My mom used the word "nice" to describe any boy who even *she* didn't think of as cute.

"Yeah, I met him."

I leaned toward the window and snatched a glimpse of Parolin standing watch.

# CHAPTER 21

As the sun rose, the quarter moon was still low in the sky, a sliver of silver like a glowing lopsided smile. Parolin turned his head in my direction, his eyes orange in the waning moonlight. I pulled back from the window and dragged myself out of bed.

"How are you feeling today, honey?" Mom asked as I lumbered into the bathroom. She clipped back her hair while looking in the mirror and took a sidestep from the sink to give me some room.

"I'm fine. Just tired," I said, raking my hand through my bed head hair.

"You need to get used to getting up early again, and we both need to get used to sharing a bathroom. I'll do my makeup in the kitchen, so you can hop in the shower."

"Thanks, Mom."

I had my own bathroom when we lived in Albuquerque. It was smaller than this one, but at least I didn't have to share. She left the bathroom with her cosmetic bag in one hand and a handheld mirror in the other.

My showers were usually quick, but when I rinsed the conditioner from my hair, I stood under the shower head for several minutes with my eyes closed, inhaling the tropical scent of my body wash and remembering the first time I saw Brell.

Flat on my back on a blanket of pokey, dead leaves, Brell's body backlit by an aura of blinding sunlight, I'd looked up at him, my mind racing and full of wonder. And now here I was, just days later, a half-race with a supposed responsibility bigger than anything I could have ever fathomed on my own. Shrugging the image away, I left the shower and dressed.

Pulling my backpack over one shoulder was disheartening yet satisfying in a strange way. I didn't want summer to end, but getting back into a regular routine could keep my mind from the fact that I needed an armed team of Landaffens to protect me. I grabbed my keys and shoved a granola bar in my backpack.

"Is that going to be enough? I can make eggs," Mom said.

"That's okay, I'm not that hungry."

She set down her coffee cup and took her wallet from her purse. "For lunch," she said and handed me a five-dollar bill.

A howl from Bay split the air.

I slipped the bill into my back packet. "Thanks, Mom. See you tonight. Love you," I said and rushed out the door.

Steam curled from the grass at my feet as the morning sun broke through the fog. Where were Parolin, Gressim, and Farnaway? The rim of trees was empty. And where was Bay?

"Laura."

I spun on my heels.

"Brell, what are you doing here?" A bow and quill hung from his right shoulder. A sword and scabbard rested against his hip.

"Aren't you happy to see me?"

"Of course, but . . ."

I looked up and saw my mother's face in the kitchen

window. She smiled and gave me a thumb's up. I waved, returning a smile.

"She cannot see me," Brell said.

"I know, but she can see me," I said, trying not to move my lips, "and she'll wonder why I'm talking to myself." I opened the driver's side door. "Come on. Climb in through my side."

Holding the top of its frame, Brell swung into the passenger seat, landing in one smooth movement. I tossed my pack in the back, and Brell repositioned his bow and quiver, bringing them between his legs to rest on the floor.

"Where are my protectors?" I asked.

"Parolin and Gressim have mounts."

"Horses?"

"Yes. They are on their way to your school. Farnaway is in the Grove. I have taken his place."

"So your father changed his mind?"

"I am a scout again, not a protector, though I did come prepared." He kissed me on the cheek.

I started the Challenger, the roar of its engine cutting through the damp morning air as we rumbled down the driveway. Brell pressed his palms against the dash and pushed back into his seat. When I reached the road, I put the car in neutral and set the parking brake. His body relaxed.

"It is my first time in a car," he said.

"Here." I pulled the seat belt across his lap.

"To keep us in place if there is an accident?" he asked.

"Yeah, but don't worry." I patted his knee. "Nothing's going to happen. There'll be hardly anyone else on the road this early, and I don't plan on going over the speed limit. It's not any more dangerous than riding a horse."

"Landaffens do not crash or fall from our horses," he said smugly.

"But they can fly from the trunk of a car." I laughed.

"A horse will do anything to avoid pain, death, and to protect its rider. Your Challenge—"

"Challenger," I corrected.

"Your Challenger cannot do that. And your natural bond with Molly is growing. I am sure you have felt it."

"I have."

"Your Landaffen self is strong." He leaned across the center console and kissed me. "I should not distract you, but you are getting too hard to resist."

"Distract me all you want," I said, and kissed him while shifting into first and pulling onto the main road into town.

I picked up our speed, throwing my car into second, then third, and fourth. Brell gripped the door handle hard while keeping one hand flattened against the dash, though I never accelerated past fifty miles per hour, which kept us well below what was legal.

The high school parking lot was half full. I parked in the last row closest to the road, and Brell finally loosened his shoulders and gave a deep sigh as I turned off the engine.

My shoulders remained stiff and square. A big inhale and exhale did little to tame my anxiety. With a quivering hand, I shoved my phone in my back pocket, yanked my backpack from the backseat, and found the scrap of paper where I'd written my schedule from memory.

"So what's the plan?" I asked Brell. "How long can you remain invisible? I'm not done until two."

"I will be unseen until that time," he said, confidently, arching his back.

"You know I can't talk to you or even act like you're there, or people with think I'm a crazy person, right?"

"Yes, I understand. It is the way things will be."

"And you'll need to crawl out my door, or people will think this car's name is Christine." I carried my joke with a laugh, but my voice cracked. Brell's furrowed brows told me he had no idea what the heck I was talking about.

"It's from a book," I explained. "Christine was a car that was possessed. It could open its own doors and turn on the radio." I bit my quivering bottom lip.

"You are scared. You are anxious. Emotions so strong they are being absorbed by the trees," Brell said. He set his hands on my shoulders. "I love you, Laura. I will not let anything happen to you, and neither will your protectors."

"Are they here? Are they at their posts?"

"Yes. I feel their presence."

"Thank you," I said softly.

We hugged, and I leaned across his upper body, ignoring the pain of the stick shift digging into my stomach.

"There may be times when even you do not see me," Brell said. He kissed my cheek. "But that will not mean I am not there watching, ready to protect you."

"Okay," I said, brushing my lips against his neck in a soft series of kisses.

"Remember, a Landaffen's abilities are weaker away from the forest. Do not leave the school until it is necessary or one of us instructs you to do so," Brell warned.

"I won't. I understand." I swallowed hard, kissed his neck just below his pointed ear, and whispered, "Let's do this."

# CHAPTER 22

"Laura!" Todd shouted.

Brell moved to walk on my right just as Todd jogged to my left, pulling his backpack with him.

"Hi," I said. Brell matched our stride as we entered the large quad.

"I want to apologize again for not meeting you here last week," Todd said.

"That's okay. I understand. How's your grandfather doing?"

"He's better."

"That's great to hear."

"Do you need help finding any of your classes?"

"No. I can figure it out. Thanks."

"I texted you yesterday. Did you get it?" Todd scratched his head.

"No. I didn't. Sorry. I told you about the reception at my house." Honestly, I'd kind of forgotten about my phone. I had hardly used it since I'd met Brell.

"Well, I texted to see if you wanted to go out sometime," Todd said.

"Actually, I have a boyfriend, so . . ."

A group of students came from the opposite direction and almost ran into Brell. He skirted away, keeping greater distance between Todd and me.

*Brrrring!*

I jumped, and my backpack slipped from my shoulder to the crook of my arm.

"That's only the first bell," Todd said. "We have six minutes to get to class, but don't worry. They never mark anyone tardy on the first day."

Brell walked ahead of us and peered around the next building. I unfolded my makeshift schedule. Fresh with palm sweat, it ripped down its center. When I looked up, Brell was gone.

"So who's your boyfriend? That guy I saw you with?" Todd asked.

"What guy?"

"The one sitting in your car with you before school."

Brell should have made himself unseen before we reached Forest View. I'll have to ask him about that. "Yeah. That's him," I said.

"I haven't seen him before. Is he new here, too?" Todd asked.

"Yeah, but he doesn't go to this school. He's home schooled."

Todd gave a shrug, then asked, "Where you headed?"

"Building four." I quickened my gait.

"So am I. I'll walk with you."

I glanced left and right, feeling as helpless as I'd felt when I was lost walking in circles in the woods. No Brell. No blurs. The girls' restroom was at the end of the next building.

"I have to go to the bathroom first. I'll see you later," I said.

"I still want to drive that car of yours someday," he shouted as I hurried away and entered.

Brell said I wouldn't be able to see him most of the time, but I thought he'd at least tell me he was going to make it hard enough for me not to see him at all.

I stared at myself in the mirror. My face wore my worry. It was pale and my lips and jaw were tight. If I hadn't been wearing makeup, I would have doused my face with a handful of water. The girls at the next sink shared a lip gloss, applying it with the wand applicator and patting the slick finish down with their index fingers.

"You okay?" one of them asked me.

"Yeah, thanks."

*Brrrring!*

"Last bell," one of them said, and they both laughed like school was a big joke.

I headed to building four, entered the hall, and ran up the stairs to room 21. My heart beat in my throat. When I opened the door, the teacher was taking roll electronically on a tablet. He pointed to a chair in the front. I sat down and gently plopped my backpack to the floor.

A chatter of voices entered my ears, words in the tone of a whisper, but resonating in my head as if they'd been spoken out loud.

"Who is that?" someone asked.

"I've never seen her before."

"She has to be new."

"She's definitely not from here."

I folded my arms across my desk, lowered my chin, and stared at the graffiti etched into the desktop. "Whack job," "DGAF", and a drawing of an erect penis. Normally I'd crack a disapproving smile.

"I'm Mr. Parker," the teacher said. "Some of you already know me."

He was the weird teacher Robert had told me about. A poster of the Loch Ness Monster, the famous photo of a curved, dark head sticking from the water, was tacked to one of the walls. A stuffed alien toy with green skin, oversized head, black eyes, and slit for a mouth sat on his desk. Above it hung a photo of Mr. Parker in a forest of pine trees crouching down next to what looked like a giant footprint in dried mud. A spaceship mobile in the center of the ceiling completed his classroom décor.

"Laura," he said. His smile was big and goofy like a clown's. He pushed the bridge of his thick, black-framed glasses further up his nose.

"Yes," I said.

He looked down at his tablet. "I see you're from New Mexico."

"Yeah, Albuquerque."

"Have you ever been to Roswell?"

"Yeah, a couple of times."

"Ever eaten at the Green Alien Café?"

Practically every kid in the class laughed.

"No."

He scratched his bald spot. "Well, the next time you're there, you gotta go. They have the best pulled-pork sandwiches in the state, and the waitresses can tell you stories about UFOs that'll make you a believer."

"Okay, thanks."

The door opened twice while Mr. Parker went over the class syllabus as he told us a story about the time he'd found a Sasquatch nest in Oregon. I glanced up both times, my heart stopping in my throat, to find some kid taking advantage of the no-tardy-on-the-first-day rule.

After class, Brell wasn't in the hall waiting for me. I spent the next six minutes searching for him in both quads, whispering his name when I knew no one else could hear me. No Brell. No blurs.

In Spanish class, I watched the clock, pretending to take notes or drumming my fingers nervously on the desk. The fifteen-minute break between third and fourth period couldn't come soon enough. I had to find Brell!

My palms burned with sweat. I doodled and picked at my cuticles, pushing them back with the thumb nail on my other hand until one of them bled. I stuck it in my mouth to stop the sting.

The teacher approached my desk, but I kept my head lowered, pretending I hadn't noticed. "Lovely, but what does that have to do with this class?" she asked, motioning to the tree I'd drawn in my notebook.

I told her that I was paying attention even if it looked like I wasn't—and I said it in Spanish. *"Yo estoy poniendo atención aunque parezca que no lo hago."*

We continued our banter in Spanish, she not believing it was only my second year taking the language, and me trying to convince her it was. She finally threw her hands in the air and told me that with my attitude, I better ace every test.

"I will," I said, and the bell rang.

I went to my locker to ditch the two textbooks I'd been given. A slip of yellow paper fell from the opened door as I pulled up the latch. It was the schedule I'd dropped when the Laramiss chased me on registration day! They were here, and to scare me, they'd shoved it through the vent in my locker door. I tossed my books inside and headed to the lower quad.

Something was wrong! Brell wouldn't have left me like this. And not for so long!

"Hey, Laura." Todd grabbed my arm as we passed. "How do you like your classes so far?"

"They're fine," I said and started to walk away.

"What's your hurry? Rushing to meet that boyfriend of yours?"

"No, why? Have you seen him?" What was I thinking? Todd couldn't have seen him.

"Nope," he said.

"Okay, thanks." I yanked my arm from his hold and rushed away.

Brell wasn't in the quad. I headed toward the far end of campus where the forest met a neglected practice field. Upon the clumpy grass sat a rusty soccer goal missing its net and an unmanned golf cart carrying a rake and trash can full of leaves.

"Brell, Brell," I whispered toward the forest. "Parolin! Gressim!" A lawn mower buzzed in the distance, tree limbs rustled from a strong breeze, and the smell of freshly cut grass entered my nose.

I dashed forward and stopped, remembering Brell's warning not to enter the woods. "Brell, Brell," I said again. But if something was wrong, I had to help him and my protectors.

With each step, slow and calculated, I advanced toward the forest, scanning left and right and looking over my shoulders. The bell signaling the end of the break rang through the stale, humid air, and I froze to reevaluate my surroundings. Shoes shuffled against pavement, lockers slammed shut, doors opened and closed, and students chattered, but those were the only sounds I heard as I cut through the first span of trees.

The forest was thick with maples and birch, their robust trunks a natural fence anchoring one end of the school. Mist rippled at the forest's rooted feet, disappearing as it wove into the sunlight. My skin prickled as the leaf canopy turned day into night, and from the corner of my eye, I saw something move.

Perched in the tree above me, his legs folded like compressed springs, the grocery-store boy stared down at me. Wearing a fresh smock and leggings, the only sign he'd been dumped from the back of my Challenger was a brown scab zigzagging across his forehead.

His mouth arched into a sinister grin, accentuating his pointed chin, and his stone-cold eyes cast an evil glint. "Krelis leachin glarius," he smirked. "De nash poshleen shanne nost." Without any hesitation or thought, I understood what he'd said.

The grocery-store boy was here for revenge, and according to my enemy, my protectors were incapacitated, unable to come to my aid.

My bottom lip quivered, and a wave of fresh anger passed into my chest, spreading to my limbs.

"I don't understand your language," I lied, my nose flaring.

"I prefer not to speak the tongue of a dirty human—even one of half-race," he snarled.

"Who are you?" My biceps pulsed with adrenaline, and I balled my hands into fists.

He jumped from the tree. "I am the one called Deveen."

My backpack slid down my arm, and I caught the strap in my hand. He lunged forward, and I whipped my backpack in his direction, letting if fly from my hand. As I ran back toward the school, I heard my backpack land with a dismal *thud*, hitting the ground instead of Deveen's deserving face.

Cranking my arms and lengthening my stride, I sprinted as fast as I could. His footsteps pattered right behind me, and his fingers raked through my hair, yanking me backward. Ignoring the pain, I twisted, ripping free and stumbling sideways, as I smacked my side against the golf cart. I tumbled to the ground.

The trash can teetered and fell, littering the grass in a mess of dried leaves.

"Keeshe," Deveen said, his squinted eyes full of retaliation and hate.

The rake wobbled on its teeth and dropped, its handle inches from my hand. Pushing up on one palm, I rose to my feet, fumbling for the rake's handle and wrapping my finger around the dry stick of wood.

Deveen leapt forward. I swung the rake like a broadsword, slicing left. He pounced right, dodging my blow.

"Where's your sword, the one—" No. He didn't deserve my respect. "Where's your sword Deveen? Oh, that's right. You're just a scout," I said and swung again, low this time, nicking his heel. He winced and fell.

Breaking into a cold run, I swung the rake behind me as I heard the sound of Deveen's footsteps growing stronger.

At the top of the ramp leading to the quad, two Laramiss protectors stood, their blond hair hanging in strands against their foreheads and swords readied at their hips. Deveen's finger fumbled to grasp my shoulder as I continued to run. I ducked, jumping from the ramp, racing through a patch of ivy. Surround myself with people—that's what I needed to do. Two students emerged from building four. It was enough of a distraction for me to snake through the doors of the building before they closed.

Mr. Parker's classroom was the first room at the top of the stairs. I could go there.

Skipping two steps at a time, I drove forward, my thighs burning and forehead hot, the rake dragging behind me. The padded soles of heavy boots reverberated through the steps close on my heels.

"Hi, Laura," Mr. Parker said as I burst inside. I closed the door to his classroom and stood with my back pressed against it, catching my breath.

He sat at his desk eating a sandwich. A banana peel lay next to a flattened paper sack and an opened can of soda. The student desks were empty.

"I don't have a class this period, so I eat lunch early," he said.

I put my finger to my lips, slowly lowered to the ground, and crawled toward him, the rake and my knees barely rising from the floor.

"What are you doing?" Mr. Parker whispered. "Shouldn't you be in class? And why do you have that rake?"

I shook my head and mouthed, "Can I stay here until next period?" I slid to a spot on the side of his desk where I couldn't be seen from the door.

"What are you doing?" he mouthed back. "Hiding from bigfoot?" He laughed, snickering in a cracked voice that turned into something like a pig's snort. He peered down at me, and his smile faded.

"You're scared," he said. "You really are hiding from something or someone. I better call campus security."

A row of old-fashioned windows flanked the outside wall of his classroom, mounted in wooden frames with peeling paint. Two of them were open, their bottom panels slid upward to meet the top sheet of glass in its casing.

"That won't help," I whimpered. I rose from the floor, jogged to the window, and flung the rake out to the grass below.

"Laura," he whispered. "What on earth . . ."

Swinging one leg outside and then the other, I held onto the sill with both hands, my legs dangling. Mentally preparing myself for the fall, I let go and landed on both feet.

"Laura!" Mr. Parker shouted as he looked down at me from the window. "I'm going to call campus security."

I couldn't let them take me to the office. They'd call my mom and I would never be able to explain this.

"Please! Don't do that. Everything is fine!" I yelled. "I believe in aliens and bigfoot," I added, hoping a little flattery would help.

I picked up the rake, snuck to the end of the building, and peered around the corner. Two Laramiss were posted at the door. I tip-toed to the other end, holding my breath as I drew closer. The other three, including Deveen, manned the double doors.

A hand clamped over my mouth! I thrashed, jerking my elbows and swinging the rake, trying to wiggle free. Ready to bite, I sealed my lips against the unknown palm and parted my teeth. A muscular arm wrapped around my waist.

"Shhh. Laura, it is me," Brell whispered against my ear.

He loosened his grip. I dropped the rake and twisted in his arm. "Where were you? Why did you leave me?"

"I heard something, went to investigate, and was ambushed. Pulled behind a building by three Laramiss and forced into the forest behind the school."

His lip was split, and a dried stream of blood ran to his chin. The collar of his shirt was torn, his sheath was empty, he held no bow, and there were only two arrows left in his quill.

"Why didn't you call for me? Scream or something? I would have heard you. I would have come after you."

"I didn't want you to come. You are much safer here than in the woods." He ran his index finger down the side of my face. "Come on," he said.

"Where are we going?"

"To the Grove."

"The parking lot's the other way," I told him as he led me in the wrong direction.

"I know, but unless they have changed their strategy, there

are Laramiss posted at the front of the school. They have broken the code. There are more than three."

"How many are there?"

"At least fifteen. We were outnumbered."

"What happened to Parolin and Gressim?"

"I do not know. They helped me escape, and as we continued to fight, we were separated."

A pair of campus supervisors sat in a golf cart near a side-entrance to the school. When they weren't looking, we skirted past them and scaled a six-foot fence taking us from the campus to the street where we re-entered the parking lot from the driveway.

"Crap," I said, smacking my hand against my forehead when we reached my car.

"What?"

"I don't have my keys. They're in my backpack, and I—"

"I have your keys," he said, lowering to one knee. He reached under the Challenger and pulled out my backpack. "You were there when I was being chased?" I asked.

"Yes, but I could not let myself be seen. Parolin and Gressim were missing, and I did not want the other Laramiss to know I had escaped. If you had needed my help, I would have intervened. But you did not." He smiled, and as his cheeks rose, I noticed one was swollen and slightly bruised.

As we drove from the parking lot, I readjusted my rearview mirror. A campus supervisor reached the top of the stairs and shook his head.

"Will the school notify your mother?" Brell asked. He dabbed the cut on his lip with his tongue and rubbed his exposed shoulder with his hand.

"I don't know," I sighed. "At my old school, they wouldn't, especially on the first day. I'd just be marked truant." I checked my phone. "She hasn't tried to call me. That's a good sign."

When we reached the highway, I increased my speed, and Brell pulled the free end of the belt to tighten it across his lap. It was almost noon. Long shadows cut across the tree-lined road and heat waves danced above the asphalt.

I pulled off the highway and entered the two-lane road leading to my house. My mother's car wasn't there—another good sign. Mr. Parker must not have reported me.

Brell stiffened his back and lifted from the seat, his eyes growing wide. "Park quickly," he said. "They are close. Laramiss soldiers. I sense two." I rolled the Challenger to a stop, and I turned off the engine. He unlatched his seatbelt. "Go now. Run to the Grove. I will keep them from finding you."

"No, I'm not going to leave without you."

"You must," he urged. "Please. You need to tell my father they broke the code of three."

"But I can help you fight."

"How? I am without bow or sword. Magic and stealth are my only defense, things you have not yet mastered. Go! Please, Laura." The arches of his eyebrows dropped, his eyes begging me to listen to him.

"Okay," I said, tears rising at the corners of my eyes. "Be careful."

I opened the door and sprinted toward the woods. I slowed to a jog and looked over my shoulder. A Laramiss solider faced Brell. The soldier pulled an arrow from his sheath and nocked his bow. Brell lifted his arms, and a swirl of dust and wind whipped the spent arrow from the air.

The soldier drew another arrow. A broadsword bit the dusty whirl of wind as a second soldier appeared, his breast plate coated dull with dust and his arm raised, ready to strike a blow. Brell stepped backward, and with fingers spread, continued to work the wind.

A wide funnel formed and grew, sucking twigs and leaves

into its eddy, heaving as if alive. A Laramiss arm flew backward, forced by the spiral of wind, and an arrow ricocheted against the current in a mad dive toward the ground.

Brell took another step backward and another. The whirlpool fluttered, its size decreasing. The tip of a sword poked through the vortex. He shifted his weight, moving to the side, and the current's speed slowed.

"No!" I screamed and ran back toward Molly's corral. She pawed the dirt with her hoof, and her ears shot forward as I opened her stall, grabbed a handful of mane at her withers, and pulled myself onto her back.

"Let's go, girl," I said. She bolted toward the dying funnel of wind. "Brell! Get on!" I yelled above the petering wind.

He curled his fingers, and the dying maelstrom renewed, spinning with an additional gust, pushing against the soldiers. And with a single leap, he landed on Molly's back.

Molly's hooves violently pounded the earth. We entered the forest. The clearing was straight ahead, and beyond that, the Grove.

A Laramiss swung from a tree as we passed, his heels kicking me hard in the ribs. I slid sideways from Molly's back, but Brell caught me with his right arm, bringing me upright again.

*Whizzz!*

An arrow shot past us. Brell pushed my head down.

*Whizzz!*

"Ahhh," Brell groaned. He pulled an arrow from his wrist and threw it to the ground.

*Whizzz!*

Molly clambered left. I shifted right, slipping from her sweat-slick coat. Brell reached for me with his injured arm and missed. I fell, dropping onto my butt and toppling backward while shielding my neck and head with my hands.

Molly planted her front legs, skidding to a stop. Brell leaned backward, countering the inertia of motion. A Laramiss soldier bounded through the trees, his bow raised and arrow nocked. Molly lifted her head, pawed the earth, and snorted as the soldiers aimed his arrow at her chest.

"Please! No!" I cried.

Brell jumped from Molly's back, catching the shaft of the arrow mid-flight in his hand. Rolling onto his knees, Brell landed in front of the enemy soldier.

"Go!" Brell shouted. Soaked with blood, his sleeve sent a spattering of droplets upon the forest floor as he motioned for me to run.

I pushed myself onto my feet.

Eyeing Brell, the soldier slung his bow over his shoulder and drew his sword. "Go!" Brell yelled. "Now, before it is too late!"

The Laramiss raised his weapon, his jaw shifting as he gritted his teeth and tightened his grip.

"No!" I screamed, rushing toward the soldier. Brell sprang upward, his body positioned to block the Laramiss from striking me.

The face of the Laramiss paled and contorted. He crumpled to the ground, an arrow protruding from his back. Gressim stepped from the trees and lowered his bow.

"There are five more coming," Gressim announced. His face was swollen on one side, and his leggings were sliced in two places, revealing bloodied cuts across his thighs.

"Where is Parolin?" Brell asked.

"I am not sure."

Brell clamped his bleeding wrist with his other hand. "Laura, you must ride Molly to the Grove."

"And you go with her, Prince Brell," Gressim said. "You are injured, and you were ordered not to leave the Grove."

"What?" I gasped. "You shouldn't have come, Brell. You shouldn't even be here."

"I promised I would accompany you on your first day."

"It was a promise I would have wanted you to break."

His sleeve was blood soaked to the elbow, and when he checked his wound and re-clamped it with his fingers, he winced.

"You have to come with me," I urged.

"I am not going," Brell insisted. Gressim tossed a dagger and bow to Brell.

"Then neither am I," I said. "I'm not going to leave you and Gressim to fight alone."

Brell hooked my waist with his good arm and lifted me onto Molly's back, and as much as I kicked and flailed my arms, I couldn't squirm from his hold.

"We need you in the Grove, Laura. It is up to you to tell my father to send additional protectors," he said.

"No! I'm staying here with you."

Before I could throw my left leg over Molly's side to dismount, Brell smacked her rear.

She lunged forward, breaking into a frantic run well past the clearing. As she reached a cluster of tall trees, another Laramiss pounced from a large maple, and the wind rang with the swing of his sword. I shifted left, but his blade hit my ribs, and I toppled from Molly's back as her mane slipped through my fingers. I fell to the ground, landing flat on my back.

I pressed my hand against my numb, warm side and looked up. Blood seeped between my fingers. The Laramiss solider straddled me, one foot of his on either side of my legs, squeezing me with enough pressure for him to pin me to the ground.

Holding the grip with both hands, the soldier steadied his

sword above me, its tip aimed at my heart. I closed my eyes and bit my lip, waiting to die.

But the piercing pain to my chest and through my innards did not come. I grunted and opened my eyes. The Laramiss offender buckled and dropped on top of me. I fought to catch my breath as his dead weight pressed against my torso.

A boot knocked against the dead Landaffen's side. The Laramiss rolled from me to the leaf bed, his body flopping and coming still, the arrow in his back bobbing.

"Brell, you saved me!" I rejoiced.

"You are hurt," he acknowledged, his bow poised in one hand.

"Yeah, but . . ." I said, lifting my shirt to expose my side. A six-inch, raised pink line rode across my ribs, no longer bleeding profusely. "It's only a scratch. I'm fine."

He pulled me to my feet. Another Laramiss soldier ran toward us. Brell lifted his dagger and leaped in front of me, the blade of his knife deflecting a blow meant for me.

"Go," Brell urged, his blade clanking against his foe's. The leaves crackled behind me, and without turning, I knew it was another Laramiss. "Go!" Brell shouted again.

I jumped onto Molly's back. She ran hard, weaving through the trees, and I wrapped my arms around her neck, leaning forward as we rode. My eyes burned, and I squinted against the wind to hold my tears. Just ahead the trees were marked with Xs. She slowed to a gallop and stopped.

"We're almost there, girl," I said, patting her neck.

Bay broke through the foliage ahead of me. He lowered his head, showing his teeth, his eyes focused on someone behind me. An arrow blazed past my shoulder. With bow raised, Parolin jumped from the biggest tree to help me.

"Parolin, you're alive," I said, hopping from Molly's back.

The cut to my side had dried closed, my shirt sticking to the coagulated blood like a bandage.

The Laramiss soldier Parolin had maimed lay on the ground, Parolin's arrow in his chest. My stomach grew sick. Bay dashed forward and secured the soldier's arm in his mouth. The soldier kicked, trying to stand, and Bay bit harder, shaking his head. Blood bubbled from the soldier's mouth, and Bay let go of the dying Landaffen's limp hand.

The crunch of many footsteps filled the afternoon air. Parolin threw his bow over his shoulder and pulled his broadsword from its sheath.

"Go to the Grove," he ordered me.

But two Laramiss burst through a fringe of trees. Parolin fought both, deflecting blows. Brell appeared next, brandishing his knife as he rushed forward to help.

"Go, Laura!" he said. "Get help!"

The pair of Laramiss advanced, striking forward, forcing Brell and Parolin to step backward. Parolin grunted, falling to his knees. Brell struck with his dagger, knocking away a Laramiss blade meant for Parolin.

But the two Laramiss continued forward, swords slashing while Brell fought, metal ringing against metal. The four disappeared into a thick band of trees. The sound of sword fighting echoed.

A twinkle from above caught my eye. I blinked, adjusting to the glare. With a running start, I jumped, reaching for the stash of hidden weapons deep within the treetops. But I wasn't tall or spry enough, and I missed my mark. I tried to climb it, but the lowest branch was too high for me to grab and pull myself upward.

Frustrated, my temples throbbing, I spread my fingers, raised my hands, and concentrated, telling myself to think like a

Landaffen. To feel the energy of the forest. Every tree. Every stone, and the ground beneath my feet. I had to harness the power of nature and let it join with my human energy. My skin tingled. My lungs expanded. My nostrils flared, and my hands shook.

A sword fell from the leaves above, its point pricking the damp soil at my feet as I grabbed it by the hilt.

Parolin burst from the thicket of trees in front of me and lunged toward a new attacker.

"Where's Brell?" I shouted.

Another opponent emerged through the trees, springing forward, sinking his sword into Parolin's side. Despite his wound, Parolin managed to pull a dagger from the strap on his thigh and plant the blade through the leather plate of his assailant.

The Laramiss faltered to the ground, his legs jerking as he staggered away and choked up blood. Parolin dropped to his back, his face grimacing with pain as his lips twisted and eyes blinked uncontrollably. I knelt, leaning over him.

"What can I do to help you?" I asked, holding his blood-stained hand.

"There is nothing you can do." He shuddered. "You are the one, Laura," he said. "You have proved that today. Save my people. Bring our races to peace and join with our prince."

"Parolin," Gressim croaked as he appeared from between two trees. He dropped to his knees beside me and held Parolin's other hand.

"Do something!" I pleaded to Gressim.

"I cannot save him," Gressim said. "His wounds are beyond the powers of Landaffen magic."

Parolin closed his eyes. His body relaxed, and his head fell to the side.

"No, no!" I sobbed.

Gressim put his hand on my shoulder. "Rise, Laura. It is

time for the earth to take him."

I rose, my legs wobbly and face hot with tears. "Where's Brell? We need to find him. Help him."

The ground shook, and I reached my arms out to my sides to catch my balance. A green tendril broke from the dirt at Parolin's feet, weaving through a thick tapestry of twigs and fallen leaves. Another vine sprouted and another, curling and twisting, probing the soft soil snake-like. I stumbled backward as each trailing plant coiled and kinked, wrapping Parolin's body in a robe of vines and leaves.

Another rumble grew deep within the earth. A tiny fissure formed and grew, cracking the ground at Parolin's shoulders. Dust burst. Rocks flew, and I watched in sorrow and awe, my hand pressed against my mouth and my breathing heavy.

Parolin's body sunk into the crevice. The ground closed, and the vines retreated.

I shuddered from fear and disbelief, my heart rate accelerating. The forest rocked in a series of quakes similar to the first. "These Landaffens are also dying," Gressim said as Landaffen magic continued to take its hold.

An intertwining of leaf and vine crawled and coiled around the Laramiss victims. The ground beneath them spurted and split, consuming their lifeless bodies. Like a healing wound, the earth heaved, and the pit resealed, returning the forest to what it was before as it had done with Parolin's dead body.

My head hurt. Pressure built behind my eyes and heat grew in the center of my chest, expanding into my arms and legs, making them tingle. My throat tightened as I threw back my shoulders.

"We have to find Brell!" I screamed. Gripping the hilt as hard as I could, I raised my sword above my head and rushed in the direction where I'd last seen him.

"No. It is too dangerous. Go to the Grove!" Gressim said. "I will find him."

"But I can't leave Molly! I have to find her!"

I sprinted in the opposite direction from which I'd come, away from the trees marked with Xs, and stopped when I reached the clearing with boulders.

Gressim ran up behind me, his bow over his shoulder and sword swinging at his side. Three fallen Laramiss lay upon the ground, moaning and contorting in pain. Bay was at the clearing's center barking next to Brell, who remained motionless. His chest plate was askew and the ripped shirt beneath it was thick with fresh blood. The knife wound was narrow but deep, a blade-width puncture through Brell's ribs to his heart.

A Laramiss jumped from the trees, landing next to Brell. "No!" I screamed. "Stay away from him." I lunged forward, and he lifted his sword. With a downward swipe, I sliced his arm and spun away from him. He tossed his weapon into his other hand, and his lips twisted into an evil sneer.

When he lifted his sword, I took a step forward and steadied my stance. Blocking one strike and then the other, I moved forward. He struck, and I countered, knocking away his blade. The Laramiss rocked backward, half-stumbling, and I raised my sword again and struck. The blade came down across his shoulder and neck, a hard hack, cutting deeply into the flesh at the base of his neck. He clamped his hand over his bleeding throat and dropped to his knees. Gressin sprang through the trees, finishing the Laramiss with a final blow.

"Brell," I said, rushing toward Bay and his fallen master. Pressure built behind my eyes.

Bay clawed the earth at Brell's feet, whining with his tail tucked between his legs, a fury of grief and passion. Molly stood under a tree with her head down.

The ground vibrated. I lost my footing and regained my

balance by shooting my hands out to my sides.

"The one called Laura," Gressim said softly. "He is gone. Do you not see what has happened? The earth is going to take him." His eyes watered, and the light in them dimmed. "Step away," he warned.

"No! That can't be," I screamed. "He gave his life for me."

My cheeks burned, and my stomach turned. My pulse throbbed in my throat, and I couldn't catch my breath. I buckled at the waist and lifted my head. Between two elder maples, a white-tipped sprout poked through the damp soil and loose cover of leaves, coiling at Brell's feet.

"Soon he too will be one with the woods," Gressim reiterated.

Sinking to the forest floor next to Brell, I became lost in the forest once again, metaphorically, my thoughts swirling as the reality of what happened became too real. I rolled onto my back and cried, staring at a square of blue sky between the treetops until a flutter of color made me turn my head.

A yellow butterfly danced in a dusty ray of sunlight, and I held out my hand as I wiped my wet cheeks with the other. It landed on my index finger, its velvety wings glistening. I sat up and crossed my legs. A tear rolled down my cheek.

"Hello, there," I said and sniffled back more tears.

With a flap, it glided from my hand, landing on the wiry tangle of roots consuming Brell's body.

The vines tangled upon him and pulled, pushing him into the earth, devouring him like a wave cresting over a mass of something inert and water-logged.

While I watched, my mind reliving life in the Grove, I gasped like I'd been reborn and taken a first breath, my whole body seizing with energy. Something spoke to me deep inside—a little voice—an unknown alter ego lying dormant until this moment.

A jolt of energy burst through my core, spreading down my arms and into my hands. Light exploded from the tips of my fingers, five beams radiating from each hand. I moved my fingers, sending shafts of white light in all directions.

Gressim gasped. "That is magic like I have never seen," he said as he watched my hands. "You are the one."

I jumped into the crevice separating life and death, the warm, steamy soil enveloping Brell's body and mine, igniting my soul with palpable vitality.

A myriad of plant shoots grew and intertwined, weaving a tapestry of stiff greenery over our bodies, crimping with each turn, budding sprouts and regrouping, continuing their duty to consume, recycle, and preserve.

The scent of spice and fresh wood dominated my senses as I lay upon Brell's breathless body and the tangle of plant life. A coil of vines sprung from below, incapacitating my legs. I kicked, fighting the plants' pull, as a spawn of newly grown roots curled up my sides, sewing my fingers closed and binding my body.

"Even so, the Landaffen force of the afterlife cannot distinguish the dead from the living!" Gressim yelled, his voice cracking. "Do not do this. Save yourself. Laura! Grab my hand." Through the supernatural fissure of plant life and tussled soil, he reached for me.

The vines about me tightened. I stole a final breath as my rib cage collapsed, and I coughed, stretching the fingers of one hand toward Brell to touch his cheek and my other hand to press upon his wound. The light from my fingers danced against the raw earth.

"Asmla lanmar una trivi, Asmla lanmar una trivi. Asmla lanmar una trivi," I chanted, using the last bit of air left in my lungs to speak. The words came naturally, though I'd never heard them or learned them before.

Heat filled my core. My body sickened, and the words I'd spoken echoed in my mind. I held Brell's face in my hands, the light from my fingers creating a solid ray of illumination around him.

I pressed my lips against Brell's, creating a seal. My breath became his, and I fought the bed of tendrils on his chest compressing his heart.

With several shared breaths, the suction at my lips collapsed. Brell gasped, his chest heaving. The plants parted, recoiling back into the earth, pushing our bodies upward, leaving him and me to lie flat upon what looked like an undisturbed plot of land littered with leaves. The light from my hands receded and disappeared.

"You did it!" Gressim stumbled forward. "Our prince was dead, but you have given him new life!"

"Laura," Brell said softly. "You brought me back. Returned my soul."

I pushed my trembling fingers through the slit in his shirt, through the drying coat of coagulated blood. The skin I touched was smooth and unmarred. "You are healed," I said.

A burning awareness of satisfaction, a sensation of pure bliss, pumped through my being and I felt truly at peace with myself for the first time.

To be of half-race! To be the one! That was my calling! That was what I was meant to do! What I'd been searching for my whole life! It is my destiny to help both of our worlds!

"The trees brought you to me," I told Brell. "And the trees are never wrong."

"Yes, Laura, you are the one. The Landaffens will survive," Brell cried. "You will lead us to peace and victory. I love you, Laura."

"I love you, too," I admitted.

Karri Thompson, a native of San Diego, attended San Diego State University where she earned her bachelor's degree in English and master's degree in education. When she's not writing novels and teaching high school English, she can be found nerding out at San Diego Comic-Con and cooking delicious meals for her family. Karri is the recipient of the San Diego Book Awards Best Published Young Adult Novel for 2014.

www.ingramcontent.com/pod-product-compliance
Lightning Source LLC
Chambersburg PA
CBHW050231110726
47898CB00007B/2105